HORN CROWN

HORN CROWN

Andre Norton

Daw Books, Inc.   New York

DAW∷sf
BOOKS

DAW TRADEMARK REGISTERED
U.S. PAT. OFF. MARCA
REGISTRADA. HECHO EN U.S.A.

PRINTED IN THE UNITED STATES OF AMERICA

HORN CROWN

1

THE RAIN FELL WITH SULLEN PERSISTENCE TO MAKE ONE'S TRAVEL cloak a sodden burden weighing upon the shoulders, even as fear can weigh heavily on heart and mind. Those among us who were simple and unlettered, who had never stirred far from the fields they tilled or the herd pastures known to their long-kin before them, muttered together of Glom the Weeper and looked upon the gray sky as if they expected moment after moment to see her two welling, tear-filled eyes above us, her sorrow hanging as heavily as a curse.

Even those who were lettered and learned could be disturbed by the thought of curses and condemnation after this exile came to us.

Were our Bard-Sages right to use their knowledge so that when we passed through the Gate, household by household, lord-kin by lord-kin, we not only left behind us our homeland, but also a part of all memory? Now we might question for a while why we had come to ride this rain-washed, dreary land. However that questioning diminished as we rode north. That the reason for our flight was dire we carried ever in our minds. Not only did Sword Brothers ready for instant alarm ride before us to scout this strange land, but a full company of them were the last at the Gate as a rear guard. With them were Laudat and Ouse, whose singing had opened that world portal and who now closed it with the clack-clack of their spirit-drums so that there could be no retreat, and perhaps, mercifully, no pursuit.

Those who rode in the van as our guides had met us this side of the Gate. They had been near a full moon-tally of days here, spying out what must be faced. Their report was strange. They told of tall hills and dales, once held by men—or else some life-form which was near enough like our own to pass for men—for our scouts had found the land now deserted, save for relics of that earlier race.

Not that the land was entirely safe. There were places here and there where other forces had been awakened and lingered, which we must take good care to avoid. However, there was much clear land waiting for the plow, hillsides rich in tall growing grass to feed our sheep, our cattle, the horses which carried our packs and pulled heavily loaded wains.

Each lord-kin moved in company, possessions well stacked, the old and the very young riding either on wagons or on the most docile of our mounts, while swordsmen and liegemen of each clan kept on alert to wall them in.

We moved at a slow pace. Sheep and cattle cannot be overdriven. Also, I think, the strangeness of this land weighed upon us, perhaps because, as we went, we sighted certain pillars or structures here and there, and, too, the sun did not make a welcome warmth or light for us.

My Lord was Garn and our household was not equal to most in either wealth of gear or strength of liegemen. Our small flock of sheep were easily numbered and we had only a single bull and five cows to watch. Relics of the old life we had brought with us filled only three wagons, and some of the younger women rode with us, many with a child before and another behind, holding to their girdles.

I was lord-kin, though not heir, being a late-born son of Garn's father's brother. Still I carried kin-shield and there were four crossbow men who rode at my command—a very small company to be sure. I was young enough to be seriously concerned with my responsibilities, and now, as I rode with my men strung out behind me at intervals, I kept to the right flank of the clan, searching among the hills for sight of anything which might move.

We had debated—or rather the Lords had, when they had come through the Gate—the advisability of this route. Only the Sword Brothers had affirmed that it led straight through a deserted land and there were none of the other people's traces near it.

It was, however, a true road—running straight, the blocks of its making showing now and again through the overgrowth of grass and plants. Our wagons jolted along it with better going than we might have found had we taken to open country.

The rain was not all that veiled this new-old land from us. There were patches of mist which hung about the crowns of some of the hills on either side. In places that mist was not the expected gray-white but had a bluish gleam, or was darker, which gave one a feeling of uneasiness.

One of the Sword Brothers spurred past me, heading from the rear guard toward the fore. I watched his passage with outright envy. They were men apart, owing no kin once they had taken Sword Oath, having no clan ties. Their skill with sword, bow, and short-spear was so well known that they carried much authority without ever having to touch steel. However, they made no demands upon the kin, supplying themselves from their own flocks and herds which the foot-brothers tended.

To be accepted into their number was the dream of most of the youth of the clans. For most that dream was never realized, for they remained always the same in numbers, adding no one except on the death of a brother.

After the passing of the rider my own overlord, Garn, came at a lesser pace, his two sworn men at his back, checking upon those of us who rode as a side guard. He was a man near as dour as this land and the weeping sky over us, not given much to talking, but with a quick eye for any failure in service, or possible cause of trouble. Silence was the best praise a man could hope for from Garn. I felt my hands tighten on the reins as his hawk face turned toward where my small company trotted. I had expected him either to voice some disparaging comment on my deploying of that part of his forces, or to check upon the rear guard who were ordered by his son Everad. Instead his horse matched pace with mine, his escort dropping back a little, until he rode stirrup to stirrup with me.

I did not expect any comments from him about the land about us, the discouraging weather, or the past. I merely waited, recalling hurriedly all I might have done lately that was not to his liking. His head turned slowly as his gaze swept from one ridge bordering the road to the other—though I did not think he was trying to see the rear riders of the Household clan of Rarast which preceded us.

"There is good forage." I was astonished at his words, though I knew that Lord Garn was one to judge well the worth of land and the uses it might be put to. I knew all those around me, I knew their likes and dislikes, their faults and virtues, and how we were allied one to the other. I knew my own part in the kin-clan, the training in weaponry which I had had, I knew—everything but why we had come into this other world and what danger we had eluded by coming.

"There shall be a council at the night camp," Garn was continuing. "Then shall be decided where we settle. The Sword Brothers have scouted well. This land is wide. Fortune may favor even those of us who have not grown so great in the past."

I still sought the reason for this frankness of speech from him. It was as unlikely as if my plodding horse had spoken. What Garn said began to sink into my mind past the surprise that he spoke so at all. A large land—open for settlement. There were near a hundred clans, most of them far beyond us in numbers of kin, stock, all which might put a lord into the first consideration. Only no lord would want to spread his meiny so thinly that it could not be easily defended. Thus there was a very good chance that even so small a clan as ours might come into land riches.

Garn was continuing: "Those of the kin-blood will be present and there will be a drawing of lots. This has been agreed upon—that there will be only one choice. Either for shore lands or for the inner ways. Siwen, Uric, Farkon, Dawuan have already spoken for the shore. The rest of us still have the choice. I think," he hesitated, "I would speak with you, Hewlin, and Everad, also with Stig, when we halt for nooning."

My agreement was perhaps unheard, for abruptly he wheeled his mount and rode to where Everad held his place in our march. He left me still surprised. Garn made his own decisions; there would be no need for any consulting, even of his heir. It was doubly startling that he would ask any advice of Stig, who was the headman of the field workers, the non-kin.

What was in his mind? Why had he mentioned the shore lands? We had had no such settlement in the past. To turn aside from long custom was not in our way of life. Still—we had come into a new world, which was perhaps reason enough to break with that custom and lead us into new ways.

I tried to remember how far we might be from the shore, which the Sword Brothers had explored only in very small part. There had been talk of harsh cliffs and reefs leading cruelly into the sea. We were not a sea-going people, though those of the four clans Garn had mentioned were fisherfolk—or had been.

The morning drizzle was lifting. Before nooning a watery, pallid sun shone. Under it the land shook off some of the brooding shadow which had made it so alien to our eyes. We camped where we were on the road, not pulling the wains away, the households strung out along its length like loosened beads on a too-long string.

Those small braziers of coals which had been so carefully tended in the foremost wain were brought out and charcoal sparingly fed into them—enough to warm pots of the herb drink which strengthened the traveler, washed down bites of journey cake. I hurried over my share that I might not keep Garn waiting.

He sat a little apart on a stool which had also been taken from the gear and waved us to less lofty seating on a strip of thick woven matting which had been unrolled at his feet. I noted that beside Everad and Stig, was Hewlin, who was the eldest of his guard, his face near as grim as his lord's.

"There is the choice," Garn began as soon as we were seated. "I have had word with Quaine who rode the shore way the farthest." He took from his belt pouch a strip of skin which had been rolled into a thin tube, spread this out so that, leaning forward, our heads close together, we could see running on it a number of dark lines.

There was one heavy black line which curved in and out, and feeding into that from one side, three thinner ways, also uneven. Two indentations of the larger line were already marked with a thick black cross, and to these Garn pointed first.

"This is the shore as Quaine has seen it. Here and there are bays which are open and this land will be taken by two of those who have already said they want only the sea." His fingertip now moved on, still along the pictured coastland, until it tapped against a much smaller indentation.

"Here is a river, not as great a stream as the others, but of good water and it leads inland to a wide dale. A river is an easy road for traveling, for the carrying of wool to market—"

Wool! I thought of our sorry herd of sheep. What did we have to market? All that was ever shorn from their backs was woven and worn by our own people and there was never more than enough for perhaps a new kirtle, a new under jerkin, at three or four years' time.

It was Everad who dared ask the question that was in all our minds: "This is what you would choose, my lord, if the lot comes to you and it is not already taken?"

"Yes," Garn said shortly. "There are other things—" He stopped short and none of us had the courage to ask what those other things might be.

I stared at the lines on the bit of skin and tried to imagine what they were meant to represent—land and sea, river and wide dales to welcome our plows, our small herds and flocks. Only they remained stubbornly but lines on skin and I could not see beyond them.

Garn invited no advice or comments from us. I had not expected that he would. He had called us together only that we might know his will and be prepared for the decision he was about to make if all went favorably for him at the lot drawing.

That river he had indicated lay well to the north, beyond the bays which he had said would be the first choices of the sea lords. I wondered how long a journey northward it would be, also how many days of foot travel it would take us. The time was spring, we should be getting into the ground the precious bags of seeds which weighed down half of our last wain if we expected any sort of a crop at all this year.

There was no telling how chill the winter seasons might be here, or how swiftly they would come, how short or long the growing time could last. Too lengthy a journey might bring us under the dark shadow of winter want, a specter to haunt any clan. Still, the choice was Garn's and no lord ever led his people into outright disaster if he could help it.

The night's council was held at the midsection of our strung out line of march, near where Lord Farkon's long parade of wains and folk wagons were in place. They had ready a fire and around that the lords sat, their blood kin behind them while Laudat and

Ouse, both pulling their gray cloaks close about them as if they felt the damp chill even more than any others, and Wavent, Captain of the Sword Brothers for this Ten Year, were in the center of that circle.

Both the Bards looked thin, tired, their faces nearer to gray in color. The opening and the closing of the Gate might have worn them close to death, but they held themselves to the task before them. However, it was Wavent who spoke.

He described again the land ahead, saying that it was uneven, lacking any stretch of plains. Rather, it was ridged by hills and between those were dales, some wide and well covered with vegetation, some narrow and stony. He also spoke of the rivers that were on Garn's crude map and of the two well shaped and open bays.

He had scarcely finished when Lord Farkon broke in: "You have said little I note, Sword Captain, of these strange places left by an Elder People—or of such people themselves. Do any linger —and if so will they not take sword to defend their own lands as any lord will do?"

There was a murmur which ran from lord to lord. I saw Ouse's shoulders straighten, almost as if he were about to rise and speak in answer. Still he did not, but left that to Wavent.

"Yes, this was once a land well held," the Captain admitted readily. "But those who held it have gone. We have found things of theirs—but in most there is no harm. In fact, there are places of peace and safety which are welcoming. But there are others, and I do not deceive you, my lords, which are pools of evil. These you shall know by the very stench of them. Also, it is well that you have no dealing with any building or ruin which you may find. We of the Sword have quartered and requartered this land and have seen nothing but beasts, have found no trace of any land holder. It is empty now; we do not know why."

Lord Rolfin shook his head, the firelight flashing from the three bits of red gem set in his helm just above his eyes.

"You do not know why those others withdrew," he repeated. "Thus we may be facing an unknown, unseen enemy here."

Again there was a stir and murmur among the lords. This time Ouse did stand, shrugging the hood of his cloak back so that his gray-haired head was fully bared and all could see his thin, lined face.

"The land," he said quietly, "is empty. Since we have come into it we have sensed nothing which we may term enemy. This night before you came to council, my lords, Laudet and I sang the warn words and lit the torches of the Flame. It burned fair, there was no stir at our invocation. There are traces of old power—of a kind we do not know—but the Flame can burn nowhere when there is war rising and evil moving in."

I heard a grunt from Lord Rolfin. He was ever apt, as all men knew, to go seeking menaces in each new place, though he could have no answer to Ouse's reassurance. It was true that the Undying and One Flame could not survive if evil ringed us round, and I am sure that I heard several sighs of relief at that reply.

Now Wavent pushed forward with his right foot a basin of bronze which Laudet had set out for him. The Captain stooped and picked this up, holding it with both hands.

"Here, Lords of Hallack," his voice becoming more formal, as if speaking ritual words, "are your choices by lot. In the Light of the One Flame are all kin-chiefs equal. Thus it was in the past, so shall it be here. Let each of you now draw by chance, for at mid-morning tomorrow we shall reach the first of the open dales and one of you may there withdraw from our journey to take up a new home."

Holding the bowl just above the eye level of the circle of lords, he then passed from right to left, pausing before each man who reached up, scrabbling fingers among the strips of hide he could not see and bringing out the lot which fortune dealt him, though all knew that afterward there could be changes made if both parties agreed.

Ouse let Wavent come well along before he followed with a smaller bowl, this one being of silver somewhat tarnished, which he offered to a handful of lords who had refused the first choosing. This we knew represented the chances of the seacoast. As he had told us he would, Garn refrained from drawing from Wavent's bowl, a happening which appeared to make his near neighbors glance at him in surprise. When Ouse reached him his hand went up forthwith and there was something of eagerness in his action though no emotion showed on his impassive face.

None looked yet upon their luck but waited until all had drawn. There were some slips left in Wavent's bowl but Ouse, though he had few takers, turned his upside down before he was well around the circle and went back to his own place.

It was only when Wavent also returned to stand by the fire that each lord unrolled the scrap of hide his groping fingers had brought him and looked down at the runes marked there—for the Sword Brothers, together with the Bards, had made these for guidance even before we had come through the Gate, and each carried clear directions for travelers and settlers.

We were eager to know Garn's luck, though he did not turn to show his drawing to his kin as many of the lords were doing. The hum of talk arose and already there were those who bargained for exchange, some wanting more pasturage, others more land for crops. We waited with what patience we could summon until at last Garn did speak: "The Flame has favored us. We have the river land."

It was a piece of fortune such as men seldom come across. That he should have drawn the very land he had marked down for his own seemed almost too well done, as if fortune (which is always undependable) had been this time reinforced by a more powerful ally.

I saw one of the Sword Brothers coming through the shadows beyond the inner circle to which the fire gave light. It was Quaine, he who had first told our lord of this possible holding. Now he joined Garn and asked: "What luck, my lord?"

Garn had arisen, the piece of hide stretched taut between his two hands. He favored Quaine with one of those piercing, near accusing glances by which he was able to reduce any man to instant acknowledgment of his orders. Yet Quaine was not of his meiny or kin, but stood easily as if he spoke but of pleasant weather.

Quaine was Wavent's age, and he had been Captain in the last Ten Time. He was, I thought, near Garn's own years, though there was no gray in his hair and his body was slim as any youth's. He walked with the grace of a fighting man who was well trained in the most skillful of swordplay.

"I have it," Garn returned shortly in answer to the question. "It is yet a long journey." He made no question of that, still he continued to look to Quaine as if he waited for some other and more important word from the Sword Brother.

Quaine made no comment and Garn glanced now from him

into the flames beyond. He was a man whose thoughts one could never read, though at that moment I wondered if he were not as well pleased with the result of the drawing as he might have us believe. I held to a small shred of doubt that this fortune came to him by luck alone, although neither Wavent nor Ouse would have lent himself to any arrangement of favor for even the greatest lord among us, and Garn was one of the least of that company when it came to wealth or ranks of kin.

"It is best," Quaine continued, "that those for the shore take trail together. There is another road leading east and then north, but it is much older and it may prove difficult passage. If you ride together then there is aid at hand should any accident occur."

Garn nodded sharply, thrusting his drawing into his belt pouch. Then he only spoke four names, making a question of them: "Siwen, Uric, Farkon, and Dawuan?"

"Also Milos and Tugness," Quaine added.

Now Garn did stare at him, while I let hand go to sword hilt without my realizing what I did until my fingers crooked hard about the metal. We might have had old memories erased as we passed the Gate, but there were some which lingered. Among the Lords Tugness was no friend to any of Garn's household. It was an old feud which had meant bloodletting once, but now it was only that we did not friend-visit with them at any season nor come to a hosting in which they had a part.

Again Garn made his question curt: "Where?"

Quaine shrugged. "I have not asked. Yours lies farthest north— the last dale we rode across in our quartering. Doubtless he will settle south of that."

"Well enough."

"We turn from the road near sunset," Quaine continued. "I will lead the Brothers for the sea party."

Garn nodded, giving no farewell, as he turned on his heel and, with the rest of us, tramped back to our own camp which was some little distance from the council place, saying nothing to us.

Though I was well tired by the journeying of the day—the everlasting matching of our pace to the slow turn of wain wheels—yet as I drew my cloak about me and used my saddle pad as a pillow, I did not at once fall asleep. One could hear the small sounds of the camp. A child was crying in a weak, fretting way where the women sheltered—probably Stig's grandson who ailed. I could hear, too, the movements of our stock as they grazed the tough, thick grass already well above the earth's edge for spring, and now and then the snort of a sleeper or a snore. Garn had gone into the small tent which was his alone. From where I lay I could see the spark of a strike light and then the thin gleam of a lantern candle. Perhaps he was again studying the lot fortune had given him.

I had thought fortune too favoring and been wary, then I had heard of Tugness's luck and believed that this was the ill part which I had sought to find. If our future holding marched with his we must learn to live in a state better than uneasy truce. This was an unknown land from whence the former inhabitants had withdrawn—the why we did not know. Though the Bards and the Scouts had stressed that there were no enemies, still there was a loneliness, a kind of withdrawal, which I, for one, felt the farther I rode. We might well need to depend on neighbors even if such lived a day's journey away. This would be the time when all men of Hallack must stand together, old quarrels and enmities forgotten.

This was not Hallack—that lay behind, lost forever. Those of our company had come to call it High Hallack, since it was a country of many hills. This it would be named in bardic memory from the hour we crossed into it.

Still sleep did not come, though the lantern candle winked out. I turned my head to look up into the night, seeking stars I knew. Then there was a coldness which crept across me, roughened my skin, and brought a prickling beneath my hair. For none of those groupings of stars was what I had known all my life. Where was the Arrow, the Bull, the Hunter's Horn? There was no tracing of any such to be seen.

The rain had stopped hours ago, and the clouds cleared. This sky was a background for many clusters and sweeps of sparkling light—but they were all new! Where had our journey through that Gate taken us? To the sight this land about us was just such earth, grass, bush and tree as we had always known. Only the stars were different. We were in a land which would support us, but we were very far from where we had been born.

I lay shivering at the sight of the unknown stars which, more than just passing through the Gates (much as we had been warned that those would influence us), brought home to me that we were indeed exiles and that we had now only our own strengths to carry us on, our own weaknesses to fight. Which lay the more threatening before us? I thought of the sea, of Garn's choice, and part of me felt excitement and a wish to explore the new. Another part of me searched for a shield against that same new and the dangers it might hold—until I dropped at last from the chaos of my thoughts and fears into sleep.

2

BEHIND US LAY THE WIDE VALLEYS WHICH NOW HELD THE PEOPLE of Farkon, of Siwen, of Uric, Dawuan, and to our right still pounded the sea as our company grew smaller and smaller. We could take heart only that the land did remain empty, though there were in plenty the remains of those who had gone before us, even at times stretches of ancient road which we followed with greater ease. Quaine and three of the Sword Brothers scouted ahead, pointed out those places of the unknown; some they would counsel avoiding, mistrusting the emanations.

There were towers, stretches of pavement surrounded by pillars, piles of rough stones, even monoliths, about which we cautiously edged. I was ever curious as to the manner of folk which had labored to set such stones one upon the other, wondering at the purposes which had led them to such labors.

The largest and most fertile of those sea-fronting lowlands were now behind us. We had been twenty days on our northward crawl. Twice it had been necessary to strike inland for near a day's journeying to find a ford across rivers, which, to our thankfulness, were lazy enough of current—at least at that season—to allow us safe crossings.

On the twenty-fourth day Lord Milos's people left us, turning westward up the throat of a narrower valley, one of the scouts riding as guide. This held no river and we were forced out upon the sea's sandy shore in order to round two ranges of steep hills which guarded it. We called farewells, made promises of future meetings come festival time. Still I think that in all of us, whether we went forward or remained in a stretch of new clan land, a loneliness grew, the uneasy feeling that one more tie with the old was broken and that we might well rue this later on.

It was true that we had drawn closer together during that long march because of the very fact that we were alone in a strange land. There remained, on the surface, none of any ancient enmity with Tugness and his people. All of us labored together to lighten wains as they crossed on the fords, to carry sheep across our saddles there, whether they wore the ear brand of our House or not. Though at night we each made our own camps, still there was visiting back and forth.

Which is how I came first to see that slim withe of a girl who rode a shaggy, sure-footed pony which bore her and two fat hide bags without complaint, though her mount showed rolling eyes and yellowish teeth when anyone else approached it. For all her seeming fragility of body, she was as strong as any lad as she went about her tasks with a brisk independence which had none of the weary acceptance of a field woman, and certainly no hint of manner of one used to the high table in a lord's hall.

It was on the third day of our northern trek that I marked her as one different from the other women who rode and were there to lend a hand, to the extent of their strength. She traveled beside a smaller cart—hardly larger than the tilt carrier which a fieldman would use to take his over-yield to market. To this were hitched two more of the same rough-coated beasts as she rode, their gray coats the same dull shade as the cart itself. Though our people have long taken pride in painting their wains and carts, no such decoration had been given this, so among our company it was more visible for that very reason.

It had a canopy, well lashed to side staves, of finely tanned and stretched hide, and it was driven also by a woman, whose kirtle and cloak were of the same prevailing gray, and who I knew at first glance to be a Wise Woman.

The pair of travelers appeared to be by themselves, attached to no lord's company. I noted that Ouse came once to ride beside the cart for a space and exchange speech with the driver, while the girl dropped behind to give him room. That the Bard chose so to single out this woman meant that she was of note among those who had the Inner Knowledge, even though she went so poorly and quietly.

I had thought that they would turn aside with one of the great lords where a larger company would give the Wise Woman full occupation tending ills and averting dangers of the spirit. However, at each lessening of our company, the two and their cart remained.

One asks no question concerning a Wise Woman. They do not call upon the Flame, yet men do not question or raise voice against them for that. Their skills are inner born and they are free to come and go, as they serve all without question. Many a fighting man, many a woman in child labor, has reason to bless their shadows and give thanks for what they have to offer.

However, if one wishes any matter enough one can learn. Thus I discovered that the girl was named Gathea and that she was a foundling whom the Wise Woman had taken for fostering and made her handmaid and pupil. Thus she was set apart and went her own way, not to be judged by the manner and customs of either the field people or those of the hall.

One could not call her comely. She was too narrow of body, her skin too brown, her features too sharp. But there was something about her, perhaps the freedom with which she walked and rode, her independence, which lingered in a man's mind. Or at least it lingered in mine and I found myself once or twice wondering how she might look with the long robe and tabard of a feast day over that slim body, in place of a shirt jerkin and breeches which were akin to my own, with that long braid of hair wound so tightly about her head shaken loose and interwoven with a silver chain of sweet tinkling bells such as Garn's daughter Iynne wore upon occasion. I could not imagine Iynne splashing through a river with a kicking sheep across her mount, one hand fast in its wool, the other beating the pony on its rump to urge it on.

When the Wise Woman did not turn inward at Milos's choice I was startled. For I had not thought that she was with Tugness's people. She and her handmaid did not camp near them at night, but rather kept their own fire a little apart. This was according to custom, for the Wise Women never lived completely in any community of a holding; they sought their own place, where they might grow their herbs and follow their ways, some of which were secret and not to be overlooked by those unlearned in their craft.

We found the beach difficult pulling for the wains and now we crawled even more slowly. That night we camped on the shore itself, with our backs to the cliff. To most of us the sea was strange and we eyed it uncertainly. Only the children went hunting shells along the edge of the waves and stood, their heads far back, watching the screaming, swooping birds who hunted their prey within the waters.

Once camp was set curiosity brought me down to where wave pursued wave, to lap and die upon the sand. The air from over the water had a richness which made a man want to fill his lungs and breathe deep. I gazed out over the darkening waters and wondered a little at the courage of those who build shells of wood to venture out on that immensity, following an art of their own, which was shield and sword against any wrath of the waves.

I caught a glint of water between rocks and went on to discover that pools were cupped by the tall stones, fed by the washing sea. Those pools had inhabitants—strange forms I had never seen, but which surprised and interested me, and I squatted on my heels to watch them for a space as they darted here and there or half hid under stones. For they were hunters all and each followed their own way of seeking food.

A splashing roused me from my study of these wily hunters and their tricks and I turned to see Gathea, her boots shed, her breeches loose from their ankle thongs and rolled up above her knees, making her way from a small reef of rock, pulling, with the full strength of her hands, a length of red, vinelike stuff from which hung great leaves dripping water. The sea vine seemed to be securely anchored, for, though she strained, it yielded only a little to her pull.

Before I thought, I pulled off my own boots and, without stopping to roll up my breeches, I waded into the wash of the water and set my hands on the slimy cord a little behind hers, lending my strength to the battle. She looked over her shoulder, a shadow of a frown at first between her sun-bleached brows. Then she gave a nod, acknowledging my offer of help, and we jerked mightily together.

In spite of the force we used that stubborn length would not give. Thus, after two such pulls, I loosed my hold and drew my sword. She nodded again but held out her hand demandingly, so I found that, in spite of myself, I allowed her to take the weapon from me, splash farther out, and while I held the vine taut, she brought the steel down, cutting the cord through in two swings. She returned to grasp the end of the vine with one hand, with the other, she proffered my sword, hilt toward me.

"My thanks, Elron of Garn's House." Her voice was low, a little hoarse, as if she seldom used it. That she knew my name I found surprising, for none of our party had had speech with her mistress during the journey. Nor was I noteworthy among my Lord's meiny. Not that Garn could boast of such a battle force as a full war band.

"What will you do with this?" I waded back to the beach and, though she neither asked for nor refused my aid, I still held to the vine and helped drag it after us.

"The leaves dried and pounded," she said as a man would discuss the setting of a plow into new ground, "can enrich the soil for planting. Also it has other properties which Zabina knows. This is a good find, taken at the best of its growing season."

I surveyed the slimy length we pulled free of the water, sand now matting down its long tendril leaves, and thought that indeed strange things must be better than they appeared.

Then she was gone, without another word, towing the weed along behind her while I rubbed sand from my legs before drawing on my boots once again. The evening shadows were well advanced and I went back to our own camp to eat and wonder what the next day would bring and how much longer we would travel on before we found the land of Garn's choice.

As I held a bowl of crumbled journey bread, softened with several dollops of stew made from dried meat, and spooned up its contents, I stopped, with the spoon halfway to my mouth, staring, as two newcomers came into the full light of our central fire. Quaine, who had been sitting cross-legged beside Garn, waved them on, though Garn himself did not raise a hand and only regarded them with a cold, level stare across the rim of his drinking horn.

Though I had seen Lord Tugness a number of times during these last days of journeying, this was the first time he had been so close that I might have put out a hand and flicked finger upon the end of his sword scabbard.

He was a short man, heavy shouldered, since his favorite weapon was the battle axe, and much practice with that had given him the muscular strength which, in another man, would have been in sword arm or thinned away by the need for agility. On horseback he was impressive; on foot he walked with a short stride which made him appear top-heavy.

Like the rest of us, he wore a mail shirt over travel jerkin, but tonight he carried his created helm, the wind blowing through his thick, ragged growth of red-brown hair. Unlike most of our race he also had a noticeable growth of facial hair, a matter in which he appeared, against custom, to take pride, and this he had trained into a fringe of beard about his wide mouth. Above that his nose was not much more than a blob of flesh so that his breath came constantly in snorts—the broken and flattened cartilage the result of a fight in his youth.

Beside Garn he slouched and looked far more like a rough blank-shield hired for some slightly unsavory task of secret rapine than a lord of lineage as long and as well songed by the Bards as any House which had come through the Gate.

Taller than his father and much sparer of frame was his son-heir, who came into the full light a step behind. He was a spear-shaft of a youth who shambled as he walked, his arms hanging. Of course, those who knew him or had heard of him were well aware he was not the staring simpleton he looked. His skill with the crossbow was a matter of comment. But he was a silent shadow of his father, having little to do with those his own age. If one addressed him he was likely to stare round-eyed and answer slowly in as few words as possible.

Lord Tugness came straight to the point, just as he would ride with axe ready against any opponent. However, it was to Quaine that he spoke, ignoring Garn, even hunching a shoulder a little as if to shut out the sight of his old-time enemy.

"When do we get free of this devil's stew?" he demanded, kicking into the loose sand, sending bits of grit flying to make sure that the Sword Brother understood his meaning. "My fore team is already neck-galled from pulling and we have no spare beasts. You have promised us land, Sworder, where is it?"

Quaine showed no sign of affront. He had arisen and stood facing Tugness, his fingers locked in the fore of his belt as he met the clan lord's stare.

"If the Flame favors us, Lord Tugness, we shall be within arrow flight of your land before sundown tomorrow."

Tugness gave one of his heavy snorts. I saw his fingers curl as if they held an axe. His eyes, under the brush of his heavy brows, demanded recognition from the Sword Brother.

"We would be on good land." Again he stamped with his boot into the sand. "This stuff gets even between a man's teeth when he eats, down his throat when he drinks. We have had our fill of it! Be matters as you say, Sworder!" His last words might almost be a threat, as he swung his heavy body about, sending sand spurting on those nearby. Behind, Thorg, his son-heir, trod with a light-footedness which might almost be that of a scout in enemy land. Also as he went Thorg suddenly lifted his head a little and I found him looking straight at me.

I was young and Garn recked me of little account, as I have well known since childhood. Still I am able to see promises which men's eyes may hold, even though the rest of their faces give no sign of feeling. I stopped in mid-bite when I caught that look from Thorg. My first reaction was surprise. Then, I hoped with all my might a moment later, I had not shown it. For why should the son-heir of Tugness, whom I had never had any reason to cross in any way, show me black and deadly hate? I told myself that I was not—that I could not have been—his enemy except that I was of my House and he of his, but I could not put aside the belief that there was more to his feeling concerning me than any formal feud. His look, then, troubled me.

There was a moon that night, fair and cold, and silver-clear. Its beam helped to hide those stars which were not as they should have been. There are old tales that the moon plays a part in the lives of men, setting upon them its touch in mind and heart, even as the sun can show its mark on skin by browning with its fire-heat. But moon power is not for men, it is a thing of the women and those among them especially who have the wise knowledge.

I had drawn a little apart from the row of men who were asleep, waiting to take their turn at night sentry duty. I rested some distance from the wains. Thus it was that I saw in the moonlight the

Wise Woman stride, tall and with a hurried step, along the sands. Behind her but a step or two came Gathea, a bundle in her arms held close to her breast, as if she carried a child or some treasure which must be closely guarded, even from the moon's rays.

North they went along the sands and I knew that no sentry would dare to speak with them, or even perhaps let them know that he saw them passing. For it was very plain that the Wise Woman was now about some business of her own craft. Yet there was one who moved in the shadows, came to a line of rocks which were the last bit of cover before the open beach.

I edged over on my side, pushed away the cloak which covered me. It was important to me, though I did not question why, that I know who it was who had followed those two up the beach and now watched their going from his own hiding place.

Though I might not be as skilled as a Sword Brother, I had hunted game, yes, and taken much training in the methods of fighting known best to us—a sudden surprise and quick attack meaning more than any sustained battle. Now, on hands and knees, taking advantage of another upthrust tooth of rock, I found a vantage point from which I could spy upon that watcher.

For what seemed like a very long time we remained so—he in his hiding, I in mine. Then he came away from his post—for the women were gone and there was nothing to be seen under the moon now but the ever restless inward sweep of the waves. I could not see his face, but by his walk I knew him. Why had Thorg followed the Wise Woman and her handmaid? He had broken custom and would have brought on him swift punishment had he been sighted. Not perhaps from the men, but the women of his own house and clan might have set upon him, as was their right. For in the things of women's knowledge no man might meddle and their vengeance to protect that right was keen and swift.

He was gone back toward Tugness's camp and I did not follow him. I was left to wonder why he had dared flout custom. He could not have an eye for Gathea—the very thought of that was enough to unsteady one. Still—

I shook my head against my own wild thoughts and dozed until I was called to the last sentry go, when dawn was not far away and I was able to see the sun rise. It was an odd rising, for to seaward rested a vast bank of clouds close to the water, yet in the early morning those clouds looked solid, like an island, as far as one could see, lying offshore. There were peaks and lowlands, and all in heavy shadow so that I would have sworn one could take boat and go out to set foot on a land freshly born in the night offshore. Never had I seen such a cloudbank and it held me amazed. Then when I heard a faint clink behind me I had sword out before I swung around, and felt foolish to see Quaine standing there, his hands once more hooked in his belt, staring as I had out to sea.

I resheathed my sword as he spoke.

"One would think that land—"

"I do not know the sea," I said. "Perhaps that is common in the dawning hereabouts."

He shook his head. "No—it is like having the far sight. Look!"

There was urgency in his voice and I followed with my eyes the hand he flung out. I had noticed that there were mountains upon that cloud land, stark against the reddening sky. Now against the side of one of those was defined more sharply than any of the other smooth contours of the cloud place, what was surely very like a keep, a square-walled fortress from which arose two towers, one a fraction shorter than the other. So complete and solid did that appear that I would have sworn the place existed. The coming of the light, though it faded the dark of the rest of the cloudbank, did not change the darkness of that blot.

It had been solid, easy to see, then it was gone! Not wafted away by the slow change and drift of clouds, but winking out, as if it were a torch of lamp which had been blown into nothingness. Still so clear was its outline in my mind that I could have taken a stick and drawn its outline on the smooth sands.

I looked to Quaine, for I was sure that this was no freak of night but something strange, perhaps a part of those wonders of this land concerning which we had been warned. Also I had so strong a feeling that somewhere the keep I had seen did exist that I was moved by a wish to search it out. I spoke part of my thought aloud:

"The keep—it—it was real—"

Quaine looked at me sharply, a look I expected mainly from Garn when I was at fault in a matter. "What did you see?" he asked and his voice was soft, like a whisper, which barely sounded above the constant wash of the waves.

"A keep, double-towered. But how could such stand upon clouds—?"

"Clouds can form many things if one watches them," he returned. I felt ashamed as might a child who sees all that lies in a songsmith's tale taking shape about him, making monsters from rocks, and magic by his own inner thinking.

Yet Quaine continued to stand and watch the cloud island until it was fully revealed for what it was. There had been no dark spot where that keep had been for a long time, and I could hear our camp stirring into wakefulness. Then the Sword Brother turned away from the sea and gazed again at me as if he sought in some way to search out my thoughts.

"This is a strange land." Again he spoke very low as if he were sharing a secret. "There is much in it which we cannot understand. The wise man will leave such alone. But—" He hesitated and then continued. "To some of us curiosity is a goad. We have that in us which must learn more and more. Only here there are no trail guides and the fool may well vanish into his folly. Walk you with care, young Elron. I think that perhaps you are one with the Burden—"

"The Burden?" I repeated without understanding.

"The wise, or those who think them so, call it that. There are others who might name it a 'gift.' It is how you use it or abuse it which counts—and how you learn what you must learn. I will say this to you—do not go recklessly in this land. It is doubly perilous to those who have more than first sight."

He strode off abruptly even as he uttered that last word of warning—a warning against what I could not tell. Nor did I understand why he spoke of a "burden" and a "gift." I was only a very small part of my lord's following, just as his House was a very poor and weak one. What I had mainly were the clothes on my back, the sword and mail shirt and helm which had been my father's before me, and a thin pack of possessions in one of the wains: a ballad book of old runes which I could puzzle out, though the runes were different from those we used today; a tunic of good wool for feast days; some body linen and a belt knife, jeweled and fancifully hilted, which had been my mother's. Certainly no burden—

As we moved out that morning I kept remembering that keep I had seen among the cloud mountains. Had Quaine seen it also? When he had asked me to tell him of my discovery he had not acknowledged it, although he had drawn my attention to it at first. The Sword Brothers had their own form of knowledge. They had explored this land before we had braved the Gate. It could be that something of what they had learned they kept to themselves, or shared only with the senior members of the council.

Still I carried with me as I rode slowly on, matching the pace of the wains, two mysteries to mull over: first why Thorg had followed the Wise Woman and her maid as if he were a spy trailing some enemy; second, what I had seen in the clouds. For a part of me stubbornly declared, past all calm reasoning, that I had seen something which was different and to be noted only because we traveled a land steeped in all that was alien to what we had always known.

Quaine was right. We did come, at last, to another indentation among the cliffs and so out into a dale which, though its sea entrance was narrow and it had no means of acting as a port, widened out well into a broad sweep of lowlands, now brilliant green with the grass of spring, such a fair country as even Lord Tugness could not fault. There his people turned aside, one of Quaine's two men riding with them.

We made brief farewells since there was no friendship between us, only the fact that we were fellow travelers from the same source. I heard our fieldsmen comment upon the rich look of the soil, and express their hopes that we would be served as well when we came to our own place. But what mattered somehow more to me was that the Wise Woman also turned her cart into the way marked by Tugness's heavier wagons. I was sorry to see that she had chosen to remain here rather than go with us.

Our own train, now reduced, rolled slowly on. Once more we camped upon the beach and this time the moon was veiled in clouds. This time I did not, when I took my watch in the early hours, see any cloud island offshore. Instead a wind drove at us, spattering salt spray at times, though we camped well about the waterline. The next morning the rain was once more upon us.

The wagons found heavy work of it. Often we had to dismount and set our shoulders to the push, or fasten our mounts with extra lead ropes to add their strength.

We were worn with the fatigue of that fight against the land itself when we rounded once more a cliff wall and found a bay, much smaller than those farther south and menaced by reefs which showed brokenly in ledges out to sea, so that it would give little welcome to any seafarers. But into it flowed a river and I did not need Garn's hail to know that we had reached our abiding place.

The cart animals made a last pull, we lifted sheep, drove cattle up along the riverbank which ran for a short length between cliffs in which sea birds roosted, the rocks stained white with the droppings of many years.

Those winged ones wheeled angrily above us, voicing sharp cries which echoed even more loudly from the stone walls about. Then we were at last through that passage and came out into a land which seemed as fair at first sight as that which Lord Tugness had claimed. The sheep and cattle fell at once to cropping the new grass and we pulled up the wains by the riverside, for the moment content to rest and rejoice that we were at last in what would be our own land—clan land for us and our blood forever more.

3

I HAD FOUGHT MY WAY UP A STEEP RISE WHERE THE ROCK BONES of the land had pushed through soil which grew thinner until it only lay in pockets, sometimes enough to give rootage to coarse grass or wind-twisted bushes. Not until I reached the top of that cliff and felt the keener wind of the heights about me did I turn to gaze down into Garnsdale.

In the woods, which looked from here like a lumpy carpeting of greenery (for spring passed swiftly and leaves doubled in size overnight), I could see those openings where trees had already fallen to busy axes, to be denuded of branches and drawn down to that place which Garn had selected for a temporary keep.

Four of the wain horses were engaged in that transport. The other six were already at plows used for the heavy work of breaking thick sod to open ground for planting. There was constant labor to which each man and woman lent their strength, whether of lord-kin or field clan. I was free this day because it was my turn at patrol along the heights. For, as open as the land seemed, and as empty, still Garn did not take for granted that it lacked possible dangers. In addition those patrolling the heights were also named hunters and anything they could add to the pot was welcome.

Quaine and his two men had stayed with us for ten days and then had gone, heading back westward in a general sweep into the unknown. Even as I played sentry on the dale ridges, so were they to patrol the whole of the western borders, they and their brothers, sentinels and guards for all the new settled dales. One of their duties was to seek out and map for us any remains of those vanished beings we had begun to call the Old Ones, they who had left this land before our coming.

One reminder of them was placed above this very valley. Though it was unimpressive—according to Quaine—compared to those seen elsewhere, still it was a place each patrol warrior watched and made himself familiar with—as I was about to do.

I went in mail, helmed, carried my crossbow as well as my sword, almost as if I were indeed prepared to meet attack, though certainly we could well have come into a deserted world for all we had seen. Now I jumped a crevice in the rocks and turned westward to begin the prowling along what we all accepted as the southern border of our new holding. So few were our party that Garn could only detach two fighting men at a time for this duty and we were expected to provide him with a full report upon our return.

There was animal life to be found here. The wild creatures were not too different, save perhaps in color or size, from those I had hunted all my life. A species of deer, very fleet of foot, had used the dale for pasturage until our coming; now fled and seldom seen. However, there was also a creature which lived in the upper rocks, nearly as large as a new-thrown foal, but heavy of body. It had wicked claws and fangs and a temper to match so that one was wary in the hunt, but it was excellent eating.

Always there were birds, some brilliant of wing, bright flashes against the sky. Another species were black and somehow unpleasant to look at. Those roosted in flocks upon the trees, screeching in rage at our axemen. When they took to the sky, they winged westward as if they sped to report the devastation we wrought in what had been their stronghold. I saw them rise now and wheel once over the forest—then speed away just above the height of the ridge.

I kept close watch on what might come among these rocks. Roff had reported from his tour of duty yesterday that he had discovered some odd tracks, deep printed in one of the pockets of earth, as if that which had made them had come to the very edge of the ridge and perhaps spied upon us. Save that the tracks were those of a large padded paw, as wide as his own hand. It might well be that he had found a trace of some native animal which was more dangerous—a hunter who would come hunting us.

Thus I had shed my boots before the climb, putting on rather the softer and almost shapeless foot coverings which hunters used, and through which my feet could feel the surface of the rock as I went, making as little noise as possible. The air was fresh and clean, and I believed that it did carry in it the faint scent of growing things, sometimes even a trace of what might have come from wind-stirred branches of blooming trees or bushes.

That there were such here I discovered shortly, for there was a dip in the westernmost part of the ridge, and, advancing with caution to the rim of that, I looked down into a cup of land which held our own trace of the Old Ones. Trees hardly taller than my own head, but old, judging by the gnarled trunks and crooked branches, were set evenly spaced about a square of pavement.

Those trees were in full blossom, their flowers being of a creamy pink-white, large and nearly flat, the tip of each wide petal rimmed with a darker pink. Many of those petals, already wind loosened, had shifted down to lie upon the stretch of stone pavement. Though the petals lay there no grass clump had taken root, nor was there any trace of moss on the stones' surfaces. Inlaid in the center of the square was a symbol in the form of a moon-shaped curve—this fashioned of a bluish stone, quite unlike that about it, which appeared to have a metallic sheen under the sun's touch. Each corner of the square was also marked by a column which rose to near my own height. These were topped by bold carvings: a circle, and then half circle, quarter circle, and a dark disc of another sort, dead black, though the others were of the glistening blue.

Since this place had been first sighted a few of us had discussed it often. Iynne, who had made a secret visit with her brother, had declared that it was moon magic of a sort and that the carvings denoted the moon itself in its four phases. She had been most excited and had spoken several times of how she wished to see it under a full moon to test if some ancient power had centered there. That she would dare such a venture on her own I doubted. Nor did I believe that any man would aid her in it. Garn's hand would be heavy and quick to punish any such rank folly.

In fact, his orders were that no one of us must even venture foot into that pocket of land. We were to view it at least twice on each sentry go, but leave it inviolate. Which was prudent.

But prudence was not always a virtue of the young, and I longed to go down to see if those symbols and carvings were inlaid metal which had survived the erosion of time and weather. Also there was nothing of a threat here. Instead, even as I stood above and watched petals gently fall upon the stone, I felt a kind of peace and a strange longing, I could not have said for what, save that it was in me. Thus I shook myself, as if another put hands on me to awaken me sharply to my duty, and moved on, though it seemed that there also moved with me the scent of the blossoms, even a faint tugging, as if the unknown would hold me back.

I was not, I had always believed, one who was given to fancies and dreams. Such could not have lasted in Garn's house without alteration of his own ways of thought. To my lord all which dealt with feeling was suspect. Now, since I had come through the Gate, I knew restlessness. I was plucked by a desire to stride out across this land without any ties, as if I were a Sword Brother, free to learn both its good and evil. I slept badly, had to fight that unease and longing, to set my hand to the work before us with strong self-discipline. It was no labor for me to patrol; rather I looked forward to my duty day with a light heart and a surge of pleasure which I was careful not to mention.

The rounds of the dale walls took all of the day, from the morning sun to the long twilight of summer, and one could not linger on the way. Now I set forth at my best walking speed, keeping to the track I already knew.

To the south the ridge was very wide, its coating of rocks bare of any growth, dark gray and somber. This wilderness of wind-worn stone could be crossed to come into Tugness's hold, but none of us went that way. To the west the ridges bordered the stream to form a second narrow throat where cliffs rose even higher, leaving a sheer drop into the water both on south and north bank. So broken were the stone walls there that one went with caution. There was no crossing of the river from above so that there were two of us who patrolled—one to the north and one to the south—usually making rendezvous at the stream cliffs and waving to one another across the chasm.

Hewlin had alternate duty this day and such was his authority I had no desire to be late in reaching the point of meeting, though afterwards we would eat our rations at our pleasure, and consider the prospect of a hunt before we returned, to descend to the valley floor.

Hewlin was a little before me, leaning back against a postlike rock. He raised a hand and I answered his salute. Also I noted that he had better luck than I, for by his feet lay one of the rock beasts, cleaned and ready to be turned over to the cook. I waved to him in a gesture of congratulation, to which he made no answer, dour as ever. Then he picked up his kill and went off. I lingered where I was to eat my ration and drink the warmish water from my canteen.

There was another flight of the black birds, winging down the passage carved by the stream, so low I could see them easily from my perch. Their eyes were a brilliant red, and there was raw lapping of red flesh about their strong black bills so that they had a diseased look which added to their unpleasant appearance. Two of them broke from the flock as they approached, to circle directly above my head, their coarse, harsh cries breaking that peace I had felt ever since I had looked upon the Moon Shrine.

One swooped straight for me without warning. As I flung up my arm in haste, its claws actually tore at the leather sleeve of my jerkin. I drew my sword and scrambled to my feet as the two continued to circle in a manner I had never before seen birds use against a man.

The glint of their red eyes was bright, their open bills continued to loose cries. Again one swooped. I swung at the bundle of feather. It eluded me easily. The other now was already on its way down to attack. For the first time I was uneasy. My defense could only be clumsy, I had no real way of avoiding those claws and beaks if they continued so. Unless I found cover. I glanced quickly around to sight a leaning stone, which should give me protection if I set my back to it, even though that would force me into a hunched position.

Those two winged furies tied me into that scrap of cover. Though the rest of the flock were gone, it would seem that these were determined to carry to the finish whatever quarrel they fancied they had with my kind.

The shelving rock protected my head and shoulders. If they

would come at me now they must fly low and in, where I could meet any such attack with a calculated swing of steel. So I waited. However, it was almost as if the flyers had the power of reasoning and were too wary to give me any advantage. Instead they continued to keep me besieged.

My anger grew. That two birds could so use a man, almost playing with him (or so it appeared to me at that moment) fueled that anger. My greatest uneasiness for some time was that their constant cries might bring a return of the entire flock. While it seemed out of all reason that birds would attack—would be able to overpower an armed man—I began to believe that these could well do so. Certainly they could if I were in the open giving them room to fly as they pleased.

I tried to think of my next move. My crossbow was slung on my shoulder but its bolts were never meant for the hunting of birds and I did not believe that I could make good use of such a weapon here. How then was I to break out of hiding, for they showed no sign of withdrawing? They might have arranged to hold me at bay awaiting reinforcements to move in, even as those hounds which the greater lords bred for the chase did with some quarry too large or dangerous for them to pull down by their own efforts.

They still swooped and circled about my rock refuge and then— so suddenly that they left me near off balance—they both shot up into the sky uttering squawks which sounded different from their hunting cries, more as if they themselves were under attack, though I could not see what would send them so away.

I waited a long moment. However, the birds were definitely gone, winging off still squawking, to follow the vanished flock. In spite of that, I kept steel in hand as I emerged from my refuge, for I could not put aside the idea that they had been driven off by no effort of mine but by something else that walked here.

In a moment I saw her.

Gathea, the Wise Woman's handmaid, stood on a taller rock so that I must look up at her. Her hands were held high as her fingers wove patterns in the air. I saw, too, that her lips moved, but I could hear none of the words.

So I saw her and behind her—

I cried a quick warning, readied my crossbow to take aim. Then my finger froze to the trigger as if I had been suddenly encased in the stone about me. I saw her right hand point to me and realized, with a rush of sheer fear, that some power I could not understand, something this girl could use even as I used bolt and sword, held me prisoner.

Still—behind her— She must be warned!

I shouted then and perhaps my fear, mingled with growing anger (because she had mastered me so) made the shout echo back from the cliffs.

Behind the rock on which Gathea stood showed the furred, fanged head of a great cat. It arose on hindquarters, planting wide, well-clawed paws on either side of the girl's feet. Its head lifting so that it could stare, yellow-eyed around her legs directly at me. It snarled and those huge curved fangs in its upper jaw looked as long and sharp as a table dagger, and much more deadly.

Gathea turned her head to look down at the beast. This time I saw no movement of *her* eyes, only that its head moved so that their gazes met and held for a long moment. Then it dropped back on the ground and padded around, to stand between us, still eyeing me, but with those gaping jaws closed. I could not doubt that in some way (perhaps the same way that she had controlled the birds) she also had dominion over this formidable beast.

Her hand gestured. I was free. But I was also wise enough to lower my weapon, offering no threat. Still the strangeness of this meeting held me where I was, almost as if I still were bespelled. The cat was a thing of wild beauty, I was willing to acknowledge that. Its coat was a silvery gray-white with a faint mottling of darker silver along the back and haunches. I had never seen its like before.

"He—he is tame—" I found words which were neither quite statement nor question. This animal had not traveled with her certainly, thus it was a beast of the dales. How had this girl discovered it in so short a time, bent its will to hers?

"Not tame." She shook her head firmly. "For that would mean that his will is broken to that of man. Such is an abomination with his kin-kind. He recognized that I mean him no harm—that I am a seeker. Perhaps long ago his kind knew other seekers and were friend-kin to them. This is a land rich in much—" Her hands went out in a small gesture as if she would gather to her something proffered which was her life's desire. I saw excitement and longing in her eyes then, yes, and a kind of joy which was wild and free. "If we do not take it harshly then we shall be repaid many times over. Only—" Now her eyes turned as fierce as the cat's—"it seems it is not the way of men to do anything but pit their strength and impose their will wherever they go."

"You—what did you do with the birds?" I did not want to argue with her. Also, I was still angry—a little because she had seen no harm in bending *me* to her will, though she denied that she would use an animal so, more at the fact that she had brought an end to an attack I had seen no way of countering in so easy a fashion.

"I—no, that is not for the telling, Elron of Garn's House. Let it be that those who live at peace with all living things and do not strive to make them slaves and servants have in turn certain authority they may call upon at their need."

"The birds are hardly servants!" I retorted.

"None of ours, no. They are servants, I think, of ancient evil. Perhaps they were once sentries. There is a covey of such also in Tugness's dale—though Zabina is seeking to discover why they watch and where they go—"

I was caught by what might have earlier seemed to me to be sheer fancy. Could birds be trained to spy, to report? If so, to whom *did* they carry news? Should Garn be warned? I thought I could see already his look of scorn if I advanced such a theory to him.

"Your Wise Woman," I said, "if she discovers—will she share such knowledge?"

"If it would be necessary for the good of all, yes." Gathea nodded. "We have seen them watch and fly, but before this they have never tried to attack. What did you do to awaken their rage?"

I was irritated that she would immediately assume that I was the provoker of that very one-sided engagement.

"Nothing but stand here—watch them fly west. They sit most days in the wood to spy upon the loggers, before they scream and fly."

"So have they done also in Tugness's dale. It may be that now they would try their strength. I would warn those you know to take care. They could well worry sheep, even cattle, to their deaths. Take an eye from a man. . . . Look to the mark you bear now."

She pointed to the sleeved arm I had raised to protect myself at the first attack. The leather was scored and torn.

Before I could answer, she leaped lightly down from the rock on which she had taken her stand. The cat, who had been blinking sleepily, arose. His head was near to her shoulder and she dropped one hand on the thicker fur which nearly formed a ruff at his forequarters.

"Do you go alone? There may be worse than evil birds—" I knew even as I spoke that my words sounded not at all firm as I had intended but rather as a weak warning which she would be likely to meet with the same scorn as Garn might show at my bird story.

"I am in search of that which is strong for what we need," she answered obliquely. "Zabina has used the Sight, but here there are veilings so one cannot work too much with the Talent for fear of awaking that which is better left to slumber. This land is, in many ways, a trap. We may not have had much choice in our coming, but now we must walk as one does between two armies, both of which are our enemies."

In spite of myself, she impressed me. We did not remember what had driven us through the Gate (it must have been fear—some disaster which had given us no other choice). Now in spite of the Sword Brothers' reassurance, I accepted that this land might also have, as she called them, traps, elements that even those scouts and warriors had not yet chanced to discover.

Still we were here and there was no going back. What came to us we must face, with steel if need be, or perhaps by believing in such messages as this Wise Woman's maid had just given me.

She was moving on, and, since her path ran the way of my patrol, I hurried after her. The cat, coming to its feet, padded soft-footedly ahead, pausing now and then to sniff at one of the rocks, though I could see no reason for such interest.

"Have you any of the Old Ones' places in your dale?"

She had her head up, turned away from me, to gaze straight ahead, and sometimes she paused, looking to her right, her nostrils expanding as if, like the cat, what she sought she could first scent.

"No—nor is it *our* dale," she returned with a sharpness which I would not allow to quell my curiosity, or my need to learn more from her—and of her. "We are no clan-kin of Lord Tugness—nor others." She frowned. "There was a need, thus we went with his people. Whether we remain," she shrugged, " that will be for future deciding. Ah—"

She flashed ahead, darting around tumbled rocks, streaking across open spaces with the fleetness of the gray deer which our coming had driven out of the dale. Before her bounded the silver cat, overleaping some of the obstructions she had to round. Because I must discover for myself what had sent her off so eagerly, I pounded after, dropping well back, unable to match her pace, weighed down as I was by my weapons and gear.

Then I realized in what direction she moved. She was heading straight for that small hidden valley of the Moon Shrine. Remembering Garn's orders, I pushed my pace. None were to enter there, he had warned. We were not to explore whatever was made by those who had long gone. But that I could keep Gathea away was a vain hope.

I called out twice. It was as if both she and the cat were deaf; neither turned head nor slowed their pace. By the time I reached the edge of that hidden place, the girl was standing between the two trees which fronted the square. Her hands were pressed tight to her breast, her eyes fixed upon that pavement, as if it enshrined some great wonder visible to her alone.

Behind her crouched the cat, this time its eyes were not half closed, but alert, also watching.

Gathea took a step forward.

"No!" I raised my voice, tried to leap over the rim, to forestall her before she ventured onto the pavement.

I tried to leap, only to sprawl backward in a tumble of limbs and body, the crossbow flying away, myself kicking to regain my balance as might a beetle which has been turned on its back.

I scrambled to my knees, flung out an arm ahead. I might have driven my fist against a wall of the same rock as lay all about. There was a barrier there—one I could neither see nor force. Now I used the fingertips of both hands, feeling up and up until I stood once more. Both my hands ran across something—something which held me out yet appeared to have let Gathea past.

When I looked down I saw her standing just on the edge of the square. To her right was lifted on the pillar that dark disc, to her left one of brilliant blue. Her eyes were still fixed in that stare and I watched her lips again move in soundless speech.

Slowly she went down to her knees, her hands sweeping out, her head bowed forward, as if she paid the most formal of homage to some great lord. Petals still drifted through the air; several fell to lie upon her head.

Her hands moved once more as she gently swept some of those which lay upon the pavement, gathering them into the hollow of her right palm. Once more her head lifted so I could see her face. Her eyes were closed and she had a listening look as if she heard some message of import which she must remember and deliver to another.

Again she bowed, but this time she held against her heart the palmful of petals. Then she arose, and, at the same time that she turned away, like one who had completed a task, the surface against which my hands had been pressed vanished.

I pushed again farther on—to encounter nothing. Still I did not leap down into the dell as I had planned to do. Here, that would have seemed more than discourtesy—an outrage of a sort. I shook my head, trying to free it of such fancies. Only I knew that these were no fancies, that what I thought was real. I dared not intrude upon the Moon Shrine, though there was no threat of evil, merely the realization that it was not for such as me. Tramping in, I would break some beautiful thing which was precious beyond my imagining.

Now I lingered for Gathea to rejoin me and it was not until she was some distance away that I understood she was headed south. Apparently she had no intention of sharing a path any farther. The cat followed her for a space, while I stood and watched her, uncertain of what to do or say.

Then that silver body again flashed up into the air in a graceful leap as the cat left her, heading westward and south, apparently seeking its own way along the rim of the other dale. I remained alone as Gathea walked steadily forward, and not once did she look back or speak any farewell.

When I finally realized that she was on her way back to her mistress I started my patrol once more. How much of what had happened would I report? Never before had I thought to conceal from Garn any part of what I had seen. Only this time I had a feeling that what I had just witnessed had not only been no business of mine, but also it was not for Garn's prying. For he might possibly order perhaps even the destruction of the Moon Shrine (yes, that crossed my mind). He detested, I well knew by now, all elements of the unknown that could not be met by physical force, and he would be angry that Gathea had manifestly found something here of power. I had, too. That invisible wall which had held for a while was certainly no dream.

The birds, yes, of those I would tell him. For it might be as Gathea had warned, those could turn against us and our animals. So we would have to be forewarned and forearmed against that danger.

Thus I was carefully building up my report as I made my way back down to the dale. At the same time I also longed to know what had been present in the Moon Shrine Gathea had paid homage to—and what other things might be found in this land—of good or ill—if one was free to go seeking such.

4

THOUGH I WAS FIRST TO MEET THE HOSTILITY OF THE BIRDS, I WAS not the last. As we cut deeper into the wood, brought out more trimmed trees to be used for the building of a long hall to shelter our small clan for at least a season, the birds gathered more thickly about the scene of our labors. Then the children who had the herding of our few sheep raised shouts of alarm, and went in, flailing with staffs, to keep deadly beaks from six newborn lambs upon whose lives depended much future promise.

Finally Garn had to withdraw men from necessary labor to use hunters' bows and keep watch with the herd. The birds appeared to have uncanny skill in avoiding even the best of our marksmen. Thus tempers grew ragged, Garn's cold displeasure ever present, as what had seemed a petty thing grew into a constant threat.

It was not until we had thinned the trees which were the strongest and the most likely to serve as good building material that we found at last what was perhaps the reason for that baffling attack. For, when one morning a giant fell beneath our axes it took with it a mass of creeper already well in leaf, flattened thick brush, to show us that the Moon Shrine was not after all the only relic of the Old Ones in our chosen dale.

Again pillars stood, having avoided the flattening of whatever had screened them, as if they had power to hold away the tree. There were seven of these, near the height of Garn himself, placed closely together so that perhaps only a hand might be slipped between the column of one and the next.

Unlike the rocks of the ridges which formed our boundaries

these were of a dull yellow stone, oddly unpleasing to the eye. Also their surfaces had a smooth look in spite of what must have been long exposure to plants, wind and rain, reminding one of a foul mud frozen into shape. Each of them bore, halfway down one side, an incised panel on which was carved a single symbol, all differing one from the other.

When our clearing exposed these to the sun there was an instant boiling up of the birds whose cries and circling of the workers were so threatening that Garn gave an order to fall back, leaving our laboriously axed tree lying where it had fallen for the time being.

Luckily, as we thought then, the birds kept up their clamor, their low flights, only for a short time. Then they flocked together, winging their way west, paying no more attention to what had been wrought. Nor did they return. Thus after three days of freedom from their noisome company Garn ordered the tree to be brought out by the aid of our horses. He did not need to warn any against going near those pillars, nor did we cut any more in that direction. We all by now disliked the sight of such relics.

The heavy work of plowing the first fields was complete, our carefully hoarded seed sown. Still we, fieldmen and kin alike, were not easy in our minds until the first sprouts showed, proving that what we had brought with us had indeed taken root in this alien soil. Now, sparing disasters only too well known to those who till the fields, we would not lack for a crop this season, small though that might be.

Some of the women, under the eye of Fastafsa, the Lady Iynne's old nurse, now keeper of the house for Garn, sought out other growing things. There were berries beginning to ripen, and certain herbs which the women recognized as stuff fit for the pot. Those stars over our heads might be strange, but this country seemed in some ways like the land from which we had come.

We had the walls of the hall raised—not of stone, rather logs dressed to the best of our ability. This first shelter was one long building which was partitioned to serve the families of the clan: a wide central space where we might eat together as did all kin and clan, at high and low tables. There were wide fireplaces at either end of the building and a third at the side of the hall, these cunningly constructed by Stig's orders from specially selected stones taken from the stream bottom where water had washed them smooth. When the roof of poles, cut and well fastened to three long central beams, supported within by firm pillars, was complete, we had a small feasting to celebrate the completion of our first shelter. Stig's youngest son was chosen to climb and fasten to the roof peak that bunch of lucky herbs the women had prepared.

For the flock and the herd, their numbers being small, we set up pole shelters. As yet we did not know how severe the ice months might be in this new land. Meanwhile, the building being over, those of us who had hunters' skills went out daily to bring in what we could of meat to be smoked over fires carefully tended for that purpose. There were fish to be taken, too, and enough were netted to fill several barrels.

In that time of steady labor we saw no others except those of our own clan. I had half expected the Sword Brothers to return. Yet none came, nor did any of Tugness's people make the journey across ridges to see how we might fare. Still, each time I patrolled in the heights—as Garn still continued to have us do—I would pause by the Moon Shrine and search for some sign that Gathea had been there.

The blossoms of spring were long since gone, and the trees about that pavement grew leaves strange to me. These were of a darker green than usual and very, very glossy; also they were vined with a color which showed as blue in the full sunlight as the symbols left by the long-vanished builders.

Twice I surprised Iynne there, gazing into the shrine as if she sought something. Each time she appeared startled by my coming. At the first such meeting she begged me not to speak of her seeking this place. It was wrong but I obeyed her wishes, not because Garn's daughter was any I might look upon as heart-lady, for we were too close kin and had been more as brother-sister for most of our lives.

Still, her secret visits to this place bothered me. Firstly Iynne was not such as went adventuring. By nature she had always been a shy and timid girl, one who found quiet pleasure in women's tasks within the keep. She was very clever with her needle, and near as good as old Fastafsa herself at brewing and baking, the ordering of a household.

I knew that Garn had sworn her hand to the second son of

Lord Farkon. An excellent match, one which would bring Garn and all the kin a strong backing. Though as yet the time for Flame and Cup had not been set. We of the kin did not wed by choice, rather to further the good of our Houses and it was much a matter of fortune how matters went after we had come to the marriage bed.

The field people were freer, though still there was sometimes hurt and suffering because one sire or another would arrange a union to make sure that there was some small advantage for both households. Once or twice I had seen Iynne at the handfasting of some field girl, watching intently the smiling face of the bride. Did she ever think of the long journey down coast which would come in due time after which she might not ever see again this dale which her father governed?

We did not talk of such things; it was against custom, but I believed that Iynne's sweet face and quiet, competent ways must earn her a favored place in any keep to which she would go. I had seen Lord Farkon's son—a tall young man comely enough, having both his father's favor and his brother's liking, an unusual combination among our people—so I believed she should be one of the fortunate ones in the end.

Why she now broke with all the rules of our people to steal away secretly to this place she did not tell me, though I asked. All she would reply was that she had to. Then she was confused and near weeping so I did not push her further, though I warned her against danger and tried to make her promise that she would not venture so again.

Each time she did so, swearing so vehemently that I believed her. Still I would find her there crouched at the edge of the pavement as though she were at the door of a chamber she would enter but had not yet the courage to attempt. The second time I told her that I could no longer believe her promise, that I would speak to Fastafsa to make sure that she was warded within the dale and could not slip away without the knowledge of the women. That day she cried, slowly and pitifully, as one who is bereft of a treasure for which there is no substitute. She did obey me, but so drearily that I felt a brutal overlord, though what I had done was to protect her.

The bite of fall was in the air soon after we completed the keep.

Together kin and clan labored as one to hurry the harvest. Our seed had done well in this virgin soil. Stig beamed at an ingathering which was more than he had hoped, as he said again and again—already making plans for the breaking of new fields in the next planting season.

Hewlin, during a hunting expedition at the far western end of the dale, came upon at, about the same time, a third sign that this land had once had other lords and people. For he followed the thread of our stream between those high cliffs, to discover a second and wider stretch of open land. There he had found trees heavy with fruit—what the birds and a type of wild boar had not already harvested. There was no mistaking that these had been planted, for they stood in order, with here and there a gap where one had died, leaving only a worm-eaten stump.

We went in a party to harvest what was left of that crop. Fastafsa and her women, Everad, I, and three of the household armsmen. Iynne did not choose to join us, saying that she did not feel well. Fastafsa left her bedded in one of the kin rooms of the keep.

We made a two-day journey of it since the passage up the cliff-walled stream was not too easy. In spring, if the waters arose as they must do, this way would be totally closed, I believed, noticing the high marking of past floods on the walls.

Once there we worked steadily. The armsmen ever on guard, the rest carrying and emptying baskets while Everad and I made short explorations into this second dale, seeing land which held excellent promise for our own future, advantages which would come if we could persuade Garn to expand our holding in this direction.

Save for that orchard of the past we found no other sign of the Old Ones, which was reassuring. Neither were there any birds here to raise grim warning. By the morning of the third day we were up early, ready to return downstream, each taking a hand with the loaded hampers so that there were always two men free with sword and crossbow. It would seem that in us there was always a deep uneasiness, no matter how fair or pleasant or open this country—as if we dwelt on the border of some enemy land. I found myself wondering why this was so. Except for the venture of the birds—and those were long gone—we had come across nothing threatening here. Yet we went as if we ever expected a surprise attack.

We returned to trouble, as if that which we had unconsciously feared had at last gathered force enough to strike full and hard. Hewlin came spurring his mount straight for us, well armored and in full war gear. At the sight, we men drew together, the women huddled behind us, suddenly silent where moments before there had been light laughter and singing.

The marshal of Garn's force drew rein, his sharp eyes flickering over us as if he sought one who was not there.

"The Lady Iynne," he pulled up before Everad, "she has not been with you?"

"No—but she was ill—she said— Fastafsa!" Everad turned his head to the house mistress who now pushed forward, her eyes wide, her face pale beneath the usual ruddy color.

"My lady—what do you say of her?" She elbowed past Everad, spoke to Hewlin with force and fierceness. "She was in the keep— I gave her a sleep draught before I went. With Trudas to sit near and see to her. What have you done with her?"

"She is gone. She told the maid that she felt better, asked her to get her a wallet of food and said that they would both take after you. When the girl returned—our lady was gone!"

At that moment my own guilt stung me. I could think of one place where Iynne might have gone. But if she had vanished just after we had left, then she must have been lost for a night and a day! I had only one duty and that was now to tell what I knew and take the consequences.

When I faced Garn I knew that my life rested in his hands— yet that was as nothing when I thought of Iynne exposed to such as the cat which Gathea might choose as a trail mate but which my cousin could certainly not hold in mastery. Thus I spoke clearly of what I had seen—of the Moon Shrine and Iynne's seeking it out secretly.

I saw Garn's fist rise, encased in a metal enforced glove. And I stood unresisting the blow which sent me sprawling, the taste of my own blood in my mouth. His hand flashed to his sword. He had that half drawn as I lay before him, making no defense. It was his right to slit my throat if he desired that in payment. For I was foresworn to my lord, and had broken blood-bond—as everyone who circled about us knew. Duty holds to one's lord and is our strongest law. To break that makes one kinless and clanless.

He turned on his heel then, as if I were not worth the killing, bellowing orders to those who were still his household. They left me as if in that moment I had lost existence, as, in a manner of long custom, I had.

I levered myself up, my head still spinning from that blow. Yet worse than any blow which Garn could give with his hand, was that which had come from my own treachery to my lord. There was no life here for me anymore; I could expect none to acknowledge me.

When I pulled to my feet I watched them start for that slope climbing to the Moon Shrine. Somehow I was also certain that they would not find Iynne there. Though I was foresworn and now clan-kin-dead there was one small thing left for me.

Nothing would return me to life in Garn's eyes, or in those of the clan. Still I lived, though I would rather that my lord had taken the lesser revenge and killed me, as his face showed that he had first thought to do. No, I could not turn back time and do as I should have done, but there was perhaps one way I could aid Iynne.

I had, in my blurting out concerning the Moon Shrine and her secret visits there, said nothing of Gathea, being too full of my own careless and disastrous action. If I could now reach the Wise Woman and her maid (they knew far more of the shrine than any of us, of that I was sure) there was a thin chance I might discover a trail to my cousin.

Nameless, kinless, I had no right to anything, even the sword I still wore. Garn had not taken that from me and I would keep it; perhaps I might still use it for a purpose which would—not redeem my betrayal—but at least aid Iynne.

Thus on foot I turned my back on the cliff and the people who followed Garn. Rather I moved seaward, planning to enter Tugness's dale by the other way and find the Wise Woman. My helm with its House badge I left lying where it had fallen from my head at Garn's blow, and with it my crossbow. Bare of head, empty of hands, staggering because my head rang, my eyes seeing sometimes two images of what lay before instead of one, I started downriver.

I spent the night on the shore. To a sea pool I crawled and bathed my aching face in water which stung like fire. One eye was swollen shut and the pain in my head was a pounding which made it hard for me to hold any thoughts—save one, that I must find the Wise Woman—or her maid—who knew most of the Moon Shrine and what power lay there.

I might well be a hunted man, once Garn found no trace of his daughter. Somehow I was sure that would be true—that there would be no trail left to follow among the rocks of the ridge. Yes, Garn's hate and vengeance might flame high. Any one of my own clan who brought me down would have his favor. If I were to stay alive long enough to do Iynne any service I must take care. Save that my head let thoughts slip in and out crazily, and I kept rousing to find that I had fallen in the sand, or was creeping in a mindless way along where waves dashed upward to wet my face, bringing me to consciousness again.

Night and day, I caught at what strength I had to battle my way on. At times I thought I heard shouts behind me. Once I wheeled about, waiting to see the sword raised again to cut me down. But there were only the sea birds crying in the sky.

Somehow I found my way to that place where Tugness's wains had turned from our road. There I leaned against a rock and fought for a clear head. To go openly into dale was to court disaster at once. Though he was no friend to Garn—or rather *because* he was no friend to Garn—he would take pleasure in offering me up to any who had followed me. It would be a sweet morsel to roll upon the tongue for Tugness, that one of Lord Garn's own close kin had played him false. An outlaw was fair game for any man, but I would be more valuable as a prisoner to be returned to shame those whose name I had once bore.

Thus I must use what craft remained in my aching head, such skill as I had, to avoid any of Tugness's people and search out by stealth the Wise Woman. I could not even be sure whether she would give me aid, all I had was the knowledge that those of her calling did not always hold by kin and clan custom, and that she might, in her role of healer, take pity enough on me to point me in the direction whereby I might serve the lady of Garn's House as I had not done in truth.

I do not know how I won into the dale. Some instinct stronger than my conscious self must have aided me. I was aware of fields, of a distant log walled building or rather a cluster of three such—unless my eyes were again playing me false. I think that part of the day I lay within a cup of rocks unknowing, though I had a confused dream afterward of a black bird which swooped to peck sharply at my face so that the pain of his assault stung deep. But that may only have been a dream. It was deep dark of night when I awoke with a raging thirst, my skin as hot to the touch as if I were clothed in burning brands.

I kept close to the edge of the cliff, where the ridge rise was steeper even than it was in Garn's land. A single thought held me to my path, that it was along here somewhere Gathea had found her way up, and perhaps so I might both elude anyone on watch around the holding buildings and fields, and also come across some trace of a way to the Wise Woman's place. For, remembering how she had held apart during our journeying, I was firm in the belief that she would not have become one of Tugness's household.

After a while in the dark when I fell and rose again more times than I could count, that fever which possessed me was victor, I took a last stumble which brought me down with such force that it not only drove the breath out of me but also sent me into a dark which was not sleep but something deeper and less easy for body and mind.

Thus it was in the end that those whom I sought found me, for I awoke by unhappy degrees, seeming to fight that awakening, to look up into a low roofing of poles woven and tied together with dried vines so that the whole looked like a field which had been harvested and only the dead stalks left. From this dangled bunches of drying stems and leaves, fastened together to form a kind of upside-down garden, autumn killed.

My head still ached dully; however that fire which had burnt into me was gone, though when I tried to raise my hand it obeyed me only slowly and I felt such a weakness as sent a small thrill of fear through me. Now I strove to turn my head. The ache became a piercing throb but I was able to see, yet only one-eyed. What I saw was that the bed place I occupied was against the wall of a hut which was far removed from the stout building of Garn's keep. Nor were there more than stools to sit upon and the hearth, on which a small fire smoldered, was of stones dabbed with baked clay. More stones had been used to form standards for boards laid across to make shelves. These were crowded with more bundles of dried things, as well as a number of small clay jars and pots and boxes of wood.

The air was filled with many scents, some spicy and good, some strange and distasteful. On the fire a large metal pot sat three-legged, bubbling and giving out still another odor, which made my stomach suddenly feel as empty and aching as my head.

There was movement just beyond the range of my vision until I managed to turn my head a fraction again, to see, in the half gloom of the room (for the only light filtered through two very narrow slits in the walls and from a doorway), the Wise Woman. She glanced in my direction and then came directly to me, her hand touching my forehead where once more pain flashed and I must have flinched, though I tried to hold back all sign of what torment that lightest of contacts had caused me.

"The fever is broke." Her voice was low but it somehow held a note close to that of Garn's harshest voice. "That is good. Now—" She went to the fire, ladling out of the pot a dipper of dark liquid which she poured into a rudely fashioned clay cup, adding thereto some water from a bucket, then two or three pinches of dried stuff she took from her array of pots and boxes.

I saw that, though during our journey she had worn the decent robes of any clan woman, now her kirtle had been shed for a smocklike garment which came no farther than her knees. Below that she had breeches and the same soft hunters' footgear I had worn on patrol.

She was back beside me, her arm beneath my head, lifting me up with an ease I had not thought a woman could manage, holding the still hot contents of the pannikin to my sore lips.

"Drink!" She ordered and I obeyed, as any child would obey the head of the house.

The stuff was bitter and hot, not what I might have chosen. Still I gulped it down, refusing to show any of my distaste for what I was sure was a healing brew. When I had the last of it and she would have risen, I managed to bring up my hand and tightened my fingers in the edge of her sleeve, keeping her by me while I spoke the truth, knowing that I must do this now that I was myself again in clearness of thought, for not to speak would be a second and perhaps worse betrayal.

"I am non-kin—" My own voice surprised me, for the words which formed so easily in my mind came out with halts between as if my tongue and lips were weighted.

She lowered me to the pallet, then reached up and loosened my hold.

"You are ill," she returned as if that fact could excuse a sin no matter how dark. "You will rest—"

When I tried to speak again, to make her understand, she set her fingers firmly across my lips so that once again I flinched from the pain in my swollen and distorted flesh. Then she arose and paid no more attention to me, moving around her house place as she counted those bundles and boxes on her shelves, now and again pulling one out and placing it back in another place as if there were a need that all be in a certain order.

Perhaps it was her brew which made me sleepy for I discovered that I could not keep my eyes open. Once more I fell into a state mercifully free of dreams.

When I awoke the second time it was Gathea who stood by the fire. The pot still seethed there and she was stirring its contents with a long-handled spoon so that she could remain at a little distance. Which was well, I noted, for now and then that liquid sputtered, and a spatter of its contents flew out and down into the low fire which blazed in answer. I must have made some sound of which I was not aware, or else she was set to watch me, for my eyes had not opened for more than a few breaths before she looked to me, withdrew the spoon which she laid on one of the shelves and came over, having brought another cup with her.

This time I levered myself up on one elbow, not wanting her help, and found that what she had to offer was clear water. I drained the full contents of the cup and never had anything tasted so good as that cold draft. When I was done I brought myself to make plain what her mistress had not seemed to understand:

"They have made me non-kin—" I kept my chin up, my eyes on hers. The shame was mine, but also how I bore it was mine and I could do that well or ill. "Lord Tugness shall find profit in sending me back to Garn. He may hold your Wise Woman at fault if she does not reveal where I am—"

The girl interrupted me and she was frowning. "Zabina is no kin-blood to Lord Tugness. What he will or will not do is no matter of hers. You are hurt, you need her help—that is according to her craft and let no one question her concerning that!"

I felt that she still did not understand. Among our people one who is not-kin is cursed and those who give shelter to such can also raise trouble for themselves. Henceforth no man or woman would speak me fair. I was the undead walking, and who would company with one who was nameless, clanless?

"It is because of the Lady Iynne—" That which had brought me here—not to beg their tending—filled my mind. "She went to your Moon Shrine. I found her there several times but I did not tell Lord Garn. Now she is gone, perhaps drawn into some evil spell of this land."

"We know—" she nodded.

"You know?" I struggled to sit up and managed that somehow, though my head felt as heavy as if helm of double iron now weighed it down. "You have seen her?" The thought that perhaps Iynne had encountered this girl and maybe even sheltered with her—though why she would do so—

"You talked when the fever was in you." Thus she dashed my first small hope. "Also Lord Garn came of himself to the dale in hunt. They rode westward afterward for there was no word of her here."

"West—" I echoed. Into that unknown country which even the Sword Brothers treated as a place to beware of—what would have taken Iynne there?

"She may have been called—" Gathea said as if she lifted that question from out of my thoughts. "She went to the shrine at moon's full and she was one who had no shield or protection."

"Called—by whom and to where?" I demanded.

"Perhaps it is not your right to know that. Zabina will decide. Now," she had gone to another shelf and brought me a wafer of bread fresh baked, with it a bowl of fruit stewed into a soft mass which only caused me slight pain when I ate, "fill your stomach and grow strong. There is perhaps a road for you—and others."

Leaving the meal in my shaking hands, she left the hut and I had no one left to question save myself. And I had no answers.

5

I FOUGHT AGAINST WEAKNESS, STRIVING TO MAKE MYSELF STRONG enough to leave this place. For I still knew that, Wise Woman or not, Zabina courted trouble by sheltering me. Lord Tugness, I was certain, was not one to be ruled by custom when it was to his advantage to move otherwise. Though all I knew of him came by rumor only, still in the core of such always lies a hard grain of truth.

My head still ached with dull persistence but I could see now through the eye earlier puffed shut, and my fingers, touching my skull gingerly, found that tightly clothed by a bandage. I had, in spite of waves of dizziness, managed to draw on my breeches, slide my feet into the softer trail boots and was picking up my linen undershirt (which had been fresh washed and carefully folded over my other clothing) when the Wise Woman returned.

She straightway crossed the small room to stand before me, frowning.

"What would you do?"

I pulled the shirt down over my head, tensed against the wince which came in answer to even such slight a touch on the bandage about my head. "Lady," I could not dare to bow, but I gave her courtesy of address, "I would be out of your house with what speed I can. I am kinless—" I got no further when she made an abrupt gesture to silence me before she asked a question of her own:

"Do you know what ill tie lies between Tugness and Garn?"

"Not between them." She surprised the answer out of me. "It is an old feud between the Houses."

"Yes. Old indeed. . . . Why do foolish men cling to such matters?" Her tone was one of impatience. She made another abrupt motion with one hand as if she so swept away what she had deemed foolishness. "It was started long before Garn's father came from the womb—being marriage by capture."

I sat very still, making no more move to press the shirt under the belt of my breeches. Though my head still buzzed, I was not so lacking in wit that I could not guess what she meant.

"Tugness's son?"

That Iynne's disappearance might be a simple—or simpler—matter of human contriving had not crossed my mind until that moment. Now it was far easier for me to accept that my cousin had vanished because of some stealthy act on the part of our old enemies than that she had been rift away through forces loosed in a forgotten shrine. But, this being so, how much more was I the guilty one! To achieve such an act Thorg must have spied long—lain in wait for the coming of Iynne—watched her movements until he could make sure of her. While I, who had been sent to patrol the heights, had not even suspected that we were under his eyes. I had been foolish, stupidly too interested in the strangeness of this land to take thought of old trouble.

The idea she planted in my mind grew fast. Out of it was born strength so that I was on my feet now. I might not have been able to face with success a battle with the unknown (though that would not have kept me from trying), but I could bring down Thorg. Give me only steel in hand to do so!

Now I said with authority that I might not have used moments earlier:

"Your handmaiden spoke of the force of the Moon Shrine; now you push my mind toward Thorg and old struggles. Which is the right?"

Her frown grew darker and I saw that she had caught her lower lip a little between her teeth as if to hold back some impatient or betraying words. Then she said:

"Thorg has volunteered many times through these days to go hunting. He has passed by on his way to the heights, but it would seem that his skill fails at times, for two days out of three he returns with empty hands. Also, he is not trothed to any maid. There were none who would accept Tugness's offer on his behalf. I have had to give him warning when I found him looking too often after Gathea. He is one who is hot now for a woman. It is a quarrelsome family and few can say good of their House for three generations or more. Also, there was Kampuhr—"

"Kampuhr?" I could readily accept all that she said save that last allusion which held no meaning at all for me.

She shrugged. "It is of no matter, save that it lies in the past. But it was enough to make men wonder where Lord Tugness truly stood on a certain concern that was of importance in its day— which is now past!"

Her eyes caught and held mine as if by her very will she would now impress upon me that this was to be forgotten, that she had made a slip she regretted—or had she? Somehow I believed that Zabina was not given to such errors, that perhaps she had uttered that name as a test for me—though I could not understand why.

"And Thorg?" I was willing to let the matter of her reasons be. It was far more important to think of the present than to delve into the past at this moment. "He now shelters in the keep house?"

She shook her head. "He went forth with yesterday's first sun; he has not returned. Before that he was gone for a full day also."

So he had had a good chance to do even as the Wise Woman suggested, either meet with Iynne and in some way win her favor, or else make sure that he knew her ways, lie in wait, and carry her into some hiding place of which there were far too many in this untracked land. Yes, that was all far easier to believe than that Garn's daughter had been spirited away by the unseen.

Thorg was a man and, in spite of any hunter's cunning he might possess, I believed that I could match him. Though I knew nothing of his skills and had seen him only a few times during our trek north, still he was human only and therefore human wits could bring him down.

What he had done was once the custom among our people and many were the feuds which grew out of it. So many, that, years past, before my own birth, there had been a solemn covenant made that the youths and maidens of the keep-kin be early betrothed. Then any man seeking to break such a bond was at once kinless.

Had Thorg believed that because we were in a new land and there were few maids (also Farkon's son being far away) he might do this thing without penalty? I knew very little of him but that could well be so. It would take days of riding for any of Lord Farkon's host to come, and Garn had only a handful of men, none of them knowing much of the broken lands to the west. Lord Tugness might make a show of joining with them just in order to set up subtle delays, insuring thus his son achieved his purpose. For, once Thorg lay with Iynne, then she was his by bed-right, though her kin would be considered sworn to Lord Farkon and he might levy on them any bride price he desired.

I could see two dales—perhaps three—locked in a bloody battle, and because of me. Had I not made it possible for Iynne to seek out that shrine, had I not gone blind myself while our enemy slunk and spied—then this would never have come to pass. Right indeed had been Garn's judgment of me.

There was nothing for me now but to seek out Thorg's trail as best I could. He would not yet be aware I was kinless. Thus if I challenged he must answer. I could—I must—kill, washing out with his blood this insult to our—no, Garn's House.

"Lord Tugness knew?" I had settled my shirt in place. Now I picked up the quilted under-jerkin which cushioned my shoulders against the weight of mail.

She shrugged, saying: "You are kinless—"

"Thorg does not know that," I answered, schooling myself to accept my disgrace. "If I can reach him first—"

The Wise Woman smiled but there was nothing pleasant in that stretch of lips. I owed her much—the tending of my wounds, my return perhaps to health, weak though I felt. Still I did not believe she tended me because of a liking for a stranger. No, it was because of her craft, to which she was pledged, as all men knew. The sooner, perhaps, I was out from under her roof the better she would like it.

"Your head needs fresh dressing—" She turned away to her many shelves, taking up a pot of salve here, some powdered stuff which lay within a box there. These she set on the lowest and widest shelf, and set to working the powder into a generous la-dling of the salve, mixing them with her fingers before spreading the result across a strip of cloth in a thick smear.

"You were lucky," she commented as she came back, holding the bandage from which arose a scent of herbs, fresh and clean. "Your skull was cracked—Garn must have a heavy fist indeed. But there is no damage within or you would not be sitting here."

"That knock was not my lord's doing—it came when I fell. This was of his hand." I touched my swollen cheek with a cautious fingertip. I remembered my helm left back in the meadowland of Garn's dale. It was my only gain that he had not stripped my sword from me then, as he had every right to do. Perhaps his anger had made him forget the final degradation due me.

She said nothing, unwinding the old bandage from my aching head to put on the fresh. Then without warning she caught my chin with a firm hand and held me, searching into my eyes.

"Do you see double?" she demanded.

"Not now."

"Well enough then. But I warn you—go upon the trail before you are fit and you will end a dead man, accomplishing nothing."

"Lady, it is because I accomplished nothing when I should have, that I am here. If I can follow Thorg, then I am returning to Lord Garn a small portion of what my folly cheated him of these past days."

"Folly!" she made an impatient sound. "Carry your burden of unneedful guilt then. Each man walks the road which is appointed to him—that may take many twists and turns. He thinks that he rules his life, he does not know that some threads were already tightly woven before he came to work upon the loom."

I got again to my feet. "Lady, you have my full thanks for all you have done for me. There is a call-debt now between us—if a kinless one can be allowed to acknowledge such. But I have an older one to Lord Garn. I may no longer be of his house, but I can still move in this matter."

"Go your own way, as all men do. I warn you to take care—but again you will be moved only by your own desires." She turned her back on me as I reached for my mail shirt.

As I made a fumbling job of putting that on (for I vowed I would not ask for her help and it would seem that she had done with me now even as Garn had done with me earlier) I saw that she had taken up from that lower shelf a bowl—not of wood or of clay—but of silver, burnished and bright. She held that in both hands, looking down into the cup of it for a long moment before she raised her head to glance once more at me. It was as if she strove to make some decision which was of importance. Whatever that might be she came to it quickly, setting the bowl back in its place.

Instead she now picked up a wallet such as a traveler might carry slung over one shoulder. Into this she began to fit things. There was the remainder of the salve which she had put on my bandage, then she made quick choices among some of her other small boxes, slipping each within, as I tightened my sword belt about me, loosening the blade, pulling it out a little that it might move the quicker.

In addition to the boxes she had stored within the wallet she now packed also journey cakes, though she added no dried sticks of meat, and I remembered that those of her calling did generally not eat flesh. There was a twist of hide also which held dried fruits. Last of all she picked up a water bottle which I recognized as the one I had carried on my last trip down the stream gorge.

"Fill this at the spring. It is good water—moon-blessed." Both the wallet and the bottle she dropped on the pallet by my side. I felt oddly alone. It was as if here, too, the curse Lord Garn had set on me held. For all her care of me, it would seem that she wanted me gone. Nor could I blame her.

Still, though I was on my feet now, and had beaten back that weakness which strove to put me down again, I could not go without more acknowledgment of the debt between us. There was only one way that those of my calling could take the full balance of payment upon them. Now I slid my sword all the way from its sheath and, grasping the blade, held it out to her hilt first. Though I fully expected her to spurn what I offered, since I was of the undead who had no right even to speak to such as she.

Zabina looked at the blade and then once more at me with that searching, measuring gaze. But, even as I had thought, she did not touch the hilt, refusing me even so little a heartening of spirit.

"We do not deal with steel and sword edge," she said. "Nor do I take homage. But what lies behind your offer, Elron—yes, that I shall accept. Perhaps in time there may come the day when I shall claim your services."

I sent the blade back into my scabbard, feeling an even greater burden for an instant or two. Then that faded and I straightened my back, pushed aside whatever filled my mind. The Wise Woman was no lord, no clan leader, but she had meant what she said, and to her at least, I was not totally outlawed and of the un-dead. I picked up the wallet and gave her thanks, though my deeper thanks were for what she had just done.

"There are things for wounds within," she pointed to the pouch. "Their uses are marked on the lids of the boxes. Do not leave off the salve and the cover for your head wound until the full ache is gone. And go with blessing—" Zabina shaped a sign which was not of that sacred Flame which the Bards guarded. However it was plain that to her this symbol was a potent one. Again I bowed my head in thanks.

I would have liked to have had speech with Gathea also—thank her for her part in taking care of me. Only she was not there and I knew that I had now been dismissed. There was no reason for me to linger.

It was past midday by the look of the sun when I came out of the Wise Woman's rough-walled hut. I could see to the east the fields and the wood-walled keep of Tugness. The Wise Woman's dwelling had been built back against the rise of the ridge and I thought that not far above must lie the Moon Shrine which Iynne had so foolishly visited.

Certainly there was the best place to begin a tracing of any trail. Garn's men must already have combed all the top of the ridge. Did they suspect also the hint the Wise Woman had given me—that no supernatural thing or previous dweller had taken my cousin, but rather she had been made captive by our ancient enemy?

If so there must now be sentries above ready to loose a bolt at any coming from this dale. They would like nothing better than to make me part of their bag.

I filled my water bottle at a stream which leaped vigorously down from the height to form a brook near the hut. Then, with the weight of that on my hip, I made my way along the foot of the ridge rise. There was a trail of sorts, made perhaps by Gathea in her comings and goings. That the shrine was of importance to her I well knew. I stood at the beginning of that and looked back, out over what I could see of the dale.

There was a flock of sheep at graze to the west. Men worked in the fields. I saw no riders and the aspect of the land was one of peace. Could I accept that as meaning Lord Tugness had no suspicion of the activities of his son? Or was this quiet all a sham, meant to deceive any who might be spying? It could be either answer and I knew so little of Lord Tugness. I must go on as one against whom would be turned every bolt and sword point were he to be seen.

Though it would perhaps have been better to begin my search when twilight veiled me from any in the dale, still there was also the need for light to view any traces Thorg had left. For it was now firm in my mind that indeed Lord Garn's old enemies had moved, since that explanation of Iynne's disappearance was far more logical.

Accordingly I took that upward path, sure that there was no better place to begin my search than the shrine itself. Had Iynne's preoccupation with that been wholly because of its strangeness? Or had she in fact been meeting Thorg secretly?

I found that suggestion presented me with a far different picture of my cousin than the one I had always had. Meek, compliant, wholly absorbed in the matters of the household—a colorless, timid girl who abided by the customs of our people—was she really just that? Or had such "virtues" been only a cloak which she had thrown off readily when she found a new freedom in the Dales? Looking back now there was little of Iynne that I discovered I knew. That astonished me as much as if a tree suddenly opened a bark mouth and spoke. She had been part of the background of my life since we were both small children, but after that, by kin customs, her life had been lived in another pattern altogether. What I recalled seemed to make her a colorless stranger.

What had it meant to her that she was promised to an unknown man without any reference to her own choice? That was custom, but until this day I had not thought much of that, for Iynne, such a decision might be another matter—a thing to fear. Had she taken some dislike to her betrothed which Thorg could play upon to get her to flout all the rules of our people? Iynne was coming alive in my mind, shaking off the shell my past way of thought had cast so tightly about her.

I won up to the top of the ridge, though I found I must take that climb slowly. Not only did I study all which lay about me as I looked for any sign that this path had been recently in use, but also my lingering weakness forced me to rest several times during that climb.

The only traces of any before me which I saw was a single track which could only have been left by that great cat which had accompanied Gathea, a paw-mark deep printed in a pocket of earth. I slipped from one bit of cover to the next, using my periods of rest to listen, though I could hear nothing, only now and then a bird call. If there were any waiting in hiding above they were keeping the silence of an ambush.

To approach the Moon Shrine from this side was easier for my purpose for there were a number of large rocks to afford cover. Whether they had been purposefully set for shelter I did not know—but their stone had not been worked.

Finally I reached the last one, from which I could plainly see the trees sheltering the sign, now so full leafed that they near hid pillars and pavement. Branches had been ruthlessly broken from one of the nearest of those trees as if to force a way. Yet only a few had been torn aside so wantonly. I believed that whoever had wanted to come at the shrine itself had lost that desire before they had summoned courage enough to achieve it fully.

For long moments I listened and waited, even raising my head high to sniff the breeze which blew from the direction of Lord Garn's holdings—north to south. There was no taint which I could detect in that. If any lay in hiding here they were very well concealed.

Then I tensed, for from between the tree which had lost its lower branches and that next to it, moved a light figure. The great cat pushed into the open to stand sentry. Its head swung about deliberately, then paused as it looked in my direction. Whether it could indeed see me by virtue of that keener sight which is given to those wearing fur, or whether it scented me, I could not tell. Only I was very sure it knew that I was there.

However, that it was here was also reassurance for me that there had been no guard placed on this spot by Garn; I was certain that the beast would never have stood so boldly in the open if it had had to face more than one man. Now I arose to my full height, moving away from the rock behind which I had taken cover. If the cat was here—could I then expect that Gathea would also appear? Or if the animal was alone, would it allow me to approach and search for the traces of Thorg and his captive, or his enticed companion?

I was right in my first guess. Zabina's handmaiden slipped, with the same silent ease of the cat, from out of the trees' shadow. As she had on the trail, Gathea wore the leather and heavy jacket of a far traveler, and her hair must have been bound tightly about her head, for she had drawn over it a tightly knit cap of the same brown-gray as her clothing. Now she stood away from the trees, also facing in my direction. Nor did she seem surprised to see me, rather it was as if she had been awaiting my arrival, impatient that I had taken so long in coming.

As I did, she carried a wallet bulging full, even a larger one than mine, and a water bottle. Only she bore no weapons, at her belt was just the sheathed knife one would use for eating or small tasks of a camp.

She watched me approach soberly, giving no greeting, as if between us there was no need for that. The cat wrinkled an upper lip, but if he meant a warning it was a soundless one.

"So you came—"

I found her words a little puzzling. Had she thought that I would not? I might never redeem myself in the eyes of my kin, but for my own belief in myself there was only the one thing I could do, and that was take any trail which would lead me to Iynne.

"If there is a trail, it should begin here," I made short answer. "This is where I found her—where he must have met her—or somewhere nearby. There would have been no other way for them to—"

"*He—they—?*" she repeated, interrupting me sharply. There was puzzlement on her face.

"Thorg," it was my turn to be impatient. "He would play old games—gain a wife and put dishonor on a House enemy."

"What has Thorg to do with this?" she wavered without turning her head, indicating the tree-hidden shrine.

"He must have seen Iynne here, led her into folly, or else took her bodily. She was easily frightened." I was not altogether sure of

that, but for the honor of Garn's House I hoped it was the truth
—that my cousin had been taken against her will.

Gathea moved forward a step or two. As the Wise Woman had
regarded me earlier that day with that searching stare to read my
thoughts, so did her assistant now also study me.

"Why do you think this of Thorg?" she asked.

"Your own mistress said it so—"

"Did she? Are you sure?" her voice came even sharper, quick
and emphatic enough to make me recall what words I had had
with Zabina. Had she actually said Thorg had done this thing? I
put remembered word to word. No, she had not said it—she had
only asked a question or two, made a statement of things past,
and the rest had been my own interpretation.

Gathea must have read that conclusion in my expression as
quickly as I reached it. She nodded.

"Zabina did not say that," the girl stated flatly. "You have put
words into her mouth."

"What she said led me to think so!"

"She is not responsible for the thoughts of one who wishes to
find an easy enemy."

"Which I was not looking for—until she spoke so!" I countered
hotly. "When I said that I would trail him she did not deny that
I had reason for my belief."

"Why should she? What difference would it make to her to
have you embroiled with another of your kind? If trouble came it
would spread only from your crooked thinking, not draw in that
which is not yours, could never be—"

I took a long stride forward, angry at the growing belief that
these two women were playing with me. They had tended my
body well. But that was of their way of life and came not, as I
knew well, from any liking or interest in me as I was myself.
When I was near healed they wanted none of me. Zabina had but
subtly sent me packing on a trail which would lead nowhere and
this girl was openly hostile. Yet, why had she not agreed readily
with her mistress's suggestion and not disowned it so readily? She
could well have cozened me on into the western wilderness on a
false trail until I was long lost.

"Where is Lady Iynne?" I thought this was no longer a time to
be mistaken about what might or might not be. There was only

one form of action left for me—that was to repair my folly in leaving my cousin prey to whatever had taken her, whether it was some man of the dales or else something worse and more feared which lurked here, an exile from an earlier and to be feared time.

"I do not know."

I believed her. Only—she might not know where Iynne was, but that she had some knowledge of what might have happened to my cousin, I was still convinced.

At that moment I was prepared to shake the truth out of her, so strong was my rising anger, the belief that I had been played with, pushed out of their way. However the cat snarled, bared fangs, so I remained where I was.

"She was called." Gathea spoke slowly. "For I watched her, and she did not come here in idle curiosity as you believed. No, within her a woman's deepest instincts were rising to the full. She was—is —of an age when the Great Lady summons womankind to ripeness. Even such as your Iynne who has all her life dwelt by man's laws and customs, will answer to women's magic, if that be strong and full enough. So she was drawn to a place in which moon-touch lay potent still. However, because she was not armored with the strength we know, she lay too open to the full flow of that."

"I do not know what you mean. She went to the shrine. Well, then what happened? She could not have vanished into the air, sunk into stone, been carried away save by a man—Thorg."

To my surprise Gathea laughed. "Shut your mind doors and bar them as you and your kind always have. So Iynne is gone and you would hunt her. Well, enough—if you have the courage. There are mysteries in this land; seek them out and perhaps you will find a thread which will lead you properly—perhaps you will not—you can only try."

She shifted the wallet strap higher on her shoulder and turned away, the cat still between us, padding along beside her. She headed west with the confidence of one who knew exactly what she would do.

6

I watched her go, certain that I would get no more out of her than she had already said. Still I knew she believed it was not Thorg who had gone wife-raiding. Convinced in part, I turned to the shrine. I came only to that thin opening between the trees which guarded it when I was shocked by the knowledge that I could not enter.

Once more I was met by a wall with force enough to shake my whole body. This place did again have invisible barriers, a defense which I had no power to breach. Though I tried, yes, I put forth all my strength to fight that which stood between me and that square of pavement.

It was not in my past training to understand such a thing. The clans swore by the Flame, paid homage to the Everburning at the proper festival. We listened to the words of the Bards who had the record-keeping of our past, and who sang of men who won battles or went down to defeat. Yet never had any one of our blood, as far as I knew, met the unseen force against which perhaps even the riders of an entire clan could exhaust themselves or be easily defeated.

At that moment I was not awed, only angry—with my own lacks, with my ignorance, yes, and with Zabina and her Maiden. For I was well assured that they knew far more than they told—*if* they had told me anything except to mislead and mystify.

So I could not force my way in to view closer a place of empty stone? Well enough. Iynne was not here. She had not returned to Garn's holding, therefore it remained that she was *somewhere*. I swung around to stare in the direction Gathea and her beast had taken. It could be that Iynne had, in some way, made common cause with this arrogant pacer-of-unknown-trails, for what purpose I could not say. I only remembered the well-filled wallet the girl had, and I thought of a supply of food being carried to someone in hiding. I could see no reason for such action on my cousin's part, but it was not given me to understand the mind of a maid, and it might well be that she had been dazzled by Zabina's teaching.

Wise Women—I searched my own memory for what I knew of them. They were healers, and had also (according to rumor) the use of certain powers. Those they were pledged to use only for good, so that no man ever raised hand against them and they went where they would as they chose. Each picked her own successor, to be trained and fostered. Once such a maid was chosen, she was straightway clanless and kinless, no matter what name or House she had been born with and into. But I have never heard of any woman taking two such followers. What would Zabina want with Iynne when she already had Gathea? Also such assistants and handmaidens were chosen when they were still small children, not when they were grown and ripe for the marriage bed.

However I was certain that Gathea, at least, knew more than she had told me, and that if I were to find Garn's daughter, it would only be through her. I turned to follow the trail she had taken, keeping close watch for the cat, since I had an idea that she might use the beast as a rear guard to make sure that I would not uncover any of her secrets.

There was no distinct trail. Still, from time to time, I found a fresh paw mark of the cat, set almost deliberately as if to lure me on. That trail did not run far along the ridge, rather almost abruptly it descended into a narrow cleft, much narrower than a valley or a dale, in the rock providing a hidden way. Then I came upon a mark which was left so flauntingly clear I began to question my own decision. Surely she whom I followed would not have left such an open guide. I reached out and pulled from a thorn-studded limb of a small bush a bit of veil—thin stuff such as I had seen Iynne often use to shield her face from the full rays of the sun.

First the paw marks and then this! They must believe me an utter fool! Only the fact that I had no other trail and I could not quite believe that the Wise Woman would ally herself and her maid with Tugness's son kept me going.

I made another discovery, that this narrow way had niches of steps set into it as if it were a stair. Old and worn, the tread very narrow, these were surely steps chiseled out of rock for a purpose. They were too regular to be any freak of nature's building.

Earth had shifted over them in some places and on those, in clear marking, were first the prints of trail boots, then, overlaying those, the paws of the cat. Thus it was no wonder that Gathea had vanished so quickly from sight, she had dropped into this way down from the ridge.

She must have moved with speed for I did not catch sight of her ahead. Now I increased my own pace, becoming more and more sure that if I could only catch up with her I might learn enough to find Iynne speedily.

The crude staircase did not descend very far, ending in a narrow way where there were two deep symbols cut in the walls, one on either side of the final step. One was a pair of upward pointing horns and the other a fantastical curving of lines which could be some runic word or sign in a language which was or must be long since dead.

I had put out my hand by chance as I reached the last step so my fingers brushed across the horns. My cry of astonishment echoed hollowly down the way ahead as I jerked back. For there had been such heat there it was as if I had tried to pluck a glowing coal from the heart of a fire's blaze.

In fact I examined my fingertips, half expecting to see blisters rising, so intense had been that pain. I sidled on, trying to keep as far from what looked no more than barren, gray rock, as I could.

Now I did sight Gathea, for no growth cloaked this way. She was well down along it, through into shadows. Shortly after one left the end of the stairway the sides of this runway sloped inward, meeting in places for a space and then opening again in a crack which gave a small measure of light.

"Gathea!" I dared to call, even though I guessed that my summons would do no good. As it did not, for she neither looked over her shoulder nor slackened her swift pace. Nor did the cat behind her pay me any attention.

Thus I was left to follow as the stinging in my hand died away, and my determination to have a straight answer from her grew.

The way of the cut was lengthy, yet the girl ahead never shortened step. Nor was I able, even though I lengthened pace, to catch up to her. Which became another puzzle, adding more fuel to my anger. Always there was the same distance between us—though she did not run and my strides were close to a trot.

There was more light ahead. I thought perhaps we were coming to the end of this hidden way. Would it bring us out at the far end of Tugness's land, or into Garn's dale? Either way I would have a second difficulty added to the first. Not only must I keep Gathea in sight, but I must also watch for any search parties as might be out.

Gathea and her cat were gone—into that opening. Now I did run in truth, fearing that they might vanish so completely that I could not find them if they entered open land ahead. We did face that, I discovered moments later.

I did not recognize what I saw before me as any part of Garn's dale. Here was no spread of grass, no easy, sloping way. Instead the land was sterile of any growth, rock-paved, with spurs of tall stone standing. These latter were set, grim, unworked, solid stone, in a circle with, beyond the outermost fringe, a second inner circle of slightly shorter stones, and within that a third. They had not the finish of the pillars I had seen at the Moon Shrine, but certainly, like the carven staircase behind, this arrangement was a work of intelligent purpose, though what purpose I could not guess. It could never have been intended for any defensive fort, for there was a man-wide space left open between one stone and the next.

I plunged forward. At the same moment there leaped from among the rocks to my right a gray-white body, bowling me over so that in a moment I lay flat, the heavy forepaws of the cat planted on my breast, pinning me to the ground, while its long fangs were very near my throat. I fought against the weight, striving to get hand to my sword hilt, even to reach my belt knife, but the beast held me helpless. Yet it did not follow up that leaping attack with any swoop of those jaws to tear out my throat.

Out of the air sounded a call, a word perhaps, but none I could understand. The cat wrinkled lips in a silent, warning snarl. Then it raised the bulk of its weight from me, though it did not back away, instead crouched as if well ready to pull me down a second time should the need arise.

I could get my hand on sword hilt now and I was already drawing blade when Gathea stepped from among the same screen of rocks where the beast had lain hidden to survey me disdainfully.

"Am I Thorg, warrior, that you hunt me?" Her voice was scornful. "Do you think that I am hiding your Lady Iynne—to her dishonor?"

"Yes," I returned flatly, and then added: "perhaps not for her dishonor, but for some reason of your own."

She must have felt safe in the presence of her furred liegeman for she laughed. And, as she stood there, hand on hips, watching me, my anger passed from hot to cold, as it has always done, making me now very sure of myself and of what I must do.

"Put up your steel," she ordered, a taunting amusement now at the corners of her mouth—wide and thin-lipped. "Be glad that you were stopped from the folly of plunging into that!" With a jerk of her chin she indicated the first circle of the standing stones.

"What harm lies there?" I remembered how the symbol on the wall had burnt my fingers, and uncertainty broke through my anger. How could one guess what dangers lay hereabout?

"You would find out soon enough—"

I thought she was trying to evade me. With a wary eye on the cat which watched me unblinkingly, I got to my feet to front her, feeling better in command of myself when I could do that.

"That," she said brusquely, "is a trap. Come here and see for yourself."

She reached out and caught my jerkin sleeve, drawing me with her to the north side where there was clear sight into the center of this stone wheel. In there a man sprawled out face down. He lay unmoving, but when I would have gone to him Gathea tightened her hold, and the cat slipped in between me and the rocks of the first wall, snarling.

"He is dead," she said without emotion. "One Jamil of Lord Tugness's meiny. He followed me—as Thorg has also done—

because he was hungry for a woman and he deemed me fit prey. Once within those circles he came not out again. I think some madness struck him, for he ran about and about until he fell and then he died."

How much of that tale could I believe? No man raised hand against one with the Wise learning. But then Zabina had also hinted that Gathea had been sought by the Lord's own heir. She must have seen my doubt for she added:

"You know not Lord Tugness and his ways. Among those who ride for his House are oath-breakers and worse. They—" She shook her head. "I do not think, nor does Zabina, that the Bards were wise when they allowed the Gate to hide so much of our past. It would seem to me that something of our own evil crept through to flower here. If so, Jamil learned that there are forces even he could not front."

Again I did not doubt that she spoke the truth as she saw it. The thing which had been that dead man's intent was a monstrous act which no sane man could have conceived. As for the Gate—I, too, had wondered if a new life without certain memories had been altogether wise. I questioned that the more now after hearing her story.

"What killed him?"

"Power," she answered somberly. "This was a place of such power as we cannot understand. Gruu here can tread those ways." Her hand dropped to fondle the ears of the cat. "I have seen other living things cross it without concern. But for my life's sake, and for the sake of that inner part of me which is more important than the life of my body, I would not venture in there. Do you not feel it at all?"

Since she watched me, and I needed to recover from the fiasco of my capture by Gruu, I moved closer to the stones, stretching out my hand. Perhaps there was no invisible wall here, but I was ready to discover one. There was not, but my flesh began to tingle as I neared the outer circle. Not only that, but there arose within me a feeling of sudden danger, that I must leap forward into that circle which was the only safe shelter from an ominous shadow I could not put name to.

So forceful became that drawing that once more I was jerked to stop by Gathea's grasp, by the cat pushing against my knees making me stumble backward. I felt my anger stiffen into a chill of sheer fear. For that pull upon me, until the two who were with me urged me back, was such a compulsion that I wanted to fight them, free myself, fly into the safety of the circle—

"Not safety—never there!" Could she read my mind or had some experiment of her own made her understand what moved me?

I was well back now, away from the influence of the stones, free —and very much shaken.

"Iynne!" I could think only what might have happened had she come this way. There lay only one body in the center of that monstrous trap but, now that I stared more closely, I saw that Jamil did not rest alone. There were bones there, gray-white in the day's light, which was beginning to fade. I do not know how many might have been before him, but there was enough evidence that what abided there still held its captives.

"She was never here." Gathea loosed her hold on me. "As I told you, she was drawn by another magic—"

I pointed to her wallet. "You have her hidden, you take her food. Does she hide from Thorg, or have you witched her with your ways so she would become like you?"

"Like me? You ask that, warrior, as if you find me less than a keep lady with her imprisoned mind, her soft body, her willingness to be driven to the marriage market as a ewe is driven to be sold to the highest bidder!" She flashed back. "No, perhaps in your soft little lady there lies a spark of the talent so overladen by years of being a keep daughter that she never realized what slumbered within until she found a place of power and that hidden part of her stirred to life, awakened from a lifetime of sleep. I do not hide Iynne and steal away to give her food and comfort. She has gone—but I cannot tell you where, though I shall try to find her. For what she discovered was wasted on her." Now there was some of the same scorn she had shown me coloring her tone. "I—I would have known how to weave, and bind and tie. I was not there when the life of the shrine returned. She was taken when *I* was meant to be the one!" Now there was anger, as cold as my own, in her voice. "She took my birthright and what she will make of it, being who and what she is, that I cannot guess. I go now not to rescue your little lady, warrior, but that I may repair the damage her curiosity has caused!"

"Where?"

"Where?" she repeated, her chin lifted. "There—" Now she swung out one arm, pointed west. "I follow no trail such as you would understand. My guide lies here." She touched her forehead between the eyes. "And here." And this time that pointing finger dropped to her breast. "It may be that I have not the power I hoped for, still I can try—one can always try."

"You believe this," I answered slowly, "that Iynne blundered into ensorcellment and was taken, that you may be able to find her. After seeing that," I motioned to the stone trap, "how can I say that anything may or may not be true in this country? But if there is a chance to find my lady and you can act as guide, then do I go also."

She frowned at me. "This is woman's power," she said slowly. "I doubt that you can follow where I may lead."

I shook my head. "I know not one power from another. I *do* know that it is laid on me as a debt of honor that I go where there may be a chance to aid Iynne. I think that your Wise Woman knew this of me," I continued. "She may have thought to mislead me with her hints of Thorg, but she gave me this," I motioned to the wallet I, too, bore, "and she did not warn me away from what I intended."

Gathea smiled with a certain stretch of lips. I disliked that more each time I saw it.

"There is one thing Zabina understands, that many times it is useless to argue when a mind is closed. Doubtless she read that yours was—tightly."

"As is yours, perhaps?"

Her frown grew sterner. "You guess too much." She turned. "If you will push into such peril as you cannot begin to dream, kinless one, then come. Night is not far away and in this land it is best to find shelter."

She started on, without another glance at me, skirting carefully about the edge of the circles, across a country which was rough going. For here had been many slides of stone, some running nearly to touch the standing pillars. Those we scrambled over (for

I was close on her heels) with care, lest some tumble of them carry us out into the influence of the trap.

The cat went ahead, much to my relief, for I did not trust him, no matter how he served my companion. We had passed that ominous set of circles, were in the rock-covered country beyond, before we found him waiting for us under an overhanging ledge at the edge of wilderness country where a few splotches of green showed, but which was mostly rocks and upstarting ridges in a chaotic mixture of broken stone.

There was no wood for a fire. Nor would I have wanted to light one in this wilderness, drawing to us—what? Garn's men, or things far more dangerous even than that lord in his rage? The sun seemed to linger, as if favoring us enough to allow me at least to mark every approach to the shelter Gruu had discovered. The big cat had vanished into that wilderness of rock, intent, I was sure, on hunting. Gathea and I ate sparingly of the food we carried and drank only scant mouthfuls of water. I had seen no trace of any stream in the land ahead, unless one of those splotches of growth a goodly distance away marked some spring or rain-catch basin.

We did not talk, though there were questions enough I would have liked to have asked. However she turned a shut face upon me, making it plain that her thoughts were elsewhere, so that for stubbornness of will I would not break the silence which lay between us.

Instead I continued to study the land lying ahead, attempting to mark the easiest path among those sharp upcrops and ridges. It was as desolate, and, in its way, as threatening a land as I had ever seen. That it had ever held life surprised me. Unless that circle trap had been built as a barrier against some coast invader, only the first, perhaps, of deadly surprises.

"This is not Garn's land," I said at last, mainly to hear my own voice, for her continued silence built the barrier higher and higher between us. If we were to go on together we must work out a way of communication so that we might front the dangers I was sure lay before us together as companions-of-the-trail at least and not as enemies standing well apart.

"It is not Tugness's either," Gathea surprised me with her answer. "This land lies under another rule. No, do not ask me whose

—for that I cannot tell. Only here we are intruders and must go warily."

Was she in those words obliquely agreeing to a partnership? At least there was no impatience in her voice and she no longer wore a frown. The sun banners were fading fast from the sky. Shadows reached out from the rocks before us as if they were hands to grasp and hold anything venturing near.

"This is a cursed land, and we're the fools for taking lordship of it!" I burst out.

"Cursed, blessed, and all manner of such in between. Still we were meant to come, or that Gate would not have opened to us. Therefore there is a purpose and a reason and it is for us to discover what those may be."

"The Gate," I said slowly. "I know that the Bards sang it open, that also it wiped from our minds the reason why we came. Why was that done unless—" My thoughts turned direly in a new direction. "Unless that was so that we might bend all our wits and strength to front new enemies here to deal with in the future not the past. Yet I wonder why we came—"

She had put away more than half her journey cake, made fast the loop latch of her wallet.

"Ask that of the Bards—but expect no answers. This land may be more blessed than cursed—"

She halted, for a sound arose into the evening air. I caught my breath. They say that the Bards, if they so wish, can sing the soul out of a man, leaving him but an empty husk. I had thought those but the idle words of men who try to add more to any story. Now the sound which arose and fell across the stone world before us was such singing as I had never heard in my life—not even when the Arch Bard Ouse sang at midsummer feasting.

Nor was this any man's voice, but rather the soaring voices of more than one woman, reaching notes as high as any bird could carol. And it came from behind us!

I was on my feet and out from under the ledge, looking back along our pathway, only dimly aware, so bemused was I by that singing, that Gathea stood beside me so closely now that her shoulder rubbed against my own.

It was a hymn of praise—no, it was a song for lovers, beckoning.

It was a trilling of victory, welcoming to safe homes those who had fought well and dared much. It was—

I could see them now. Women, yes, though their faces were mostly hidden by long hair, which stirred about them as if blown by a wind I could not feel here. Was it only long flowing hair which covered their slender bodies—or wore they robes as thin and frail as these locks which blew through the air? Silver was that hair, silver their bodies. They were far from me and yet as each one paced, singing, facing me, I thought that I caught sight of bright eyes, fire-bright, for they were the color of ruddy flames, which held steady sight in spite of the veiling of their hair.

Hand and hand they went, yet with a space between each of them as they circled—and there was another circle behind them and beyond that. Three circles! I uttered a small sound of my own.

Where the stone pillar of the trap had stood, that was where these singers now trod their way. Did I still see the pillars, or had twilight shrouded them? The silver bodies, the spinning hair, had a light of their own, thin and wan—

Still they wove their way singing. Peace and happiness, love, longing fulfilled, life everlasting, but life of a new kind—a wondrous kind. One needed only to go to them and all this would be given. Sweeter, lower, more enticing became that song. I moved yet I had not willingly or consciously taken those steps. But I must go—

Again I was thrown with painful roughness into rock, this time rolling over with the force of the blow which had sent me down. Then a second body joined me and we struggled together in a tangle of arms and legs until a large and heavy furred weight landed crosswise, pinning us both to the earth.

I smelled the strong breath of the cat, heard the rumble of a growl, so low it was more a vibration through his body than an actual sound. The singing held high and true, but our struggles to throw off Gruu were useless.

Then I heard Gathea's voice through that heart-wrenching singing. Her face was so close to mine that her breath was warm on my cheek as she spoke.

"Fingers—in—ears—lure—"

I felt her squirming, and guessed that she was doing just that, thrusting her fingers into her ears to block out that sound. Half dazedly, for my head was beginning once more to ache woefully after this second assault, I, too, loosened my arms, though I did not struggle to free myself, so sealing out that singing with my fingers.

Gruu however did not stir, nor did Gathea attempt to free herself from where she lay half over me, the beast pressing us both down. I could smell the scent of herbs, sharp and clean, which must come from the hair which had shaken a little loose in her fall and now lay with the braid end close to my nose.

Guessing that this was a second part of the stone trap, and that it was an even more dangerous lure than the first, I strove to shut out sound, to concentrate on other things, such as how soon we might get away from this ever-present peril, and how many of such plague spots we might be apt to meet with in this unknown land.

Very faintly I could still hear the singing, and it dragged at me, making me want to squirm free, to seek out those singers. Then, slowly, it died away. Perhaps we lost ourselves in a daze, for I cannot remember well what happened until there was the chill white of moonlight across us.

Gruu heaved himself up at last. I felt bruised and sore from being flattened so on against the stone and was slow in drawing to my knees, so Gathea arose before me. She faced into the full rays of the moon and I saw her hands move in what could only be the gestures of some ritual.

It was a very bright moon, making the stone around us either silver or dead black, as shadows dictated. I dropped my hands from my ears. The night was so quiet I could only hear a whisper of sound from the girl as she recited words not meant for me to understand. I drew a little away from her and stood to look back at the circles of stone. They looked very far away, just as the singers had seemed so much closer. And they were only that once more—stones set on end for a purpose which I did not like to consider. The singers of the evening were gone, only the moon hung over us as Gruu pressed close to Gathea with a rumble of purr louder than her whisper voice.

7

"MORE OF YOUR TRAPS?" I DEMANDED, SHAKEN IN SPITE OF MY efforts to appear well in control.

"Not *my* traps." However her tone was light. I believed I saw a shadow of excitement on her moonlit face. "Sirens—yes—and meant to lure." Now she flung her arms wide. "What wonder lingers here? Who wrought such spells and sorcery? What they must have learned—beyond the simple knowledge we have always thought so great!" She asked those questions not of me but of the night. It was as if she had come eagerly to an abundant feast table and could not begin to choose what was to be first sweet or appetizing taste on her tongue.

Perhaps because she was already touched with learning beyond the control of rules and customs, this was indeed for her the opening of a door. Only for me it was otherwise. Save that I could not deny that my wariness of mind, my uneasiness of spirit, also held within seeds of curiosity.

We heard no more in the night and she had set Gruu on watch, assuring me that the great cat was far more likely to detect any danger than the most acute of human sentries. I had to agree that it was his quickness which had saved me once, and perhaps a second time, along with her, from the traps. Thus I did sleep, and if I dreamed no memory of that dream reached past my first awakening, to find the sun already throwing beams across the sky.

Gathea was seated cross-legged a little beyond, her back to the sun as well as to the dales where our own kind strove to shelter. Her head was up as she studied the broken land ahead, and I read into the tense angle of her shoulders the same alertness as would grip a hunter before he started on a warm trail.

Under the sun the land looked even more barren than it had when the moon had laid the silver of light, the dark of shadow across it. There were small gullies riven in the bare rock, as well as stretches which were as smooth as pavement. However, I was very glad to see, no standing stones which were more than those nature herself must have set on end and then smoothed through long seasons of sand blown by the wind.

This forsaken land was so empty that I doubted Gathea's quest, unless I had been right and she knew well enough just where Iynne hid because she had aided her to that hole herself. However, I knew enough to keep still on that suspicion and lend myself to the devices of the Wise Woman's girl, even if she meant only to confuse me, though some stubbornness within me argued that Gathea was more intent on traveling on into the unknown for her own reasons than she was in Iynne's plight or my own part in that.

I wondered, too, if the Sword Brothers had ridden this way during their exploration. If so they had certainly made it safely past that trap of the standing stones.

"Which way do we go?" I asked in a carefully neutral voice as I sat up.

Gruu had vanished again. Much as I mistrusted the beast, for I was not used to companying with an animal out of the wilds that manifestly had some form of communication with my companion, at the same time he could offer defenses which I believed we might need.

"Westward," she replied. Nor did she turn her head, but spoke almost absently, as if her mind already ranged well ahead of her body.

Once more we broke our fast in silence, and then arose to cross that broken land. At midmorning, as far as I could guess by the sun, we came upon one of those cups of green among the stones which did indeed house a spring—a boon, for two others we had earlier investigated had no water. Here water rippled forth, ran for a short distance, and then was lost in a stone hole into which water poured.

There were two trees of reasonable size here and a number of bushes, from which started birds and some furred things which streaked across the ground so swiftly that one could not catch good sight of them. The bushes had been their reason for showing, for the branches were heavily laden with fruit—larger than any berry which I knew. These were rich, dark red in color and some had burst open from the full strength of their own sweet flesh, or had fallen to the ground where they had been pecked and gnawed.

Gathea broke one of the globes free, lifted a piece of its skin with a fingernail, sniffed long at the inner flesh and then set the tip of her tongue to the break. A moment later she drew it all into her mouth and was chewing lustily. While I, depending on her knowledge of growing things, followed her example. After our long journey across the broken lands and the sun-heated stone nothing tasted so good. These provided both food and drink and we helped ourselves until we could eat no more. Then we gathered handfuls to be carried with us, cradled in leaves which Gathea pulled from a plant that grew at the border of that very short stream and fastened together with small thorny twigs. I took both her water bottle and my own, emptied what little remained in each, rinsed and filled them until there was only room to pound in their stoppers.

We had passed no more relics of the unknown people during the morning. The farther we had withdrawn from the circles, the emptier this land appeared, the more my spirits recovered. When I had finished replenishing our water supply I hitched my way up to the top of an outcrop which helped to shelter the pocket of the spring and, shading my eyes to the sun's glare, strove to pick out ahead the easier of the ways which might be offered us.

During the morning the distant line on the horizon had not only risen but grown still more sharply outlined against the cloudless sky. I thought that it marked heights—perhaps even mountains. But my inner uneasiness grew. I did not care how long a head start Iynne had had, surely she could not have come this way without any supplies or aid. Had I been deceived when I had been in a manner lured away from my first belief that she was taken by Thorg? No one who was not well hardened to the trail could have beaten us this far. While Iynne had been much shielded all her life—even during our trek north when she had spent all her hours of travel within that wain which had been made the most comfortable for her alone. Garn was not in the least soft of speech or manner, but he valued his daughter, if for no other reason than for the alliance her eventual marriage would bring to his small house—he would risk nothing concerning her.

Having decided that she could not have come this way alone, I determined to have plain speech once again with Gathea, and slid down the rock, pushing through the brush to where she was washing her hands in the running water.

She did not look up at me but she spoke, startling me:

"You turn again to thoughts of Thorg. You believe that I do not know—or care—what happened to your keep lady. Not so!" Now she did raise her head to stare at me, a fierce light in her eyes such as I have seen a hawk wear when it surveyed its own hunting territory and thought of the swift flight, the final pounce, which was to come. "I know this: There was power in the shrine which would be an open door—at the right time. Why do you think I sought it? I—I was meant to take that path! Your lady gathered up a harvest which was to be mine! She is a fool and will not know or understand what she had chanced into. But she shall not have the good of it—no, she shall not!"

"I know she could not have come this far alone," I pushed aside her heat of voice. "She was not one who could trail so. Thus—I must have missed some sign or—"

"Or you think I have misled you? Why? She has what is mine. I will have it! If you can take her back—then I shall rejoice. I tell you she meddled ignorantly and we have yet to find the end of a trail which may never touch on the ground of this land at all!"

Gathea arose and shook the water from her hands, then ran her damp palms across her face.

"There were no signs of any mounts—" I held stubbornly to my own thought.

"There may be here such mounts as you cannot begin to dream of," she snapped. "Or other ways of travel. I do not think that the door she found open gave on this land before us—but that its source does lie ahead."

Because I had no answer for myself, I again had to take her word as we went on. There was no sign of Gruu. If the cat still accompanied us, he either scouted before or ranged at some distance beyond our sighting. However we were not far alone from the cup of the spring before we came to a way which was some relief against the straight beams of the sun whose glare on the rocks struck back at us with a heavy heat like that of an autumn fire.

There was another cut in the broken lands, this a narrow valley. No water ran here, but as we dropped into it we found that in places the stone walls arose to arch across the way and there was cooler air, which now and then puffed full into our faces, as if a wind deliberately chose to make our way easier. Also the floor of this cleft was free of any falls of stone from the rim and ran almost as straight as a road westward. I searched carefully for any sign that this had been made by intent but there were no marks on the stone to suggest that man or some other intelligence had wrought this.

Gathea strode forward as if she knew exactly where she was going, and there was a need for haste. I went perhaps more slowly, keeping not only an eye on the edges of the cliff well above our heads, but an ear to listen for any sound which was not made by the pad of our own trail boots.

Perhaps because of that extra awareness I sighted what I might not have noticed had I trod in the dales or along the trail we had come from the Gate. It was neither sound nor sight, but rather uncurled *within* me, as might a thread of thought which I had not consciously summoned. It is difficult to describe an inner awareness that has no visible existence.

Had I walked under the sun I would have thought that I was dazzled by the heat, my mind affected enough to see those mirages which travelers are supposed to view in desert lands—often to their destruction if they are beguiled to leave the trail. Only there was not enough heat here. In fact, the farther we advanced, the more the cliffs above drew together to shade us and the oftener those wandering puffs of air came to cool our bodies.

Still—can a man form pictures in his mind alone? Scenes which were not born of memory or from some tale he had heard many times over so that the descriptions which are a part of it take on reality? I did not know—save this, which began to linger in small quick snatches of inner sight, was from no dream of mine, and certainly not out of memory.

Twice I closed my eyes for the space of three or four strides.

When I did so I *knew* that I did not walk on naked rock in a desolate land. No, I marched with purpose along a way well known to me and there was an urgency upon me that some task hard set must be carried through, lest evil come. Nor did walls of rock rise on either hand. I saw, from the corners of my eyes (or seemed to) brilliantly colored buildings among which people moved—though I had only a flutter of shadow to mark them. When I opened eyes again I was in the cleft—and—still—that other half-sight was also with me.

Whether Gathea experienced that same strange overlay of one with another I did not know. Nor did I want to ask. There was sound in my closed-eye place also. Not the sweetness of evil such as the singers in the night had used to draw, rather this was a kind of whispering—if one could hear distant cries or orders or urging to action as *whispers* instead of shouting.

I think I was caught in that maze of one world upon another passage for a long time. For suddenly, when I roused, there was no longer the other scene about me; the sun was well to the west and our cleft opened out into a wide valley as green and open as the dales behind, appearing to be a land in which enchantment had no place.

Animals grazed some distance away. One, on the outskirts of that herd, raised a head on which branched horns glinted with a sheen as if they were coated with burnished silver. It was larger than the deer we had seen in the sea-girt dales, and its coat was paler, a silver-gray, marked with lines of a dark shade about the forelegs.

It gave a bellowing call and then was gone with a great leap, the rest of the herd dashing after it. But not swiftly enough, for out of the tall grass flashed a furred hunter that could only be Gruu. He brought down a younger buck, one with far less of the horned majesty of the herd's leader, killing it by a single well placed blow.

Thus, as we came up to the cat, he was licking eagerly at the blood, raising his head to stare at us and growl.

There was a goodly amount of meat and I found myself eager to set knife to it, to build a fire and toast strips which would be better eating by far than the dry journey cakes. However I knew better than to dispute with Gruu over the prey he had himself pulled down.

So I hesitated but Gathea went forward quickly, the cat allowing her to come near. She stooped and put her hand on the head of the dead creature, touching it lightly between those silver horns, as she spoke aloud:

"Honor to the Great One of the herd. Our thanks to That Which Speaks for the four-footed that we may eat—we take not save that which is freely given."

Gruu raised his head also and sounded forth a roar as if he added to her words. She turned and beckoned and we did share Gruu's kill—taking only that portion which we would eat that night and leaving the rest for the cat. Nor did I attempt to hide the fire I built, collecting wood from some trees nearby—for there was a feeling here that the night would not hold danger.

Gathea opened the second pocket of her wallet and brought forth a small bag fastened with a drawstring. Into the palm of one hand she cautiously sifted some of the contents with such care that she might be measuring sigils meaning great good or ill. Then, with a sudden toss, she threw what she held into the midst of the fire I had fed into a steady blaze. There was a puff of smoke —bright and searing blue—and with it a strong odor which was of some herb, though I was not schooled enough in such matters to be able to name it.

Having dropped the retied bag upon her knee, the girl leaned forward and, with small waves of her hand, sent that odorous smoke wafting first in one direction and then another, until it had blown, obedient to her coaxing, north, south, east, and finally west. She had, as we searched for dead wood under the trees, stopped often to look upon bushes and trees still alive, and had finally cut from one shrub a length near as long as my sword. As I had gathered my spell to put my spark snap to it she stripped the leaves from her trophy. Now she picked that bare wand up, to pass it back and forth through what smoke still lingered.

Having so held her switch into the vapor as long as it might be noticed at all, she got to her feet and began to move around the fire, marking out in the soil, for I had chosen a bare place near some rocks (perhaps the last remnant of the hard land through which we had come) on which to establish our camp. Gathea drew a circle and, beyond and enclosing that, she made the sharp angles which formed a star. Into each point she shook a drop or two of blood from the butchered deer, adding a pinch more from her supplies, in the form of some withered bits of leaves. Having so wrought she returned and sat down across the fire, planting her wand upright like the pole of a lord's banner—save that no strip of emblazoned cloth fluttered from its tip.

I would ask no questions since it had been increasingly irksome that, each time I had done so after this journey of ours had begun, she had been condescending and spoke as if in her way she was far more learned than I could ever hope to be. Thus I accepted in silence that she had once more used some ritual of her craft to put safeguards about us, though it puzzled me, for, since we had come into this open and goodly green land, I had felt no alarms, rather that we trod in safety. This was to prove once more that I indeed walked blind among open pitfalls.

Night drew in as I watched the sun disappear behind that line of heights which was now even more manifest to the west—their upper crowns forming sharpened points against the sky.

Since Gathea remained silent, I did the same, though I was startled into an exclamation as Gruu sprang upon us suddenly, seeming from out of nowhere, taking shelter also by the fire.

I had earlier cut and smoothed a number of spit sticks and on these I skewered sections of the meat, setting them so to roast at the fire's edge, the juices trickling down to bring small bursts from the flames. The smell of the roast was mouth-watering and I waited impatiently for the flesh to be seared enough for us to taste, tending my spits carefully to brown well on all sides. This was an old hunter's ploy taking me back to the days before the Gate—though my memory was misty.

At length I handed my companion one of the sticks with its sizzling burden and took another, swinging it a little in the air to cool it enough to mouth, though Gathea sat holding hers as if she had no great interest in it after all.

I thought at first that she watched those singularly jagged looking mountains, and then I realized that her gaze was limited to a point nearer at hand. As far as I could see nothing moved out in that open valley since the deer had fled at Gruu's attack. Not even a bird crossed the night sky.

Still I would ask no questions, but ate stolidly, chewing the meat with that relish which comes best when one has not tasted such for too long a time. Gruu lay at ease on the other side of the fire, his eyes near closed, though he still licked now and then at one paw. If anything moved beyond he had no interest in it.

The dark came very quickly after the sun had vanished, that last striping of the sky overspread by dark clouds. I thought a storm might be on the way and wondered if we would not better search for cover—even so limited a shelter as that stand of trees from which we had brought our wood. I was about to say that when I saw Gathea's whole body go tense. At the same time Gruu's head came up, his eyes went wide as he, too, stared outward—and westward—into the twilight.

There was no singing, no weaving of silver shadows this night. What came upon us did not entice, it hunted on soft feet—if it had feet at all—moving in over the open plain. Gruu's hair stiffened along his spine. He no longer lay at ease, but drew his limbs under him as if he prepared for a crouch to spring. His lips wrinkled but his snarl did not sound aloud.

I do not know what my companions saw, but in my eyes it was as if sections of the shadows split one from the other, fluttering, some even rising from the ground as if they leapt upward and landed on the earth again, unable to take to the air as they desired to do. They were only darker blots against the twilight, which came so quickly. However, it was plain that they came, in their queer leaping way, closer to our fire, and never had I felt so naked and defenseless.

In truth I had drawn my sword—though what use that might be against these formless, half floating things, which appeared to well up from the grass-covered earth itself, I could not sensibly say. However, my action brought for the first time quiet words from my companion.

"Well done. Cold iron is sometimes a defense, even though one cannot use directly its point, or sharpened blade. I do not know what these are—save they are not of the Light—" And the way she said "Light" made me realize that what she spoke of was not a matter of seeing but of feeling—true as weighed against false.

Gathea reached out and laced fingers around the wand she had set in the earth, though she did not pull it free of the soil, rather waited, even as I did, holding my sword hilt. The dark looked very thick to me. I could no longer distinguish movement by eye. Only, in a queer way, new to me and frightening (had I allowed it to be so), I sensed that outside our star-girt circle there was that which paced menacingly, strove to press forward, and was denied.

What did reach us first was a kind of hunger backed by confidence, as if what slunk beyond was as competent as Gruu in bringing down whatever it had cornered. Then impatience followed, as it met a resistance it could not master—surprise, growing anger that anything dared to stand against *it*. I knew it was there, I could have turned my head at any moment to face it, as it—or them—made the round of our protected campsite. Still I had no idea what form these besiegers took, nor how dangerous they might be.

Once more I was startled, as, into the outer edge of the firelight there flashed for an instant a hand—or was it a claw?—withered, yellowish flesh stretched tightly across bone. It could have been either, as I sighted it only for an instant before it jerked back. The sight of it aroused all my instinctive fear for, unlike the silvery singers of the night before, this clearly advertised its evil by its very look.

Gathea pulled the wand from the earth with one easy movement. She dropped the far tip to point to the star angle directly before her where she had sprinkled the blood and placed the broken bits of dead leaf of herbage. At the same time she spoke, not to me, but commandingly, in words I could not understand.

There was movement from the spot to which she had pointed. It seemed to me that the ground itself began to spin, shooting upward part of its substance. As she began to sing, louder and faster, so did the whirling become a twirl of movement, a pillar of flying dust particles growing solid.

Then there crouched in the point of the star a figure which in a crude way was human. At least it had two legs, two arms, a trunk of body, a round ball of head perched thereupon, though it was such a thing as a child might fashion out of mud in play, crudely done. When it stood erect, Gathea brought down her wand in a sharp slap against the earth and uttered a single loud cry.

That thing which had come out of the ground ambled forward, stumping on feet which were clumsy and ill shaped. However, it was able to keep erect and move with more speed than I would have believed that such an ill-wrought body could show.

"Quick!" Gathea looked now to me for the first time. "Your knife—cold steel—to secure the doorway—" Her wand twitched across the ground to indicate where that must go.

I unsheathed my knife. Still keeping my other hand fast on sword hilt, I tossed the shorter blade as if I played some scoring game. It thudded true and stood quivering, hilt uppermost, set well into the earth at the very spot which that shambling figure had just left to go into the dark.

Gathea now seemed to listen—and I did likewise, finding myself even keeping my own breathing as noiseless and shallow as I could so that I might hear better. No night bird called; there was nothing to trouble the silence beyond our circle. But I sensed that that which had earlier tried our defenses was gone—if only for a space.

The girl did not relax. Taking my cue from her, I did not either. The cat at last gave a sigh and blinked. But if Gruu was satisfied my companion was not.

"Not yet—" It was as if she admonished herself, refused the comfort of believing that her sorcery was successful.

"What you made—" I felt that I could go no longer without asking at least some of the questions nagging at me—"did it lead away what waited out there?"

She nodded. "For a while it may play the quarry for those—but it may not last long. Listen!"

Perhaps this was what she had been waiting for. There rang through the night, echoing as if we were in some great cavern and not under a cloud-filled sky, a cry, a wailing, so filled with malice and the promise of evil anger to come, as to bring me to my feet, sword point out, ready to fight, though I could not see what enemy had sounded that call of fury.

"Do not, for your life," the girl said, "go beyond the circle. It will return—and, fooled once, it will be twice as ireful."

"What is it?" I demanded.

"Not a thing which can be brought down by that," she nodded to my sword, "though steel is rightfully its bane. But only as a defense not a weapon for use. I do not think that it can be sent on a second fruitless hunt. As to what it truly is—I cannot put any name to it. I did not even know it might come. My precautions were taken because this is a strange land and we had spilled blood. Blood is life—it draws the Dark Ones where they are to be found."

"You used it to seal us in."

"As I said, blood is life, from it can be conjured counterfeits, though those would not move or have being in the day. They, too, draw from the dark. Now—"

Her wand came up once more, pointing even as did my sword. Those things which prowled were back, weaving back and forth where we could not see—only feel them. Twice claw-hands swung in at the edge of the star point where my dagger stood, only to jerk back again. But they could not pass and I felt raised against me the growing heat of an anger as hot in my mind as the fire was upon my body. That emotion pressed, sought, battled to reach us with a dark and ugly hunger flowing as a high warning of what we might expect should it win inward.

Gruu arose, threw up his head, and gave such a roar as made my head ring. I thought at first it was an echo of his cry I heard, until it was repeated from afar. Then I could not mistake the ring of it as it sounded a second time. I had heard such before but never as full toned and holding the notes so strongly. So did any lord's marshal sound his warn horn at the edge of a neighbor's land!

Out in that blackest of the night there was another now—and he sent forth his challenge.

8

FOR THE THIRD TIME THAT HORN RANG. I BELIEVED I COULD HEAR, under the edge of its echoing, another sound which was between a bay and a squawl—certainly made by animal. Gruu answered fiercely. He patted first one clawed paw against the earth and then the other, as if he were leashed and wished for release—to be freed to attack in the dark. Gathea took a step forward to rest her hand on the beast's head. He looked up at her, showing his tongue between his openly displayed teeth in a dire grin.

Though the horn did not sound again, I saw a flash of light through the night, and heard a crackle as if someone had harnessed the power of lightning itself, had fashioned it into a weapon. The dark was so thick that flash came and went before I could catch any sight of what lay about. The flash hit again, and again, as the clamor of what might be a hunting pack drew closer.

I could not see, but I could sense. Whatever had besieged us was now at the back of the circle, cowering with us between it and what coursed through the night, using a weapon of flame, urging forward some hunting "hounds." So it continued to cower until Gathea took a hand. She faced about. Her wand arose once again as with its tip she wrote upon the air.

Symbols appeared, curved up and down—green those were—and yet blue—as water mingles such shades along the shore of the sea. Out spun the signs, not fading, rather flying as might small birds released to be free. They gathered outside our defense lines to hang in the air.

There was no audible snarl of rage but a sense of burning anger strove to strike us. Then that was gone, as suddenly as if a door had opened and closed. That which had striven to reach us was now shut away from our world.

We heard a rushing in the night which sounded as if a company had divided, one part going to the north, one the south of our defense. Then that, too, was swallowed by silence. I felt an emptiness, through which one could hear the clear, clean rustle of wind across the stand of grass but nothing else. Gruu settled down —this time dropping his head to rest upon one curve of leg. Gathea, her wand still in hand, curled beside him, leaving to me the other side of the fire. The girl pillowed her head on the cat's shoulder, her eyes closed as if she—and we—had nothing more to fear. Still I sat, reliving all that had happened this night. It seemed to me that when I had staggered out of Garn's dale—no, even before that, when I had first looked upon the Moon Shrine— my life had begun to change; I was no longer the same Elron who had ridden through the Gate, liegeman to a clan lord, knowing nothing much beyond the duties of my place and the security of my standing with my fellows.

I should have been stricken more deeply by Lord Garn's blow, which had not only marked my body but had cut me off from all the clan. Now that act appeared of little consequence. I had come not only into a country that those of my blood had no knowledge of, but there was a part of me which said: See, I am kinless, yet I am not a nothing; I have walked with danger and faced squarely that beyond reckoning.

Yet no skill of mine had saved us. That, too, I must face. Gathea's talent had come again and again to stand between both of us and disaster. Such an admission was not a pleasant thing—or an easy one—for me to face honestly.

Perhaps my discomfort arose because I was used only to the women of the keeps—the clan maidens whose skills were in the ways of common living which I knew instinctively that Gathea scorned. She was unlike any maid I had ever known, as I had realized since our first meeting by the sea. One could not say to her: This is not your battle, let me stand forth to defend you as is the rightful custom. I knew a kind of shame because I knew I did not want to grant all due her, or admit that in our journey so far she had borne the brunt of action.

Gathea's desire to reach the west, the hint that she had given me that Iynne had somehow intervened between her and what was rightfully hers, power connected with the Moon Shrine, that I now accepted. Much in this land one must accept blindly, even though it was beyond all man's experience, perhaps even a Bard's tale.

I wondered what hunter had moved in the dark out there to bring us aid. Had he answered Gathea's summons? Or was he already afield seeking that evil which had crawled about our camp? Man, I felt, he was not. Why did I even think "he," save that my training said that the chase as well as battle were for my sex alone? He or *it*—

Such things I thought—or tried to arrange in some pattern—as I fed the fire, though I had to let it die a little for lack of fuel. I kept watch because those thoughts so troubled me, and I played ever with the hilt of my sword, for the solid feel of that gave me a sense of linkage to that other me who had been so sure and certain, before this land of many mysteries had engulfed our people. How much time passed I do not know. The sky remained heavily clouded, though no rain fell nor storm arose. There was not even one of those strange stars to be sighted. We had our small fire and the circle. Beyond that lay a thick darkness without a break—curtaining us securely in.

I heard a soft sound and glanced at the girl and the cat. Gruu's eyes were open, regarding me in his searching, weighing manner. Then he blinked, turned to look once more into the dark. Thus it came to me that the beast was signaling in his own manner that he would now take sentry duty, leaving me to rest.

So I stretched out, though I kept my sword bared, the hilt under my hand, using twists of grass which we had brought for kindling for a pillow. The bandages I had worn over my wound seemed tight and the skin beneath them itched. Sleep came in spite of that minor discomfort.

I awoke as if I had been called. Yet I did not know who did the summoning, for Gathea still lay with her head pillowed against Gruu, and the beast's eyes were open, watching. Our fire had burned away, but its light was no longer needed. The lighter gray of predawn let me see, as I sat up, what lay immediately about. There was movement out there in the grass, grazing animals.

The deer made lighter patches against the growth on which they fed. Farther yet from them larger beasts also fed, none approaching us. I got to my feet, sheathing my sword. Curiosity now stirred in me. I wanted to see what tracks whatever had besieged us might have left, so I might guess at its nature. Also—I wanted to know if the hunter in turn had left any readable sign of his passing.

I went to that star point where my belt knife still stood and pulled it free, wiping the blade on a wisp of grass before returning it to the sheath at my side. Then I stepped out boldly beyond the protection Gathea had woven, to look around.

There was a dark mass some strides distant, toward which I first turned—lumps of earth, moist enough so they clung together after a fashion, but not enough to give the heap any true shape. I stirred the mass cautiously with the toe of my boot and the lumps shifted, breaking apart. This must be what was left of that earthen image which Gathea had called up to fool the attacking evil. Nothing but earth; I could not understand how it had been given not only shape, but semblance of life. What had she said? That blood was life. There was our familiar ceremony of the first fall hunt when a certain portion of the kill was hung in the open to drip and dry and remained untouched save by the birds—an ancient rite of offering we of the here and now no longer understood.

I squatted near that mound of earth, searching the ground about for tracks. There were several indentations that I measured with a forefinger as I tried to imagine what manner of thing had left them. I thought I had seen either a claw or a withered hand attempt to reach us over the barrier last night. The clearest of those prints was more like that of a claw, if such a foot or fore appendage possessed five distinct toes.

Also I believed that it had gone on two feet. The creature must have been of considerable size, for not only was that print larger than the hand I stretched just above it, but it was deep pressed into the earth. I followed the trail and found here and there enough other prints to assure me that the thing or things (for I could not tell whether this sign was left by one or more) had indeed encircled our camp.

Now I cast farther out, seeking any track left by those others—

the hunter and his pack. Of those there were no traces, even though many stretches of bare earth lay in the direction from which that horn had sounded.

So puzzled was I by that lack of trail, that I continued farther and farther away from our campsite, searching the ground. Thus I came upon an unsavory thing. Insects, even this early in the day, had found and were buzzing about what looked to be a bloody lump of flesh. I stooped close enough to see that what lay there was part of a clawed appendage such as I had seen in the firelight. There were only two of the long claws still attached, as if the thing had been badly mangled, and both ended in talons as sharply pointed as my knife. The remains of the covering skin were a yellow-white and shriveled. I disliked the sight of it so much that I tore loose a clump of grass, planting its roots and earth on top of the trophy. It would seem that our hunter had had some luck in his sport after all.

"Elron!"

Gathea waved to me and I went gladly enough—pleased that I need no longer force myself to go hunting other traces. Nor did I mention my find when I reached our campsite to discover she had already started upon a meal, including some of the cold meat from the night before, and had set out my wallet for me to do likewise. As usual she had little to say. I wanted to choose among many questions—for to reveal my own ignorance irked me more and more. If she had knowledge which was of value to us, I reasoned, then she should share it without my constant probing.

Thus I waited, chewing irritation along with my food. The supplies Zabina had given me were fast being exhausted. I trusted that the herds on this wide valley land would continue to provide us food, though it might be well if we halted long enough after some kills to smoke meat for future use. There must be water nearby and that was even more important than meat. Perhaps Gathea was also preoccupied by such practical matters.

She lifted her head to stare out along the deep grass until a furred head arose into sight—Gruu, licking his lips, a long green feather caught upon his ruff as if he had varied his dining this morning. The girl and cat met eye to eye in an exchange I could not share. Gruu began to trot away in a general line more to the north as Gathea caught up her wallet, taking also the wand from the night before.

"There is water—that way—" She broke silence for the first time as I fell in, a little behind her, she trailing the cat. Here the grass grew near waist high, hiding most of Gruu, so we marked his passing mainly by the wild waving of that cover. There were birds in the air. I watched those warily. Could that claw-foot-hand have come from a winged thing? I was sure that our besiegers had indeed covered the ground by limited attempts at flight when they had closed in on us last night. Also there were those other unwholesome black creatures which had caused trouble in Garn's dale and which might well lair or nest near here.

But those I saw in the sky here were true birds, drab of color. They appeared intent on circling above the grazing beasts. Perhaps they fed on insects which the trampling of the herds disturbed from the grass. The way Gruu took suddenly became a real trail, deep slotted and marked with hoofprints—undoubtedly a much used way to water. This footing was rough but we were no longer whipped by the grass, some blades of which had edges sharp enough to cut the skin. It was not long until we came to the top of a steep walled declivity in which ran a stream of river size, the mid-current of which, judged by ripples, flowed quite swiftly. This flow probably originated in those heights which hedged the western sky, and it swirled with a lacing of foam around rocks.

We descended cautiously to make good use of the abundance of water. I left Gathea with Gruu by a clump of brushes, going downstream to a stand of rocks jutting out into the water. There I stripped eagerly, splashing the water over my body. The bandage about my head grew wet and I dragged it off, touching my cheek and forehead gingerly, though I was sure that much of the swelling had gone and my wound was well on the way to healing. I washed and wrung out the bandage, being prudent enough to roll it carefully, certain that in this land it might prove to have future value.

Gathea greeted me upon my return with a slight frown and a demand to let her see the cut upon my head. Having surveyed that searchingly, she admitted it was now closed and healing so I might go without cover over it. She had made a change in her own appearance, for her hair, still wet in spite of what must have been valiant efforts to wring and toss it dry, hung in a long, lank tail down her back, and she had bound it back with a bit of leather thong.

We would have liked to have used the stream bank as our path but the waters were swollen enough to wash the banks high, sending us climbing back to the grasslands above. However we did then parallel our march along the cut in which it ran.

Gruu, having led us to water, drunk his own fill, disappeared. I was certain that my companion had some means of communicating with the cat even at a distance and could summon him at need.

Those clouds which had masked the moon and stars from us last night had not been much dispelled by the sun which had arisen, only to be visited with a lowering mist which hid all at a distance in a haze. The herds kept well out on the grasslands. Perhaps they had their regular time of day for seeking water, for none approached as we tramped through what looked like a wilderness country. But I had learned ever to be on guard here.

I noticed that Gathea still carried her wand, holding it in her left hand as if it were as important to her as my sword was to me, even though it was only a straight branch cut from a thicket. At length the continued silence between us grew as oppressive as the day under those clouds, and I broke my resolution to leave any communication to her to ask:

"That which bayed at us in the camp—that which hunted—you have heard of their like before?"

She shook her head, a single sharp jerk. "I do not know what either was—only that the nature of one was of the Dark. Thus it could be met by those devices which are a protection against evil. Of the hunter—" she paused so long that I thought she would not continue before she said: "Perhaps it was also of the Dark, but it was no friend to that which strove to reach us. Its nature—that I could not read. We deal with both Light and Dark, but there may be those in this country that are neither, or that can be both at will. I know—so little!" There was unhappiness in her voice. I wondered if she meant her words for me at all or if they were only a cry against her own lack.

"Oh, I have a measure of the talent," she added, "otherwise I would not have been trained from first childhood by Zabina. Like knows like even if one looks upon a babe in the cradle. Also I know that I have in me more than Zabina can bring to flower or fruit. I learned of her in the same way that you, who know yourself to be a swordsman, were once put to fence with wooden blade among the younger boys. She has called me impatient, a fool, and foreseen dire disaster for me because I push and push to know more. But the moment I came through the Gate—then it was as if I had set foot on a homeward path which I did not know before could exist—there lay ready to my hand such wonders as those of Zabina's craft have only touched upon in dreams! This," Gathea flung forth her arms wide, on her face a fierce pride and hunger, "this is a place which *I* have dreamed of though I knew it not. I went to that Moon Shrine for the first time as if I had walked its path all my days. What was there welcomed me as daughter and handmaiden. Therefore," and the fierceness of her voice matched her look, "can you not see what your dainty keep maid has robbed me of? She, who has none of the talent in her—or else it is far buried under training of custom and of House—reaped where I was meant to harvest! Much good shall it do her!"

"You have spoken in riddles all along," I returned with matching sharpness. "What *has* happened to the Lady Iynne?"

She glanced at me over her shoulder, for she always kept a stride or so in advance, as if impatient. Around her sun-browned face there were loose tendrils of hair which had dried and now blew free, giving her a less severe and remote look.

"A gate of sorts opened." Her reply was tense. "Oh, not into another world, like that Gate which brought us here. Rather it is a way of finding another and more powerful shrine elsewhere—in the west—for the places of power left here are largely emptied, or whatever once filled them is much enfeebled and drained. To the Moon Shrine I brought knowledge which was a key, but the lock was old, it had not been turned for perhaps hundreds of seasons. I worked the ritual—I called down the Moon—I—" She raised her free hand and laid it between her breasts. "*I* did this! Then I was delayed on the night when there should be an answer and your reckless lady walked in where she should have feared to set so much as the toe of her slipper. Thus she gained, and I lost—"

I thought of Lady Iynne caught in some trap—for it must seem so to her—ensorcelled in a distant place. Though how she might have been so transported I still did not understand. Fear must have caught her—it might be enough to strike her wits from her. Realizing this I turned on the girl with me.

"You knew that she was visiting the shrine, still you did not warn her!" I accused.

"Warn her? But I did! Only there are calls against which no warning will hold unless the hearer is so trained, so staunch in spirit, that he or she is armed and armored. Iynne is a woman, a maid, so she, as all of the clan folk, was and is Moon's daughter. Moon magic rises in all women, though most deny it. Or, feeling it, do not understand that one must work with it and not against it. She has been so sheltered, so bound about by all the shall nots and do nots of a keep that she answered that call in spite of herself every time she stole away to look upon that shrine. You might have kept her in bonds, by door locks, but the quest already worked in her and her first visit there locked her in its power."

I glanced about at that wide plain of the valley, at the hills beyond which were hidden now by mists, so that now and then a dark bit of them loomed against the sky, only to be hidden once again.

"You believe you can find her." I did not make a question of that, for I was sure that she thought she could.

"Yes. For it is *my* magic that she dabbled in and—look you!"

She paused then, turning to face the north. On her out-held palm lay balanced the wand, and she stared at it with a tense concentration there was no mistaking. I looked from her fixed eyes to the wand and then I saw—

That tree branch, lying on her flattened palm where in no way she could control it by some trick of hand, began to move. It had pointed north and south, now it swung slowly but unmistakingly so that the narrow tip of the wood length indicated the misty heights westward.

"You see!" she demanded. "That which I summoned and worked so hard to gain has grown within me. It pulls me on, so that I may be truly whole as I was meant to be! Where I go— there will she be."

I had seen her do so much, I did not doubt she believed entirely in what she said. Perhaps this was no different from the other strange things in this land—that I should follow a maid who was certain she sought high magic, and that it had the strength, not only to call her, but to take another to it.

We found no traces of any other powers within that valley, only the herds of animals which kept their distance. It took us two days to cross that expanse and each night we cleared a patch of earth for Gathea to make a safe camp with circle and star. There were no visitors out of the dark. On the second night the moon was clear, the clouds were gone. Gathea had stood then in the full light of silver glow and sang—though I could neither understand the words nor remember them after. Between us an unseen wall grew thicker. This was no place for me, a man and a warrior; I was her companion on the trail by sufferance only.

At midmorning of the third day we entered the foothills of the heights. Now Gathea picked her way slowly with halts to allow her wand to point the way. There was no mistaking its swing, enticing us on into a broken country where the tall grass disappeared and outcrops of stone, gray, sometimes veined with dull red or a faint yellow, were more common. Though we had left the river behind us as its source lay farther north, we discovered mountain springs—or rather Gruu nosed them out, just as he hunted and we ate of his kills. I began to feel that we had traveled for seasons across land which was barren of any but animal life.

Now we discovered a valley leading back into the hills where there was more vegetation, stands of dark trees, which I thought curiously stunted and misshapen and which I did not like the look of. That night when we camped Gathea was so alive with excitement that she could not sit still. Time and time again she was on her feet, staring up that valley way, muttering to herself, slipping the wand back and forth through her fingers, as if to remind herself of what must be accomplished soon. Gruu, too, was uneasy, pacing around the fire, his eyes turned in the same direction as the girl's, as if he searched for a possible source of trouble.

"Feel it!" Gathea threw back her head. She had not bound her hair in the tight braids again since we had left the river; now I witnessed a strange thing. Those loose tendrils about her face lifted of themselves, not blown by any breeze (here the air was heavy and weighed upon me). Perhaps it was otherwise for

Gathea, as, in turn, the ends of her longer strands of hair stirred also, as if her whole body soaked up some force which then manifested itself so.

She held out the wand, and, I will swear the Blood Oath of the Flame, I saw upon its tip a star of light dance for an instant.

"Here—I am *here!*" She shouted as if standing before a keep gate where she had every reason to call for entrance and could not be denied.

Then—

Gathea began to run. So startled was I that, for a moment or so, I did not move. Then I caught up our two wallets, for she had dropped hers, and started after her. Gruu had bounded ahead, a silver streak, weaving a path among the trees where she had already vanished. Into the night I pounded after, though it appeared that, though I tried to keep directly on Gathea's track, I had not chosen well. Trees' low branches made me duck and swerve (they had not obstructed the progress of those other two). I ran into one trunk which I had not seen even a moment earlier, nearly stunning myself, and bringing a fresh ache to the old head wound.

Branches caught at me, tripped me up, struck me hard blows, until, afraid to lose Gathea in this place and never to find her again, I had out my sword, slashed and cut to clear the way as best I could.

The crash of my own passing covered any other sounds. In truth, I was afraid to stop and listen for fear I would be left so far behind I might never catch up with her.

There were things roosting or living in those trees which added raucous squeakings and hootings to the disturbance I made. Twice something flew directly into my face, once scoring my bruised cheek with either bill or talons. I tried to protect my face with my arm as I chopped a path. Sweat flowed down my face, plastered my too-well-worn undershirt to my body. It was stifling under those trees and I gasped for breath, yet I fought on.

A fight it was. I began to believe that these trees possessed an awareness of who and what I was and were determined to prevent my invasion. I fancied I heard faint cries, as from a distant battle. I was near overcome by the heat and my own exertions. Still I kept on because something in me took command and sent me forward, until at length I stumbled up a last hard slope, nearly losing my balance, breaking past the last thorn-studded limb of a tree into the open.

9

I HAD REACHED THE CREST OF A RIDGE BARE OF ANY GROWTH, THUS could look some distance ahead. There was no sign of either Gathea or Gruu—only bare rock. Not too far away a cliffside led upward again. I listened, wondering if cat and girl still struggled as I had to fight a way free of the trees and if I had outpaced them. There came no sound to tell me that was so. They might have been snatched up bodily or perhaps vanished through one of those "Gates" I had come to distrust.

Slowly I advanced across the open. The moon was on the wane; it offered just light enough to see the ground, where I tried to pick up some track left by either girl or cat. On this ledge of stone there was little hope of that.

So I approached the cliff's foot to see what had not been visible from afar. Deep cut into the surface of the stone was a series of regular holes large enough for hands and feet. However, I could not believe that Gathea had taken this path with such speed as to be out of sight completely before I had reached the end of the wood. Surely, I would have seen her still climbing!

Like a hunter who has lost the trail, I cast about. If she were yet in the wood, then to go on would serve no purpose. Finally I had to accept that she was indeed beyond my finding—unless I tried that rude stairway.

Slinging the straps of both wallets over my shoulders, making sure that my sword and belt knife were well anchored in their sheaths, I began to climb. It was not easy, for I discovered that the spaces between those holds had been designed for someone taller than myself, so that I had to stretch to reach each hold. How Gathea might have managed this ascent confused me.

Doggedly I kept on and up, testing each fresh hollow before I shifted my weight. My fingers scooped deep into dust filling those pockets, so I became convinced that the girl had not come this way. However, I determined to get to the top and from there gain a wider view of the countryside.

Breathing hard, I pulled myself over the lip of that cliff, to stare ahead at what faced me. This was not the top of the rise—rather a platform ledge which had been leveled by the work of some intelligence.

What dominated that space towered so above me, that I had to hold my head well back to view it in entirety. Great skill had gone into its making. At the same time the very finish of that skill suggested that whoever, or whatever, had conceived such a portraiture had been of an alien turn of mind, perverse, ill-tuned to consort with my own kind.

The represented form, which had been cut from the cliff's face so deeply that it was enclosed in an arched niche, stood erect on hind feet. However, it had only its stance in common with human beings, for it was clearly avian in form, and just as clearly female— blatantly so. It went unclothed, unless a wide and ornate collar could be considered covering of a sort.

The slender legs were stretched far apart, and its hands were outstretched from the ends of upper limbs, reaching forward, while the face beneath an upstanding crest of tall feathers was barely like my own. There were two eyes, but these were overlarge and set slanting in the skull; also they had been inlaid with red stones, perhaps gems, which glowed in the dim light as if they carried at their core a spark of burning fire.

Those reaching hands were claw-fingered, taloned. Looking upon them I thought of that lump of torn flesh I had buried back on the plain, though these were not mere skin and bone as that had been.

The expression the unknown carver had given the face agreed with the menace suggested by those claws, for most of it was a great beak, slightly open as if to tear, while the whole of the upper part of the body stood framed by wings which drooped, only a quarter open, behind each thin shoulder.

Between those arching legs a dark hole had been left as a doorway into the cliff. As I crouched where I was, staring, from that black archway wafted an odor which was rank and foul. Some beast of unclean habits might well lair there. My gaze kept, in spite of me, returning to those red eyes. I had a growing uneasy feeling that something watched me.

I did not accept that Gathea had gone into that hole. This was no Moon Shrine with a feeling of peace and well being. No, this was as threatening as the Silver Singers, or those crawlers in the dark who had menaced us in our first camp on the plain.

Slowly I arose, and, with a real effort, broke the bond of gaze those eyes had laid upon me. I would not take that door the thing guarded. There must be another way ahead.

It was then I discovered I was averse to turning my back on that carved figure. The sense of a waiting intelligence had been so well caught by the sculptor I could believe that, stone or not, it only remained here at its own choice. Thus I moved along that wide ledge crab fashion, so I could both search for another path and yet keep a wary eye on the leering bird-female.

Here were no more carved handholds to aid my escape. At the northern end of the smoothed ledge there was, however, a break in the cliff which might afford me a way to climb beyond.

I had no more than reached that promising crevice and was giving a last wary look to the figure when there was a stirring within the dark hollow between its legs. I swung swiftly about, my back to the wall and my sword out. There was a rustling, and then a loud hoot.

Into the wan light crawled a thing misshapen and hunched. It crouched for a moment before pulling upward to stand on clawed feet. Unlike the figure which guarded its lair it was a male and much shorter—near bone thin, still it possessed the same talons, the same beak.

The head turned on crooked shoulders (it appeared to be deformed when compared with the statue—and closer to the alien even than that). Only its eyes were as red and glowing—and utterly evil!

Those wings sprouting from its shoulders did not open to the full as it came about to face me squarely. The creature seemed to use its pinions as a balance as it leaped at me, making for me, talons outstretched and ready. At the same moment it let loose a deep scream.

Now fanning the wings, it attacked. I was ready with my blade. Whether the thing had ever been fronted by a determined fighter before I could not tell, but it left itself open to my counterblows as if it had expected no opposition at all.

The cutting edge of my sword struck true, between the rise of one wing and the thing's throat as its talons shredded the straps of the wallets, grated and scraped along my mail.

That head flopped onto the other shoulder as great gouts of dark stuff sprouted high, some drops hitting my hand, to sting my skin like fire. The creature stumbled back, striking fruitlessly into the air with both armored forepaws, wings now fully extended and beating hard so that their activity lifted it from the ledge and it was actually airborne. I thought that blow must bring death when it fell just as I aimed it, but it appeared far from ending our duel.

The head now dropped onto its chest, attached still to the body only by a strip of flesh and cartilage. Blood spouted fountain high about it as the creature came again at me. I might have to hew it to pieces to stop its attack.

Once more I struck, this time bringing the blade down across one of those raking forepaws. The edge again cut through, so that claw fell to the stone before me. Only—from the corner of my eye I saw, as I prepared to face the monster's third rush—that severed hand now took on life of its own, crawling toward me as if the fingertips were legs of some noisome insect.

A great gout of blood from the severed wrist (which the thing still held out before it as if it yet possessed the missing talons to rake me down) spattered on my sword hand. Again flames not only licked my flesh but seared deeply. I kept hold of sword hilt by sheer will, through the path which continued to eat at me.

Perhaps this creature which would not die sensed or already knew my torment for it whirled its maimed arm in the air (keeping its body beyond my reach) spattering the dark blood outward. Flying drops stung my cheek; more brought flaming agony to my throat where there was no helm guard to protect me. I feared for my eyes when a third gout struck high on my cheekbone.

Still, in spite of my seared fingers, I attacked once more, coming in low so that the next shower of blood fell on my mail-covered back and shoulders. Protected thus, I struck upward into the belly of the thing, then leaped back, its blood running down me, living fire where it touched flesh.

There seemed no way of killing it. That ripping blow which had opened its body from ribs to crotch only added to the blood flow, as if I had broken through a filled water skin. I could not believe that the thick liquid which flowed so steadily, which spouted afar, would so long continue to drain from that thin body, as if, beneath its outer hide, this creature was hollow, filled only with blood. For its attacks it visibly depended more and more on wings for support. I must dare the spouting poison from its hurts to slash at those. Then I nearly lost my balance, skidding forward into the slippery pool of blood. Furiously I struck down at what had so near tripped me, caught on the point of my sword the living hand, to flick it away, even as the creature moved in, arms still outstretched, though surely, with its head dangling so upon its breast it could no longer see me.

In a way that attack by the crawling hand had saved me by sending me off to the side. For the thing fluttered to my right, near enough for me to risk a blow at the other wing. Again steel sheared straighter than I dared hope.

My attacker fell away, still flapping the maimed wing, the other one fanning air with great sweeps. That one-sided effort dashed it into the side of the cliff, and it went down, sprawling forward. I leaped to strike the second wing, then stabbed downward between its shoulders.

A moment later, breathless, I reeled back against the cliff myself, watching in dull horror as that mutilated thing strove to rise, to come at me. While the full tide of its poisonous blood spread out and out I cringed away from the deadly pool.

I thought the thing was helpless now. However, had it been the only one of its kind in the statue-guarded hole? There was no movement within, but if this creature was nocturnal its fellows might be already afield. The sooner I was away the better, though to try to climb the cliff with more winged monsters arriving to pluck at me was risky. I could only hope to be allowed to reach the top without another fight.

Letting my fouled sword hang from my wrist by its cord, not daring to allow the blood near my flesh, I wiped my blistered hand hastily against my breeches. The splashes which had struck my cheek burned with increasing agony.

Catching up the wallets by their sheared straps, I knotted them to my belt, turning with all haste to the crack in the cliff's surface. Fortune had decided to favor me, for, not far above, the crack widened out far enough I might edge my body into it, leaving very little chance for any other winged attacker to grasp or tear. The creature I had wounded was not dead. Still it flopped about, as if it would come at me.

The sight and the sound of that floundering body gave me fresh strength for escape, made me forget the pain in my hand as I hunted for holds to draw me up. My need to escape, to find some better defense than this tissue in the cliff face offered, lent me both the strength and speed to win to the very crest of the heights.

Here was a second gift of fortune. For on the plateau was a stand of trees. Toward those I went at a stumbling run, sure that the winged things, if more of them came, could not reach me beneath that roof of branch and leaf.

Even as I had forced my way through that wood below, so now I thrust forward into this one, eager to win undercover. At last I hunkered down between two trunks, grabbed handfuls of leaves to cleanse my sword as best I could, before opening my wallet to hunt out those salves which Zabina had packed for me. Breathlessly I rubbed sticky stuff first across the back of my hand and then along cheek and jaw.

Gradually the pain eased, and I only hoped that the creature's poison was assuaged. Of that I could not be sure, for I began to shiver with a cold which was certainly not of the night. Also I retched and retched again, so shaken with nausea that my head whirled. Nor could I hold myself upright without clinging to a tree.

Maybe that poison also reached my mind, for I kept slipping into a daze during which all I saw was the cleft, scuttling up it that severed hand, still trailing blood, sent ahead like a hound to hunt for its master. Then I would become alert and aware, knowing dimly where I was. Yet I looked about me for that crawling thing, listening for a scrabbling sound announcing its coming.

I must have drifted in and out of such horrors for a lengthy time, for when I roused from a last dream in which the hand confronted me and I was too weak to draw my sword against it, day had arrived to lay patches of sun here and there on the ground, for these trees were not so tightly banded together as to shut out that welcome light. Thirst made an ache in my throat, and I drank from my water bottle, which I held with shaking hands.

The stench of those now dry stains which covered much of my mail front and back again brought sour bile rising in my throat. When I tried to get to my feet I discovered I must cling to the tree. My hand bore a brown brand across the back, which cracked when I moved my fingers, making me grimace with pain. I had no idea of where I would go, save that I must find water to cleanse my clothing and mail and see again to my hurts.

Where in this wilderness I could find any spring or stream I did not know, but maybe fortune would not turn her face from me now.

Insects buzzed out of nowhere to plague me, drawn, I supposed, by the odor which clung to my clothing. I staggered from one tree to the next, lingering at each to hold for a moment or two, fighting for strength to carry me on, until, at length, I wavered into the brightness of the full sun at the edge of that copse to stand blinking, gathering more energy to forge ahead. I was somehow sure that the creature I had tried to slay, or its like, was of the night, and that the day would favor me while I could put distance between me and its ledge lair.

There were more heights to the west, but I had headed north to keep under the cover of the trees. Now I hesitated, still steadying myself against the last trees, while I sought to map out a new path which would not tax further my remaining dregs of energy. Grass grew here in ragged patches between bones of rocks that pierced the earth. The slope was upward and did not look too hard to climb. Thus I took that way, for I was sure that I could not gather strength enough again to fight a cliff.

I was some distance from the trees before I noticed that I walked on what could only be pavement, smoothed blocks of stone set with such skill that even the earth could not be seen in the cracks between. This trace was not wide enough to be a road such as would accommodate one of the wains of the clans, but it would have provided easy riding for mounted men. For me now it was another stroke of luck. I still went slowly, having to pause now and again, resting out those dizzy spells which struck without warning, causing stabs of fear.

This paved path—I did not name it "road"—ran north for a space. Then, like the land to my left, the western heights, arose higher and higher, and into a gap between two pinnacles which towered, sky touching high, on either hand.

The shade in that cut soothed my aching head, though there seemed no relief for my burning throat. In spite of the heat of the sun I had been shaken all during that journey by waves of chill, sometimes so strong that I had to halt and steady myself against some convenient rock until they passed.

This gap way was wider, though only the centermost portion was paved, a clearing open on either hand so that none of the loose rocks neared any portion of the block strip. Had it been tended as a precaution against ambush by those who might travel here? Thinking that, I became alert to what lay about. There might well be more of the winged things spying on me from some crevice aloft. Thus I pushed my strength to carry me as far as possible for as long as daylight held.

I no longer thought of Gathea or Gruu. Having my own danger to face, I needed to concentrate on the here and now.

Again my lost road sloped upward, but so easy was the incline that I could keep to a hurried pace. Also a clean, cool wind blew here, pulling away the stink of the dried splotches I was forced to carry with me. I came at last into what was undoubtedly a pass, and so could look down at what lay beyond the first bastion of the western heights.

The descent looked far more rugged than the ascent had been. But there was one boon: those who had made this way had marked the summit of their road with a basin of stone into which spouted a steady stream of water. I stumbled rather than strode to it, going to my knees and stretching out my hands to let the sharp, snow-cold liquid wash across my seared skin.

Nor could I withstand further temptation. Though I laid my sword ready to hand I freed myself from my mail shirt and under jerkin, rubbing both down with handfuls of wet sand from the bottom of the basin, dipping up more water to lave my face, to wash away all the signs of battle. The raw places on my face and throat stung and burned. I anointed them again with the salve—trusting that I was doing right. The brownish scab on my hand sloughed away, leaving a red band like a broad scar where the skin still pulled as I flexed my fingers.

Having rid myself of the poison stains I had been forced to carry, I was able at last to stomach some food. Once more I rinsed and refilled my water bottle, sitting cross-legged by the basin and studying, as I drank deeply, the world before me.

Below lay an odd patchwork of land. Parts I believed to be desert for they showed harshly yellow and white under the sun, with no relief of green to rest the eye or promise better traveling. The road marked out as a ribbon of lighter rock turned south, hugging the side of the heights as it descended, following what might have been a ledge hacked back in the cliff side. The sheer labor of such an undertaking impressed me. I knew what difficulty it was even to prepare a packed-earth way for travel from one dale to another —a plan discussed among the lords on our way north but dismissed because it would require more manpower than even the largest of our clans could hope to muster. Yet here the side of a small mountain had been routed out and those blocks laid with a nicety beyond the skill of any but a master builder. How long had it taken, and what lord or ruler had had need of such a thing that he could assemble enough men to carry through the task?

The road ended once more in a patch of trees of which I could only see the tops as a billowing of greenery. Not having a distance glass, I could not tell if the way broke free from those on the other side. I debated as I rested whether I should go on or stay where I was for the night. Was I still so close to that dangerous cavern that I might expect more of the winged people to search me out? Could I even make it all the way down that long road to the trees? And what of trees in this unknown country—could they not also shield new dangers?

At length the thought of a possible attack by the winged ones in greater force spurred me on. My rest by the spring and food and drink had strengthened me. If there was moon tonight, even a waning one such as shone the night before, it would be my aid. I looked to the horizon in all directions to see if there was any hint of clouds and saw none. Surely I ought to be able to camp at the edge of that wood below.

With a much firmer step and a sense that I had made the wisest decision, I set off down that long incline. As I went I thought of the Sword Brothers, wondering if any of them had chanced this way, and what they had made of the creature I had fought, or of the Silver Singers—the hunter in the dark— What wonders had they chanced upon that they had not spoken of, or only learned of after they had led us to the lands along the sea? Once, I had envied their chance to explore, to search out the strange in new lands. Now, alone, I found the exploration far different from my wistful dreams.

The road carried me at a good pace, never dipping too steeply, running as if designed for traffic that needed steadiness of foot. Thus it led for quite a distance south again, taking me well past the cliff I had won my way up earlier. The rock was the same as I had seen elsewhere—gray broken by red and yellow veins. However, the pavement was of different stone altogether and must have been brought from elsewhere, for it was of a gray white and thus stood out sharply against the darker shade of the cliff.

I had descended perhaps a third of the way between the pass and lower country when I noticed that those blocks over which I trod were no longer smooth. Instead, set upon or in each one in such a way that the foot of the traveler must fit square upon it was a symbol. Some of these were black, a thick, inky black which reminded me unpleasantly of the color of the flying creature's blood in the moonlight; others were a faded red, again not unlike *my* blood had it been shed and soaked into the stone.

The symbols themselves were very intricate and I found it difficult to view them in detail. Once one's glance was caught by some portion of the pattern, the eye was held and one's gaze carried forward, in and out, around about. I jerked my attention swiftly from them, avoiding their complexity. At the same time I had the old feeling that the reason why they had been so set was to establish the strength of those who used this way, that they might tread underfoot some sign of power which they found wrong and evil. But that may only have been a fancy and I tried not to allow my imagination to roam too far.

It was enough that the color was distasteful and I did not want to be reminded of what it represented, so I soon kept my eyes resolutely away from those patterned stones. Not all the stones were so marked. Often there were long sections of clear blocks and it was on those that I paused now and then to rest, to look down at the treetops, which appeared to remain obstinately well away from me.

That clean wind which had been refreshing in the pass was lost here. Once or twice a breeze did reach me—blown over, I believed, that section of land which was desert, since it was hot and dry. When I did head west once again, I made up my mind, I would avoid that portion of the country.

Head west? With Gathea gone and no guide, where was I heading? For the first time (I had so concentrated on escaping from the place of the winged things) I realized I had not thought of what would come next. If Gathea had really the secret of the Lady Iynne's fate, she had given me no clue. To flounder around in this wild country seeking a trail which might not even exist was sheer folly.

Still, what else was left for me? Westward was the only hint I had, and westward I could go. For me, nameless and clanless now, what other fate remained? I chewed on that bitterness as I walked another space of the symbol-set blocks and then—because the twilight was closing in—I broke into a trot which, at last, brought me to the end of the descent where the road spun on into the wood. I hesitated, trying to make up my mind as to whether I should continue on into that shadowed place with night so near.

10

I PREPARED MY CAMPSITE WITH CARE, BREAKING OFF BRANCHES, which I leaned against stout limbs I had driven into the ground, fashioning so a roof to hide me from sight of flying things. Whether the winged creatures could track by scent like other hunters I could not tell—but I would light no fire in this country to attract any prowler of the dark hours.

Remembering what Gathea had said concerning the power of cold iron against the unknown, I drew my belt knife and set it upright in the earth before my shelter, while my bared sword lay ready. The girl's wallet I put to one side; my own I explored for food, which I must ration carefully.

My headache had returned and the pain of my burns, though the salve had assuaged that somewhat, was still enough to keep me wakeful. I watched and listened.

The wood near my camp was not silent. There were small noises, a thin cheeping now and then, the rustle of leaves and brush as if the life sheltered there had come awake by night and was now going about affairs of its own. Once, there came a hooting from the sky and my hand tightened quickly about my sword hilt. However, if one of the winged people passed he or she had no interest in me.

Always my thoughts were busy now with what had happened since the night before when Gathea ran into the wilderness. I was convinced that in some way I had missed whatever path she had followed, forcing myself to accept the fact that it would only be by fortunate chance that I might ever pick up her trail again.

In spite of my struggle to keep awake I dozed, awoke with a start, only to fall into a new snatch of sleep. Still I listened and held guard, eyes and ears alert.

What I would do in the morning I did not know. To return up that road to the pass was not to be tried. I had been highly fortunate in my first encounter with the winged people. I could not hope for more luck in a second. My best chance was perhaps to journey along the foot of the heights seeking traces of Gathea—or perhaps of any Sword Brothers who had earlier ridden westward. My spirits hit a desolate low as for the first time since Lord Garn had exiled me from the clan and House I realized what it meant to be utterly alone. There was no worse fate, I decided in those night-dark moments, for any man. My hope of reaching the Lady Iynne was, I made myself accept, a dream which bore little chance of realization since Gathea had vanished.

Still, I remained stubborn enough to vow that my search would not be over until I was dead—for I had nothing else left to me.

The night was long, my broken rest was short. However, nothing approached my lean-to, as if I were invisible to anything which prowled or hunted in the dark. With the coming of dawn I ate again, only a few rationed mouthfuls, mended the carrying straps of both wallets, and, slinging those upon my back, set out once more, my guide still the blocks of the road.

Those led me into the wood, where the branches of trees met overhead to form a ceiling, keeping out much of the sunlight. Once more the blocks were clear from encroachment of growth. In fact, so bright were they that they appeared to give off a dim radiance of their own. Nor were there any here which were marked with those disturbing symbols.

The road, however, did not run straight; rather swung right or left from time to time to allow full growth space to taller and thicker trees. Their bark was smooth, of a red-brown, while their crowns were lifted high, with few branches below.

I came a good way along before I noted that those trees also differed in other ways from their fellows. For, when I skirted about them, their leaves (which were a brighter green and seemed as fresh as the first tentative sprouting of spring) began to rustle—though no breeze blew. At the third such reaction to my passing I halted to look up. No, I had not been wrong. Those leaves immediately above my head were more and more in motion—almost as if they formed mouths by rubbing together, calling or else commenting on my presence.

Had the poison which had struck me yesterday disordered my wits? I tried to think that was so—far more believable than that trees talked, were sentient beings.

I felt no fear, only a dull wonder. Nor did I move on, though had one of those mighty limbs come crashing down it would have meant my death. Still more violently the leaves rustled. I began to truly believe the sound was indeed speech—though alien to my own.

The rustling now, I decided, sounded impatient, as if my attention had been sought and I had not made the proper response. So deep was I caught in that fancy that I spoke aloud:

"What do you want of me?"

The leaves above twirled on their stems, rustling as if a gale had closed about this tree, sending it into a frenzy. Even those weighty branches swayed, as a desperate man might toss up his arms to attract the notice of some heedless sluggard.

There was a shimmer in the leaves as they tossed, giving me a queer sense that they were not leaves any more but flames of greenish hue such as might spring from a thousand candles all set alight. Green they were, but they also now sparked blue, and yellow—and a deeper violet—until I stood beneath a web woven in an unknown pattern which hung above me as might a fine tapestry in some rich keep.

That light flowed downward, or did it drop from leaf after leaf as they might fall with the coming of winter? I found that I could not look away as they—or the pattern of light which they emitted—swirled about me.

I was no longer in the wood. Where I stood then I could not have said, save it was a place in which my kind had not walked and was unknown. The bright swirl of color wove tighter about me. I felt no fear, rather awe that I could see this, which I understood was never meant for eyes like mine. Then that web parted, drew to either side like a curtain, and another faced me.

One hidden part of me knew a flash of uneasiness such as comes whenever a man faces the utterly strange. Yet the rest of me was waiting, wanting to know what was expected of me. There had been a summons of a sort, of that I was aware.

She was tall and slender, this woman whom the leaf colors had now revealed to me, clothed in a shimmering green which I could see was formed of many small leaves which never lay still but flowed about her, showing now her slender limbs, now a single small breast, now her shoulders, or thickened again until she was hidden from throat to ankle.

Her hair hung free but it did not lie still upon her shoulders, long as it was. No, it played outward in a nebulous cloud about her head, swaying and twining, loosening and tightening, even as the leaves of her clothing moved. It was also green, but of a pale shade touched with threads of red-brown here and there. Red-brown also was her skin where and when it showed in contrast to her garment, smooth—

Against that, her great eyes, which overshadowed the rest of her features, were a brilliant green like those gems cherished by our wealthiest lords. As brilliant, and of a harder luster, were the nails on the hands which she raised now to tame the weaving of her hair.

She had such beauty, strange though it was, as I had never believed could exist, as I had never dreamed of—even in those dreams of the body which came to any youth when he passes into manhood. Yet I could not have reached for her with any desire fiery in me, for there was no bridge between us that I might cross. I could only look upon her as a wondrous thing like a flower of perfect blossom.

Those huge eyes reached into me and I had no defense against such sorcery, nor did I want any. I felt the touch of her mind, far more intimate than any touch of hand or body.

"Who are you who travels the old way of Alafian?"

Not speech, but thought. Nor did I shape any answer with lips in return. Rather it was as if her asking set my memory alert and I found myself recalling vividly, with detail which I thought forgotten, all that had chanced with me since I had come into Garn's dale.

By no will of my own did I remember. Some things I wished I

had truly forgotten—but of that there was no chance. I remembered and she learned.

"So—"

My mind seemed sucked dry, though I did not even resent that she used me so. In a dull, dim way it seemed only right that I thus vindicated to her why I intruded in a land which was hers, where there had long been peace, where my very coming had broken a slumberous, happy rest.

"This is not your place, half-man. But your seeking will drive you still. And—"

Her thought withdrew for a moment, leaving me strangely empty, feeling even more that burden of loneliness which lay on me.

"What you would do—that will drive you. Your need is not of our choice, nor can such as we mar or mend. Seek and perhaps you will find more than you now expect. All things are possible when a seed is well planted. Go in peace, though that is not what you will find, for it does not lie within you."

Again her thought withdrew. I wanted to cry out for her not to leave me. But already the shifting curtain of light closed between us to move in a dizzying pattern, breaking into sparks which flew apart with a burst of light which left me blinded for what seemed a long moment.

Once more I stood beneath the tree, my feet planted on the ancient road. No leaves rustled above me. The tree was quiet as if the life which had filled it had withdrawn. Lying at my feet was a single leaf, perfect in its shape, a bright green, as gemlike as the lady's eyes. About its edge ran a line of red-brown like the trunk of the tree, or like her body which had shown so fair.

Some vision borne out of bodily weakness? No, that I did not believe. I stooped to pick up that one perfect leaf. It was not a tree leaf, or at least not like any I had seen or fingered before. There was weight and thickness to it, a leaf which had been carved out of some precious stone my people did not know, a leaf which would not wither, powder at last into dust, as do those which fall in an ordinary woods.

I loosed the pouch fastening of my wallet and carefully set that leaf within. For what purpose it had been given to me (for I believed firmly that it was a gift) I might not yet know, but it was a treasure which I would ever carry with me.

For a while I could not go on. I stared into that tree, until my longing at last died in the realization that what I had seen would not come again. Horror I had met on the ledge of the winged creatures; here I had met beauty, a vision which tugged at me powerfully and might never now be satisfied. In this land one swung between fear and awe, with no safe middle path.

Still, I went on down that road which wound in and out among those trees, but now no leaf voices called to me. I wanted to be away from them, for even to sight one made me aware of a loss which was an ache, not of the body, but of some inner part of me.

I did not stop to eat, though I hungered, only kept doggedly on, until, at last, I emerged from the wood into open land again. There I left the road, for that still held northward and it was westward I believed I must go. Not too far away another line of heights reached skyward, while the land before me was overgrown with brush and scattered trees. Beyond the fringe of growth something caught my full attention.

A *keep*—here?

Stone walls, a tower—the building was so much like those which even the Gate's power had not erased from my past that I could believe I had returned to the land of my birth, save that no lord's banner flapped in the wind above that tower, no signs of life were to be seen about its walls.

I wondered once more what had led the Bards to open the Gate for us into this world. Had indeed people of my own kind once before come this way? What had we fled? Why need the knowledge of that be erased from our memories when so much else was allowed to remain? This I looked upon now might well be the hold of any of the greater lords; it was more impressive certainly than Garn's. If it had not been built by those of my own blood then it had been the abiding place of some so like us that we might find allies here, kin in part.

The very familiarity of that fortress-hall drew me. I set a faster pace to push through the brush. There had once been fields here. Stone walls, some of them tumbled into mere scattered rubble, cut through grass and shrubs so that in my headlong path I had to climb, seeing what could have been stunted patches of grain already sun-warmed to a yellow for harvesting.

I caught a handful of the bearded heads and rubbed them in my palm, then chewed them as I had done with the harvest of fields I had known since childhood. They had a familiar taste. How close were the worlds which the Gate had bound together? At least this untended harvest would testify that seed grains which our landsmen had brought with them would grow here, promising better for the future—*if* the alien life did not battle against us, for invaders and strangers have no homestead rights.

As I chewed on that mouthful of grain I walked on toward the building ahead. The closer I got the more it appeared to be one of our own homesteads. I believed as I studied it that those who had built here had also had need for defense, since there were stout walls, windows which were narrow and well above the ground.

Only, the massive gate was not only open, but had broken free of one hinge, half of it hanging askew, allowing free entrance, making it plain that this was a deserted place. The stone from which it had been built was not native to the heights behind me, for it was of a plain rose-red displaying none of the somber veining of those rocks. Also it glinted here and there in the last rays of the sun (fast being shut off by the stand of highland beyond) as if bits of burnished silver were entrapped to give it alien beauty, belying the plainness of the structure into which it had been wrought.

Over the gate where that door hung open was a panel which flashed with even greater brilliance. Just so might the insignia of a House be set in the grander keeps of the clans, save that this was wrought into the form, sharp against its background, of a cat, silver and white like Gruu himself. The creature did not snarl defiance against any assault as one might expect by its placement —rather it sat upright, its tail curled about so that the tip lay snug over the forepaws.

Green eyes (as brilliant as those of my lady of the leaves) had been set skillfully in the head so one could not escape the half belief they had life, that this beast surely saw all who passed under its niche. Why, I could not tell, I brought up my right hand in a warrior's salute to that motionless sentry who had kept faith for so long.

I pushed under the cat's perch to a large inner courtyard. Directly facing me stood the bulk of the structure, topped by the tower, which would certainly house, not only the great hall for the assemblage of all who sheltered here once, but also the private apartments of the lord, the armory, and the special storerooms, while around the inner side of the wall were clustered smaller buildings—stables, storehouses, and some which must have been for dwellings of landsmen and servitors, barracks for my lord's meiny, and the like.

There was no sign (save that drooping door) that time had rested any heavy hand here. From the outward show, one of our clans might well have marched within to make a home in greater comfort than they would certainly know for a score of years in the sea-girt dales. Always supposing that they did not bring down upon them such enemies as the winged ones—or those Silver Singers of the night.

I went boldly. Perhaps because this was so like a dwelling of my own people, I did not have the uneasiness which had ridden me ever since I had followed Gathea's guidance into this sorcery-shadowed land. The door to the tower structure was wide open and there was a blanking of blown earth and winter-withered leaves against it to testify that it had been more than one season since any had sought to close it.

Over the arch was a broad band of smooth stone, a half circle, on which there stood out, with the same boldness of the gateway cat, a series of runes. Warning? Welcome? Clan name? I might guess but I would never know.

Again I passed on into the great hall. What remained of furnishing there was also stone. There was the dais with high-backed seats of honor—four of them—each of a sleek green stone, their backs carven with an intricate design, the details of which I could not distinguish from a distance. There was a table of the same stone, and then, running partway down the hall to make that upper table a bar across its top, a second board—this of rock matching the walls.

The place lay mainly in shadow, since the windows were high set and small. Still, near the tables I could see a massive hearth, smoke blackening up its chimney throat, nearly of a size to take a section of one of those giant forest trees. This was topped with an

over-mantel supported on either side by sitting cats which out-
topped me in height. That was again carved with runes which
glinted brightly in spite of the lack of full light.

Curiosity, together with that odd feeling of familiarity, kept me
exploring. I found chambers above, reached by a stairway set in
the wall behind the chairs of honor. Those were bare, though two
had fireplaces with carven mantels and rune signs. Perhaps once
hangings had veiled the walls, but there were none left. Nothing
lay on the floors but dust in which my trail boots left the first
marking perhaps for years.

I found the kitchen, again furnished with stone tables set out
for the convenience of long-vanished cooks—the wing holding this
running out to join the wall on the other side of the towered
inner keep. Here there was a cleverly set pipe spouting water into
a long trough, something no building of my own people had ever
had. I tasted the stream, found the water cold and sweet, and
drank deeply. Then I returned to the hall, determined that here I
would camp this night.

With the coming of dark another wonder was revealed. I had
earlier noted that the runes above the fireplace had seemed over
bright in the general gloom of the long hall. Now, as that grew
darker, they in turn grew brighter. When I examined them as
closely as I could (for the panel was set far above my head) I
could see there were small scenes carved in and among those,
coming to life with the runes.

I made out pictures of hunts. Still, there were no hunters who
might be termed men. Rather cats crept, leaped, brought down
the prey. And such prey! I had no difficulty in identifying the
winged thing I had fought on the ledge. And that was the least
strange of the enemies pictured there. To look upon them was
warning enough against venturing on into this country. Unless
passing years had brought some end to them.

There was a serpent (or at least one first thought "serpent"
until I saw the thing better) with a horned and tusked head
reared high enough to prove the head was not mounted on a reptile's supple length, having instead a human torso, sliding into
scales once again where a man's lower limbs might join his body.
Its outstretched hands held two blades with which it menaced the

cat seeking to attack it, as if it were a swordsman well versed in battle craft.

Again another cat fighter reared its own head in victory, its mouth open to give vent to what I thought might be just such a roar as I had heard Gruu utter. Under his mighty forepaw, pinned flat, a smaller creature which looked to be a mass of bristly hair leaving one rootlike arm which still strove to bring knotted talons of fingers to bear on its captor—or slayer.

That these representations were accounts of real past battles I believed. I considered the recklessness with which I had set out into a land which still abounded perhaps in such monstrosities. Also I remembered both Gathea and my lady Iynne at that moment, though there was nothing that I might do to help either, until I could come upon some clue as to their path.

There was no wood here that I might light a fire in the vast cave of the hearth, but I sat upon its stone to allow myself that small portion of food I had put aside for the next meal, thinking that tomorrow I would doubtless find good hunting. For surely any animals that grazed would be drawn to the fields to call that grain. At least I might drink my fill of water and that I did.

Having eaten, I once more went up the length of the hall which was now filled with shadows, so that I drew aside now and then from some darker clot, as I would for people gathering to talk and await the coming of the lord, his signal for the evening meal. In spite of the dusk it was to me a goodly place, one which I would have been full proud to make my own—were I a lord with a clan to house and an old proud name to hold in honor. But I was kinless, nameless—and my life was as like to be as empty of all such in the future as this hall was now; a shadow clan was all I might ever hope to head.

Yet when I had come to the high table I stepped boldly onto the dais and passed along the row of chairs seeking those four set in the middle. The openwork on the backs of those bristled with no horror scenes of cats and prey, but rather was formed by mingling of fruit-bearing stems and tall grain stocks, each bordered by flowers. Those made me think again of my leaf-clad lady and wonder of what manner of folk she was. Or had it been the spirit of the tree itself which had so confronted, weighed, and judged me?

Bold again I pushed to the fourth of those chairs and seated

myself, discovering that indeed they had been fashioned for someone like me physically. Hard though that stone was to the touch,
yet it did not seem uncomfortable to sit upon. When I placed
both elbows on the table and supported my chin on my hands to
look down the length of the hall, I saw that here, too, there had
been symbols set into the surface of the table itself, gleaming
enough so that I could make out their curves of design. I dropped
my right hand, on which still showed the brand the blood of the
winged thing had left upon me, as, with fingertip, I began to trace
the line of the symbol which was before me, my flesh running
smoothly and swiftly along the curves and sharp angles to another
curve again. Idly so, and why I could not have told, I traced that
three times—

Three times—

The lines grew brighter. Perhaps my action had cleared them of
clogging dust. I could see other sets, each of which lay before one
of the high seats, but none of those was as clear as this.

Somewhere—from out of the very air itself—came sound. It was
like the deep note of a horn. Yet there was also in it the beat of a
drum. Or was it a call of many voices joined together into a single
lingering note? I only knew that I had not heard its like before. In
spite of myself I shrank back from the table, braced both hands
now on the carved arms of the chair, staring out into the hall (for
that had grown very dark), hunting the source of that sound.

Three times it was repeated. The last time I imagined that an
echo, or a reply, had followed from farther away. The dark (I
could not even see the gleam of those pictures above the fireplace
now though their radiance had fought the general gloom from the
first) closed in deeper, thicker.

I had a giddy feeling that the whole building into which I had
dared intrude was in a state of change, that, though I was now
blinded, strange things were happening all about me. My grip on
the arms of the chair was so tight that the edges of carving cut
cruelly into my hands. The dark was thick—complete. I was falling, or flying, or being drawn, into another place—perhaps another
time from which change there was no escape.

11

IF THAT BLACKNESS WAS SOME WITCHERY, THEN WHAT I AWOKE
into was not a dream, though I wanted to believe it was. I was
still in the chair of honor at that table but I looked down a hall
which was alive with company—enough to fill it, vast as it was.
Still, when I tried to focus clearly on any of that throng they appeared to veil themselves against my direct gaze. Thus I could
only make out but a hazy outline of a form, perhaps the muted
color of a robe or jerkin. Never did I see a face clearly. Also I was
left with a strong impression that, while many of those forms were
like my own, aliens moved easily and companionably among them
—some beautiful, some grotesque.

It was plain they feasted and that this was an assembly for a
reason of importance. This I sensed rather than heard. There was
sound in the hall but so muted, so far removed from my own
hearing, it was more the murmur of sea waves breaking on distant
shore.

I leaned forward, striving to center upon just one face, hold
that in my sight until I could be sure of the features, but there
was always that veiling. Then I turned my head to the right, to
see who occupied the chair at my hand's side. There was indeed
one there, a woman whose robe was the amber of ripened grain.
But her face, the rest of her, was only a blur. When I looked to
my left I was sure that my other neighbor was a man, but more
than that I could not have told you.

Still holding tightly to the arms of my chair, I waited for them
to mark my coming, perhaps for the sorcery either to break into

nothingness, or else change, to reveal them fully. Yet neither happened, save that those hazy forms moved, sat, ate, raised goblets to drink, spoke in murmurs, and remained within a world of their own which I could not enter, only watch.

One thing only gleamed in sharp brightness—the runes on the tabletop directly before me. They were fully in *my* world and my eyes kept returning to them as I became more and more confused by vision into which I had been plunged. By a great effort I loosed my hold upon the arms of the chair, stretched forth both hands to touch those symbols. If they had ensorcelled me into this state of being, then perhaps they would free me from it again.

I had to summon up my will power to straighten my forefinger, hold it once more above that lettering. Just so had I traced the runes, mark by mark. Three times. What would happen if I wrought so again? I set my teeth and began. Under my touch that inscription was cold as if I had plunged my finger into the water of a mountain spring. So—and so—and so—

Once, twice, three times, I made the gesture, keeping my attention fully on what I did. Then my ears opened—I heard voices—no longer as a distant hum but loud and clear. Though what language they spoke—it was none of mine.

I dared to look up. The hall, all those within had been also given reality, emerged from shadows to full substance. There were men and women, feast-day clad with a richness which I had never seen in any lord's hall among my own kind. They did not wear emblazoned tabards such as my people kept for occasions of state, rather robes and jerkins of soft, clinging stuff colored as brightly as meadow flowers. There were gemmed girdles, broad jeweled collars, the flash of rings on moving hands.

Their hair was dark, and that of the ladies dressed high and decked with jewel-headed pins, or coronets so begemmed it was as if they had drawn the stars out of the skies to bedeck themselves. Circle crownlets the men wore also, but those each bore a single large gem over the forehead and were of gold or silver, or a red metal I had not seen before.

Among them were others, even as I had thought. I saw near the high table a woman who was surely of the same race as she who I had met among the trees. There was a man—or so I thought him—who wore no jerkin. But there were two begemmed belts crossing on his breast, and covering each shoulder with a wider span. His skin was furred, his features were covered by a soft down, while from his forehead there curled up and back horns of a red shade which matched the glint of his eyes. I was sure that I saw the arch of furled wings standing above the head of another farther down that board. But as I tried to catch a closer look at what I feared might be one of the monsters, I was startled by a touch. A hand rested upon mine.

"Has the spring wine bemused you, my lord? You stare as one who has not feasted here before."

Her voice was soft, yet it carried easily through the louder sound of all over voices. I turned my head slowly, to see clearly her who sat at my right, who had spoken words in my own tongue.

She was dark of both hair and skin. Even against my sunbrowned flesh hers showed darker still, and I was sure that her coloring owed nothing to the touch of heat or wind. Tall she must have been, for I had to look up a fraction to meet her eyes. Those were brown also, the ruddy brown of that amber which is so highly prized by my kin. But her brows were black and straight above her eyes. She possessed the authority of one well used to command. The amber which I had noticed through the haze was a mantle which she had flung back now that she had put out her hand to mine. Under it was a robe of the yellow shade of ripe-to-cut grain, fitted to a body which was generous of breast, but narrow of waist. Between her full breasts rested a pendant which was also of amber, though the chain which supported it was of black and amber beads alternating. The pendant was formed like a shock of harvested grain, bound together by a vine from which had burst fruit in lusty ripeness.

Her hair had been brought up in a coronet of braids, and, instead of the gem flashing crowns or pins the others wore, there was only over her forehead another amber piece, larger but of the same design as her pendant, supported by a circlet of ruddy gold.

I was so bemused in looking at her. Yes, and in feeling in myself a response such as was certainly not fitting for this time and place—that I had not answered. She was—I could not find words as my thoughts flitted in a crazy fashion to a vision of a field prepared for sowing (also other and less innocent things as my body responded to a growing excitement).

She smiled and her smile was an invitation that drew me so that only my will held me in my seat. Nor did she take her hand away from where it lay on mine. It was a teeth-setting determination to keep from seizing upon her fingers, drawing her to me.

Her eyes changed and there was surprise in them. Then more than surprise, recognition. In that moment I was sure she saw me as what I truly was—not one of their company at all, a stranger caught in some sorcery and so brought among them.

Now I could not have moved even had I allowed myself the wild drive for action which tormented me. Those amber eyes held me. She lifted her other hand to clasp the pendant at her breast. I waited to see her anger grow, to have her claim me imposter, enemy—thief of some heritage which could never be mine.

Instead she only studied me. There was now speculation in her eyes. Her fingers, touching me, moved, closed about my wrist in a grip which I do not believe that I could have thrown off without full exertion of strength. I would not have believed that any woman could hold me so.

She spoke, her words again reaching me clearly under the cover of the babble about us, with a snap of order which I could not have disobeyed.

"Drink!"

There was a goblet at my left hand. Since she did not release the hold on my right I perforce raised that to obey her. The goblet, oddly enough in that place of such wealth, was carved from a solid piece of dark wood. In high relief upon the side was the head of a man, or one close to a man—though the eyes were slanted and there was a wry kind of amusement cleverly suggested by both those eyes and quirk of the lips above a pointed chin. The head of curling locks was crowned by a circlet in the form of deer horns, while the cup was filled near to the brim with liquid which, as I raised the goblet, began to seethe and bubble. Still I could not escape doing as she bade, and I drank.

The liquid was not hot as I had feared from seeing the action within—rather cool. Still, as it went down my throat it spread warmth—warmth and something more. It fired my blood, strengthened my desire.

I had kept my eyes on my companion above the rim of that cup as I drank, and I saw her smile slowly and languorously. Then she laughed a little, her right hand continuing to stroke the pendant between those breasts which flaunted more and more their ripeness, their firmness—

"Well met, well be!" She spoke again. "There is some power already in you, man from years ahead, or you would not come among us." She leaned closer. From her body, or garments, though I was sure that scent arose from her firm flesh itself, came a fragrance which made my head spin dizzily. For a moment I found I could not put down my cup, nor loose my other wrist; I was held fast prisoner while she played with me.

"It is a pity," she continued, "that our times do not truly lay one upon the other so that you could realize that present desire of yours. But carry this with you, straying one, and give it to the proper one at the right time and the right place."

She kissed me full on the mouth. The fire of that touch ran into me, even as the wine had filled my body with another kind of warmth. I knew at that moment that no other woman could be to me what this one might have been—

"Not so," she whispered as she drew a little away from me. "Not so. In your own time there will be one—I, Gunnora, do promise this. She shall come and you will know her not—until the proper hour. You have drunk from the Hunter's own cup. Thus shall you seek, until you find."

Her hand on my wrist moved my fingers now. I was retracing those runes, whether or no, but backwards. Three times I did so. Once more she was but a haze, still I could not shake off her hold. Three times more. Then again the dark and my passage was ended. Had that been through time itself, or space?

I still sat at the table. But the hall was cold and still, and the dark of night was heavy. I held something in my left hand and I could see by the defused light of those shining runes that I held a goblet. The rune light awoke a gleam of silver on its side. Out of that other place I had brought back the Hunter's cup. My body also knew well the need which had been awakened in me, and for which there was no answer in the here and now.

"Gunnora?"

I said her name aloud. The sound of it carried emptily down

the hall. There was not even an echo in return. Then I pushed the cup aside impatiently, laid my head forward on my folded arms, my cheek pressed against the runes, knowing, without being so assured, that these would not work for me again.

Three days I stayed in the keep, sleeping before its hearth, sitting now and then in the high seat of honor trying to recall every small moment of that time when I had been allowed to look into the past. I had never had a woman, though I had heard in many tales of Garn's meiny much concerning such experience. It was our birthright that this need did not come in early youth. For that reason perhaps our families were small and it was easier for clan lords to make marriages to their own advantages and that of their heirs.

Now I was ridden by new dreams, and, knowing that I must go unfulfilled, I fought to turn my mind to other matters. Hunt I did, and managed to snare creatures coming to feed upon the grain. That, too, I harvested in a rude fashion, ground awkwardly between stones, and sifted into gritty meal to store in the box Zabina had used for journey bread. The meat I took I smoked as best I could, preparing supplies for when I moved on. For I knew I must leave this place, even though part of me wanted to linger— to try again to master the runes.

I desired nothing so much in my whole life as to join the feasting again, this time for good. Save that I understood that even with the aid of sorcery I could not so bridge time. During those days I thought very little of my quest for Iynne, my hunt for Gathea. Both seemed far away, as if a curtain had fallen over that part of my past, severing me from life before, from the person I had once been.

On the fourth morning, however, I roused, knowing, as well as if my amber lady had ordered it, that it was time for me to go. I could moon no longer over what might have been. Though I held very little by her promise that I would be eased of my hunger by any now living. She was too vivid, too much within my thoughts.

Reluctantly I left the keep soon after dawn. West must be my way still. However, after I was well beyond that deserted keep, I suddenly changed. I might have been caught in a feverish sleep and was now healed of my distemper. Again that old urgency came to life—the need for finding some clue as to where Garn's daughter had gone, and where Gathea had also vanished.

Once more land was wild and held no trace of any former dwelling, not even a road before me. I took as a guide a sighting on one peak of the continuing heights, one which resembled a sword blade pointing upward into the sky. Toward that I made my way with such caution as I could summon, for now that I was away from the deserted keep I was unsure of every standing stone, every cluster of brush which might conceal an ambush. Yet there were only birds high against the sky, and the ground under my feet bore no sign of track. This might be a world free of any life save that which grew rooted or winged.

On the second day I came to the first slope of the peak toward which I had marched. There was food of a sort to ration that I had roughly smoked or brought with me from the forgotten fields. I had come through a patch of bushes heavy with berries which I had found both food and drink. Gathea's wallet I had not opened, still I bore it with me as if I were to meet her within each hour that passed. My own grew much leaner.

Haze gathered about the peak, not far from sundown. The mist descended like a slowly lowered curtain, wiping the heights from sight as it fell. With that in view I decided to camp for the night and not attempt to win beyond until I had the aid of the morning's sun.

Thus I searched for shelter until I chanced upon a pocket among rocks where I could crowd in, my back well protected as I faced outward. Nights in this eerie land were periods of endurance which I faced unhappily. Though I had heard nothing during the past ones since I left the keep to suggest that any hunters prowled. Still I slept in snatches and it seemed that my body ached for a chance to rest the full night through with no care for any sentry duty.

Though there was dead wood tangled among the bushes and the trees which grew here and there, I set no fire to be a beacon. Rather I half sat, half lay, my back against the rock, staring out into the gathering shadows. As ever when I let down my guard there crept vividly into my mind the picture of that keep hall as I had seen it as a dream of that long ago feasting time. Why had they gone, those who had gathered there? What blight had fallen to leave their fine hall an empty ruin? I had seen no signs of war there. Had it been a plague, a threat from afar which was so potent as to send them into flight?

I started, gasped.

Had I heard that with my ears? No, that cry had been an invasion of my mind. I hunched forward on my knees, striving to draw from the fast coming night a clue as to who had so summoned help and where they, he, or it might be.

Again that plea shuddered through me. From behind—from the mist-veiled mountain! But who? I pulled around and up to my feet, staring up that wall of rock. There was a wink of light now visible in the night, though it was but a formless splotch through that mist. Fire? It did not have the color of true flames. A trap with that as bait? I could remember only too well those silver women and their wooing song among the rock circles.

For the third time came that frantic, wordless summons. Caution told me to remain where I was. But I could not shut out that plaint by covering my ears. It found its way to my very bones. Nor could I stand against it—for it seemed to me that strange though it came, it was cry for help from one of my own kind— Gathea, Iynne—? It could be either or both, a power that had come to them out of this sorcerous country.

I left my frail suggestion of safety and began to climb. The wind came down slope, striking against me. On it was an odor— not a stench of evil nor yet the musky sweetness which I had associated with Gunnora, with the Moon Shrine, and its pallid flowering trees. This I could not put name to.

Though I knew that I was a fool to venture thus into the night, still I could do no less, but I could go with caution, and a wary eye and ear. So I did not hurry blindly, but set my feet as carefully as I could, waiting tensely between each step for another of those pleas to reach me.

The splotch of light held but there was nothing else now. Nothing unless one could give some name to that sensation of awaiting some significant action, some demand which grew stronger and stronger with every step I won up slope.

Luckily there were bushes here which I could grasp when the slope became steeper, using them to haul myself farther and higher. I reached the outer edges of the mist and that clung as a clammy cloak about my body, settling in drops of moisture on my face. Yet it had not put out that light in the center of its curtain.

I stopped short every few steps I won, to cast about. I was blind, but I was forcing my ears to serve me. There was a chill to this fog as if it were indeed sleet of late autumn instead of a normal mist. It seemed also to deaden sound for I heard nothing.

The light neither dwindled nor grew, but remained as a beacon —a beacon to summon—what? Me? I might well be only caught in the web meant for another. Yet I could not bring myself to turn aside, even now when that call no longer reached me.

Then—

Out of the very ground at my feet there arose a form near as light as that ghostly fog. It reared tall and I could not mistake that soft rumble of growl. A mountain cat— Gruu?

I paused again, hand reaching for sword hilt. This lurker was surely as large as Gruu, and, if it were a nocturnal hunter like many of its breed, then even steel and my best efforts might be very little to halt any attack.

Once more it growled, then it turned and was gone into the mist which swallowed it instantly. Gruu! Surely that had been Gruu or I would not have gone unchallenged. Which meant that Gathea was up there!

I made the rest of that climb in a scrambling run, wanting to call out her name, but fearing that if she were in trouble I would alert whatever held her captive or besieged. Again the white-silver cat awaited me as I plunged on into a circle of light.

That radiance arose and spread out from an object resting on bare rock—a ledge level enough to have been cut from the mountainside by purpose. I could not see what made its core. At that moment I was more intent upon the form which lay limply beside it, over which the cat crouched, using his rough tongue gently across a cheek.

Gathea it was. Something had dealt harshly with her. The stout trail clothing which she had worn was in tatters, so that her arms, showing the red marks of deep scratches, were bare near to the shoulder, and even her breeches were shredded into strips which were held together by knotting one rough length onto another.

Her hair was a wild tangle around her head, matted and twined with bits of stick and dead leaf. While her face was only skin laid thin across the bones, and her hands, bruised and scratched, were as skeletal as those claws of the winged thing I had fought.

I knelt beside her, my fingers seeking out the pulse of life, for so limply did she sprawl that I thought perhaps what I had caught had been her death cry, and that she was gone before I had reached her. Gruu drew back a little and let me to her, but his green eyes were steady on me, as if he would challenge my tending.

She was alive, yes, but I believed that her heart fluttered weakly and that she perhaps had come near to death. I needed my supplies. There was water, and that I dripped first upon her face and then, steadying her head against my body, I forced the edge of the small pannikin I carried between her lips and trickled what I could into her mouth. Looking about that eerie pillar of light I could see no sign of supplies, but remembering Zabina's instructions I crumbled some dried leaves into the pannikin and swirled water about with them. The aroma which came from the mixture was fresh, pungent, with a clearing rush of sharp scent. Again I steadied her against my body and was able to get a mouthful of the herb liquid then another into her. Her eyes opened and she looked up at me.

There was no recognition in her gaze; she was one who saw into other worlds, beyond me, through me— Still I got her to drink all of the restorative, then I crumbled a handful of coarsely ground grain into more water—making a lumpy gruel which, using a small horn spoon, I got into her and which she did chew and swallow. Yet never did she seem to see *me*, or even appear to realize that someone tended her.

For the first time I raided the wallet which had been hers. In one box I discovered more salve which, working as gently as I could, having lain her down by the light, I anointed the worst of the blood-encrusted scratches so deeply lacing her arms and legs.

Gruu watched me intently as ever. Before I was quite done, he arose and faced outward into the night, his head up, as if he either listened or scented some peril. Restlessly he began to pace back and forth, keeping, I noted, between the two of us and the mist curtain which hedged in the small clear pocket about the flame.

Then he voiced one of those roars with which he had challenged the creatures of the night. Before I could move, he leaped out to vanish into the fog. I could hear the sounds of a mighty struggle, grunts, shrill cries, which certainly had never broken from Gruu's furred throat, last of all a gurgling.

I stood over Gathea, my sword out and ready. Yet nothing came through the mist until Gruu himself paced back. There was a dark spattering down his chest, and more blood dripping from his large fangs. He sat now, unconcerned, by the light and started to clean his coat of those traces of battle, licking and then hissing with disgust. I at last took that folded bandage I had carried with me and wet it with my water.

Approaching the cat I ventured to wash the worst of the thick clotting from his ruff where a long trickle had matted deeply into his fur. He suffered me to do this, and I did not wonder at his disgust at his own attempt to clean himself, for what I sponged off did not seem like true blood, was instead a thicker, noisome stuff with so foul a smell that I nearly had to hold my nose as I ministered to him.

Gathea did not regain full consciousness—at least she still did not appear to note that I was with her. However, I was able to get more of the grain gruel into her, spoonful by spoonful, and I made certain that her many scratches, though deep and red and angry-looking, were not real wounds. How she had won this far without supplies and what was the nature of the light which glowed by us remained mysteries. I began to believe that she had collapsed from sheer lack of food and exhaustion. Yet that strange summons which had brought me to her had been of such a nature there must have been more than just weakness of body to make her cry for aid.

With Gruu as sentry I felt more at ease than I had since I had left the keep. The cat lay now by the fire, licking his paws, seemingly wrapped in his own concerns. Yet I was sure he could be trusted.

I made the girl as comfortable as I could, her own wallet for a pillow, spreading over her the travel cloak I had kept as a roll across my shoulder. Shaking the water bottle beside my ear I guessed I had used its contents freely and I must find a mountain spring by morning—perhaps Gruu could help.

Stretching out an arm's distance away from Gathea I allowed fatigue to claim me. The light still burned as high as ever, but it did not dazzle the eyes. There was a softness in its gleam which did not shine too strongly.

I was in the light, the very core of it. There I awaited an unfamiliar intelligence. First it challenged me; there came an abrupt demand—unvoiced. From whence had I come and what would I do? At that there flashed into my mind in answer (though that was not of my calling) the symbol my amber lady had worn, the sheath entwined with fruitful vine.

My unseen challenger was startled, so much that mind picture alone might have struck a telling blow. Yet there was nothing in me which wanted battle between us. I felt no enmity toward that which had so peremptorily demanded my right to be where I was. This ability to build in such detail a mind picture was new to me, yet it seemed right. No longer was my vision only the pendant, that altered, to become a true sheaf of harvest, the fruit wound around the stick possessing real life, so that I could have reached forth a hand to pluck each globe from the burdened vine. Though I could not see her, I believed that behind me at that moment stood my lady of the keep. Though I longed mightily to look and see if that were so, still I could not turn my head.

That which the fire in the mist represented gave way. An impatient arrogance which had filled it when it would not only weigh me, but would judge me to my fate, faded. Instead there was a questioning—tinged with astonishment—not because of me but for the coming of her who was so standing to sponsor my actions.

I felt forces sweep around me, through me. Questions were raised and answered, and I understood nothing. Save that, in some manner, I had been made free of a road, though the power behind the fire was still resentful and grudging. Then I was given, at last, the boon of deep sleep which my aching body craved.

12

I LOOKED UP INTO AN UNCLOUDED SKY, PULLED OUT OF A SLEEP so deep that my body felt stiff as if I had lain so for a toll of seasons upon seasons. That which had drawn me into wakefulness continued.

Speech clear and strong, then a period of silence, as if the speaker waited for an answer. Followed by speech once again. The strange words singsonged with that rhythm our clan Bards used upon formal occasions when either House history or some fragment of the Laws were recited. However, I could not understand one of those fluting sounds which must be words.

I turned my head. Gathea no longer lay as I had left her, but sat cross-legged in sunlight. It was she who spoke, addressing those unknown words to the air, though even Gruu had vanished leaving only emptiness.

A fever may plunge anyone into a condition of seeing, speaking or acting so. That was my first thought, that she was held in a strong delusion. Nor did she turn her head when I sat up abruptly. Was she fevered indeed or trapped in some new witchery?

Before her, as she sat so, was that which must have provided the guide fire of last night. As I looked upon it I wanted to scramble up, away, drag her with me—if I could. For there, wedged between rocks holding it upright, was what could only be a portion of the wand she had fashioned under my own eyes from a tree limb.

A third of it was gone. Even as I looked another small section broke away—became a fluff of ash carried off by a puff of breeze. There was no other fuel—nothing save that fire-eaten rod.

Still Gathea sat and spoke, waited for an answer I could not hear, then spoke again. At times during those waiting intervals, she nodded as if what she alone heard made excellent sense. Once or twice she frowned, seemingly in concentration, as she strove better to understand an admonition or advice. So real were these actions that I could well begin to believe the fault lay within *me*, that I was deaf. Just as that speaker remained invisible to my eyes.

Though I wanted to reach out to her, my hand was stayed by a strong impression that this indeed was no illusion. Or if so, it was mine not hers. At last she gave a sigh and the angle of her head changed. She might now be gazing up to someone who had been seated on a level with her, but had now arisen. One of her hands lifted in a small gesture of farewell. Still her eyes followed the invisible one who left us.

Only then was I able to move. When I caught her lightly by the arm, she started in real surprise. However the eyes she turned to me were knowing—they saw me, knew me.

"Gathea—" I spoke her name.

Her frown became a battle flag of rising anger as she jerked back.

"You have no right spying—" she flared.

That impatient gesture she had made to free herself from my hold sent my wallet swinging. The clasp, never strong since my battle with the winged creature, burst open, and there fell out, to roll across the ground, that cup of the Horn-Crowned man which I had brought out of the deserted keep; from its interior in turn the gem-leaf of the tree woman since I had put these two marvels in keeping together.

Gathea's eyes dropped from me to that cup which came to rest against her own boot, the horned head uppermost, to the leaf bright in the sun. They widened into a stare of sheer astonishment, then centered upon that head as if it were alive.

She retreated farther, still staring at the cup as I reclaimed the leaf. I saw the tip of her tongue appear between her lips to moisten the lower one. There was no anger in her face now. What I read there was surely the beginning of fear. In a voice hardly above a whisper she asked:

"Where did you find these?"

"They were gifts," I answered deliberately. "The cup given me by a great lady who read for me something of the future."

Gathea did not raise her gaze from the cup. Beneath the sun-browning of her face a pallor spread.

"She had a name—this giver of cups?" That whispered question was even thinner. Her unease was plain by the way she turned swiftly to seize upon what was left of her wand, holding that as a man might hold a sword when fronted by an enemy.

"Her name was Gunnora," I replied. Some trait in me was satisfied by seeing her so shaken. As if, in her present state, I could reach her—whereas before she had been far removed from me in spirit, even though she was only a hand's distance away in body.

Once more her tongue crossed her lips. Now she glanced from the cup to me. There was a beginning of calculation in that look, or so I read it. She might earlier have dismissed me with little concern. Now I had taken on a new value.

"What is her sign?" That was no whisper. She rapped the question out as if she had a right to demand a quick answer.

"A sheath of grain bound by a fruited vine." I never would forget anything which was of that lady who had sat beside me in another time, and perhaps even another and stranger world.

Gathea nodded. "That is so, but—" She shook her head like one who is at a loss. Then she raised her eyes full to mine. There was that in them which searched, yet was still rooted in unbelief. "Why—why did *she* give this to you? And where did you find her? There was no shrine—" The hand holding the wand arose to her breast as if she hugged, like a shield, that reduced symbol of her own dealing with the unknown.

"I found her in no shrine," I repeated, picking up cup and leaf, putting one within the other again. "There was a keep, old and deserted. Through some power I feasted there with those who once held this land. My amber lady was one of them, but she alone knew me for what I was, and gave me this."

"But she did not tell you—" Gathea's eyes narrowed. Her awe and wariness were fast fading. If I had been of importance to her moments earlier, I was now losing that standing. "No, it would seem she did not. Still you have the cup, even if you do not know how to use it—and that has meaning in itself."

I was irked by her swift return to her usual assurance, to that domination she had held, or sought to hold, over me ever since we had come into this western land.

"She gave me one other thing," I said. "Which I am to use in the proper time—"

Gathea's gaze traveled on to the wallet into which I was fitting the cup once again. It was my turn to shake my head.

"No, it is not the leaf—though that I had also of a lady who had power of her own. You have your secrets, these I hold as mine." Nor did I ever then intend to tell her of that kiss and what my amber lady had said concerning it. I was no wooer of this witch maid. Whatever dream might have sprung, or would spring, from out of my memory I would not share that! Instead I moved on to make my own demands:

"What have you learned concerning Iynne or your moon magic dealing? With whom did you speak just now?"

Gathea gave a slight movement of the shoulders which was not quite a shrug.

"What I seek—" she began, but I interrupted her with new confidence:

"What *we* seek. I will find my lord's daughter if it can be done in this land of many surprises and mixed magic. Have you any word from your invisible friend as to where our path must run?"

I was sure that she wanted to deny me, to turn and walk away. Yet I was as certain that she could no longer treat me so. I might not know what power issued from the goblet which I carried, but the fact that it was mine at all plainly made her reluctantly consider me as a trail companion she could not ruthlessly leave behind.

"Past the mountains beyond—"

I looked deliberately at the heights before us, my head moving so I could view those lying to the south on to the ones rising in the north.

"A wide land for searching," I commented. "Surely you are able to narrow our wandering better than that!"

For a long moment I believed she was going to refuse. Her frown was back, and she held the wand almost as if she would like to lay it across my face. Such a rush of anger reached me that it was as if the blow had truly been dealt. A moment later wonder started in me that I had been able to sense so clearly her emotions. Though acts of anger such as Garn's blow (which had made me as nothing among my own kind) were open, still I had never before felt within me anything like this understanding of another.

I unslung the second wallet—her own—which I had carried for so long, held it out to her.

"Yours. You will find all untouched within. The strap has been mended."

My action appeared to distract her anger for a moment. Gathea took the wallet, holding it almost as if she had never seen it before. A deep score was cut across its surface where one of the talons of the winged creature had slashed.

"That was done by a flying thing." I made my voice casual.

"Flying thing—the Varks! You have fought with a Vark!"

"After a fashion. Though I wonder if they can be truly killed, at least they take a deal of killing if they are." I recalled that severed hand which had crept toward me like some monster possessing separate life of its own. "It would seem you have learned more of this land since we parted. Enough at least that you can give name to that—and what else?"

Once more her face was unreadable. "Enough."

Enough? Well, I would push her no more now. Instead I continued briskly:

"Where do we head across these mountains? Still due west?"

Gathea gave a low whistle and Gruu slipped into place between us as if she would go only so under his escort. She looked sullen, and, had I had my will I would have turned on my heel and left her then and there. Only she was my guide to Iynne. And, for my own inner honor, I must do what I could for one who carried the blood of my own House—since in part it was my carelessness which had led my lord's daughter into danger in the beginning.

We climbed in silence, Gruu in the lead, as if the great cat knew exactly what path to take, though I could detect no sign that there had ever been a way here which had been followed by more than perhaps his own kind. The mist had cleared entirely. I could look back upon the land below, stretching out even to the edge where the deserted keep stood. I wondered if Gathea had passed through there; if so what had been her experiences, though I was in no mind to ask her. She had raised a firm barrier between us, and, for now, I was content to have that so.

Steep as the slope was it did not tax us as that first height on which I had found the lair of the Vark. Now and again I did glance up into the sky to see if we might be observed by such an enemy. However the day was bright and clear and nothing moved above.

We did not try to scale the sharp set peak, rather Gruu brought us in a way around it, through a crevice so narrow at times that we had to turn sideways to win beyond. Then once more—at nooning I judged by the sun's height—we came out upon another ledge able to look down and out upon a new land.

What lay behind us was a mixture of desert and wilderness, a harsh and desolate country. What lay ahead was richly green. There was no mistaking the distant glimpses of what could only be towers, the slim white markings of roads. Gathea stood surveying this before glancing at me over her shoulder.

"This is guarded land—"

I grasped her meaning. She was declaring that she alone might have the power to continue. Well, that I would test when the time came, though the rich look of that territory ahead suggested that if Iynne had, in some way, found a refuge here she might well be in better case than I had feared.

Now my companion swung farther around. "Do you not understand?" Her tone held a hiss like the sound Gruu might make in warning to any who thought to take a liberty with him. "You are not prepared, there are barriers here you cannot hope to cross!"

"But ones which will fall easily before you? Perhaps manned by the invisible?"

She tapped the wand she had clung to during all our climb against the flattened palm of her other hand. Her gesture was one of impatience and irritation. Then, seeming to come to some decision, she added:

"You cannot begin to understand. It would take years—long seasons of time for you to unlock the doors between you and the proper knowledge. I have been schooled from childhood. Also I was born of stock which had held certain powers from generation to generation. I am a woman and these powers are entrusted alone to those who can stand under the moon and sing down the Great Lady! You are—you have nothing!"

I thought of Gunnora, of my amber lady, and of the cup which plumped the wallet hanging from my shoulder and my jeweled leaf. Thus I did not accept the belief that only a woman might be akin to what ruled here.

"You think of steel—of a sword—" Gathea continued so swiftly one word near broke on the next. "This place has weapons you cannot begin even to dream of. I tell you there is no place for you! Nor can I aid you. All my strength I shall need for myself—to carry through what I must do. Your kin-lady took from me what was mine, what I have birthright to! I shall get it back!"

Her eyes were as fierce as those of an untamed hawk. I saw that she gripped that wand so tightly her knuckles stood out in pallid knobs.

"There is a time for swords, also for other weapons. I have not said that I do not believe in your powers—or in the strangeness of this land. I have had my own contact with that." My hand went then not to sword hilt but to the bulge in my wallet.

She laughed. There was scorn in the sound. "Yes, the cup of the Horn-Crowned One, but you do not even know the true meaning of that. By ancient tradition he who wears the Horn Crown holds power only for a season or so, then his blood, his flesh, go to enrich the fields, to be a fair offering to the lady—"

"To Gunnora?" I asked and did not believe her.

Gathea stared. "You—you—" It was as if so many words boiled in her throat that they choked her into silence. Then she turned, began to descend with such reckless speed that I hurried to catch up as well as I could, lest she slip to end on rocks below. While Gruu flashed past me, crowding in ahead of her at last, to stand rock still keeping her where she was until I joined them.

"Shall we go," I asked her, "together?"

I knew that she longed to deny me, to continue that headlong dash as she had done when she had lost me before the crossing of the other range, save that the cat would not move and she had no room to push past his bulk.

"On your own head be it!" she snapped. Once more there lay silence between us until I broke it, since I had decided that this warring of words was of no service to either of us.

"It may be true that you shall find welcome here. Was it with one of the guardians of this way that you held speech with air only before you? Only I am pledged to find Iynne, since that is a kin debt. That I shall endeavor to do with every bit of strength I can summon. Perhaps a sword is no answer, I do not know. But I am only a warrior—"

Why had I said that? For nothing else had I ever chosen to be. Yet now I felt another need beginning to move in me. What had been said to me concerning a seed planted—which would grow? I was no Bard, that I knew. So, what did move in me to reach forward eagerly, longing to test the secrets of this green land ahead? More than just the search for Iynne spurred me, I realized. I had a desire, a thirst for learning what lay here—what I might of such people as I had seen during my vision in the lost keep.

"You are a man!" She made of that statement an accusation.

It was true that Wise Women had no dealings with marriage. They were known to hold to virginity lest some of their power be lost in coupling. Perhaps deep in them they harbored a contempt for all males, such as I read into her voice now.

I laughed. "That I am!" Again I remembered the rousing warmth of my amber lady's kiss. But if this lean-flanked, sun-browned girl thought that I lusted after her, having seen Gunnora, she was very wrong. "In your learning you would deny everything to me because of that? You speak of the Horn-Crowned One and his sacrifice—how is it that I have heard nothing of *that* in all my years? If it was once the way of life, it certainly has not been for seasons uncounted now. Among the kin—"

"The kin!" she flashed. "We are not among them. Yes, much has been forgot. I did not begin to dream how much, until I passed the Gate. Then I was like one being let out of a tight prison into an open world. I have begun to learn, but I am only on the first part of the path—a path you cannot think of walking. Go back, kinless one—you cannot hope to stand—"

"We shall see what I can or cannot stand," I returned, as sharply. She had flung that last insult at me knowingly, meaning to wound, reminding me once again of the need for restoring my own pride. More than ever I knew that I must continue or be damned in my own eyes.

I wanted to know what invisible presence she had met with on the mountain land. However, if she would not tell me I could not force it out of her. As I faced her squarely I saw the fierceness fade a little from her eyes, then she looked down at her wand, twirling what was left of that about in her hands.

"Why will you not let matters be—?" she asked in a low voice. "You push, you pry, your very presence here may lead to defeat. I could turn this on you—" The end of the wand flipped a fraction in my direction. "Only if I use my gift so, then the force would strike back at me. I cannot send you away, I only ask that you go. I have spoken ill of your Lady Iynne, but accept this: when I find her I shall do all in my power to free her from a tangle, which she invited in her foolishness, and return her to her own life. I can do this, being who and what I am. You cannot—"

"Because I am who and what I am?" I asked. "I may surprise you still. Shall we go?"

She shrugged and started the descent again, this time at a more sober pace to suit the roughness of the way. For on this side the peak was far more precipitous than had been the other. Here were places where it was necessary that we aid one another in finding hand-holds, or steadying over drops.

There was no more speech between us, but our hands met readily enough when it was needful. Finally we reached better and easier ways which brought us into that green land. Here there were a number of those same trees that had been in that wood which had seemed to harbor the spirit woman I had met. There was no brush growing beneath them, only patches of moss. In pockets of sun, flowers bloomed—mostly white, faintly touched on petal tip with either rose or a green-yellow, so perfect one might have thought them fashioned from gems.

Perfume hung in those sunlit glades which Gathea did not cross directly. Rather she passed about the edges, being careful not to touch or disturb any of the flowers, while I was content to copy her example.

However, I noticed that she made such detours hurriedly and never looked at the flowers directly. Once when I fell a little behind she turned and beckoned me on. Pointing to the flowers, she said:

"They are dangerous—to us. There is a sleep lying ready in their scent to drug the traveler, give him strange dreams."

How she knew this I did not understand, for their like I had never seen. But a Wise Woman has much knowledge of growing things and perhaps Gathea could sense from her training what carried danger within, even though she had not seen them before.

Gruu had vanished, speeding well ahead of us after we had found our way down the last slope. We had not stopped for nooning meal and I knew that what lay left in my wallet was not enough to carry us far. I was hungry and I began to cast glances about us as we went for either game, or some growing thing which would fulfill our needs. Save that there were neither to be seen in that wood.

At length we came from among the tall trees and their attendant glades of flowers, into a forest more natural to me, for these trees seemed closely akin to those I had known on the other side of the Gate. We had not ventured far within that section before we chanced upon a game trail on which were the fresh hoof prints of deer.

Still Gathea made no move to halt, but I was heartened to think that when we did camp we might have fresh meat to roast over a fire. As she continued a pace as swift as the obstructions of the wood would allow, I became restive, and, at last, broke that silence which seemed to be of her choice.

"I have food of a sort," I said abruptly. "It would be best to eat."

I believed that she had been so busied with her own thoughts that my words came as a startling surprise. Now she did pause and her hand went to the latching on the wallet I had brought her. She looked around. Nearby lay a mossy trunk of a tree that she chose as a seat. I dropped beside her and brought out my bag of grain now three-fourths empty, and a small portion of smoked meat.

She had unlatched her own supply bag and had a handful of dried fruit, two very stale, dried journey cakes. How had she fared during those days we had been apart? Had Gruu hunted for her or had the trail she followed been better served with fruit?

"None of that," she shook her head at the meat I offered. "I do not each much flesh within this land. And if you are wise you will not either. In fact, it would be better by far for you to bury that."

She looked upon the meat with aversion. "Things—hunters—can be drawn by the very scent, old and dry as it is."

I considered what she had said. It was true she must know far more of this country—perhaps through some report from her invisible friend—than I did. Thus it would be wise to be governed— up to a point—by her advice.

With a sigh, I grubbed a hole in the soft earth beside that log, dumped in my meat, and covered it over. I made do with part of a cake and some pieces of the fruit she had offered me, setting aside my coarse ground meal for the future. It was peaceful here, and, now that we had settled and there was no longer the sound of our passing to act as a warning, I began to hear the small noises of the life which must inhabit this place.

Down one of those trees flashed a creature with a plumed tail to act as a balance. It had a long narrow head, and very keen eyes which it kept upon us as it came. The thing squeaked in a high note and appeared to have no great fear of us.

Gathea made a small twittering noise. The animal retreated up the trunk for a short space, then halted, peering down at her with an intent stare. From the wealth of teeth it showed, I believed that it certainly had no fear of hunting and it must do well for itself as its body was plump, its fur shiny and soft.

Again it squeaked. I could not put aside a belief that it had answered, in its own way, my companion. Again it flitted down the tree trunk, leaped a last portion, to land on nearby, then ran fearlessly to the girl who held out a piece of dried fruit. The forepaw with which it reached was more like a hand than a paw, and it used that appendage with as much dexterity as a man might use his five fingers.

It chewed at the morsel, swallowed. Then it squatted, its tail flaring back and forth, snapping from side to side, and loosed a volume of squeaking. Plainly it was talking after its own fashion, and I rapidly changed my estimate of its intelligence.

Gathea twittered and then shook her head regretfully. Whatever news or message the creature had brought was plainly not to her understanding. At least she did not know *everything* about this land. Its squeaking ended in a squeal which held a note of alarm. Then it was gone, a red streak back up into the branches of its chosen tree.

The wood became still—too still. Gathea swept the remaining food back into her wallet, latched that. Then she leaned forward a little, plainly listening. I could catch nothing but the silence, but that in itself was a warning. I could have liked just then to see the silver head of Gruu rise above the bushes, being very willing to trust the cat's sense concerning enemies. That some inimical force was now moving within the wood I had no doubt at all.

I got to my feet as quietly as I could, then tensed. There came a loud call—and *that* I had heard before. It was the croaking of those evil-looking birds which had plagued us in Garn's dale. They could not penetrate the cover of the trees which roofed us over; still I was very certain that they knew we were here. Also they did not come in to attack, but rather waited as might those hounds a hunter loosed on a trail. We had been discovered, we were about to be the prey of some force, and an evil one if those birds obeyed his, her, its commands!

13

GATHEA STOOD BESIDE ME, HER HEAD HELD HIGH. I SAW HER nostrils expand as if, like Gruu, she depended upon sense of smell. If she picked up such a warning it was denied me. Rather I listened to the calling of those birds and then I gazed along the aisles between the trees. Of the great cat there was no sign, though I wished that he had remained with us.

Because I needed some hint for our possible defense I rounded on my companion, determined to get a straight answer from her.

"What do those call? Them I know and have seen before and they are surely evil."

She met my demanding gaze and I could see she was shaken.

"The Wings of Ord." Her voice reached me nearly overridden by the clamor from the skies.

"And this Ord?" I pressed her.

Gathea shook her head. "He is, I think, one of the great Old Ones—I—" Her eyes dropped to the wand which she still held, and then once more she looked at me. "There is that I can do— for my own safety—but whether it will also hold for you. . . . Bring forth that cup!"

So sharp was her order that I obeyed without stopping to think. The face of the Horned man looked up at me. Some trick of the light shifted in here by the leaves gave it a change of countenance, made it appear for a moment or two as if those silver eyes had come to life, regarded me measuringly.

"We should have wine—" She looked about her as if a cask might suddenly appear from the air itself in answer to her need.

Then she scrabbled within her wallet, brought out several small pieces of fruit which I recognized for long dried grapes, hard and black.

"These—into the cup!" She held out her hand and I scooped up those dried balls (there were seven of them I noted) to drop into the hollow of the goblet. "Now water—no, it must come from *your* flask!"

Upon the dark balls I sloshed what might have measured three mouthfuls of water, wanting to save our supply since I did not know when I could replenish the bottle.

Some new sense arose abruptly within me. I was grasping the cup with both hands, near level with my chin. So holding it I also turned it, that the liquid it held washed back and forth across the long dried fruit. A poor substitute for wine, perhaps—only, maybe a firm desire in such straits would equal the lack.

"Look at *him!*" Gathea's voice was taut. "Think of *him!* Think of wine, a toast to the Hunter. His pledge cup has passed to you. Perhaps that means that you have favor. But this is a sort which no magic raised by a woman can summon. Think of wine—the taste of it—pledge your service to *him*. Do it—and speedily!"

I did look at that face under the stag horn crown. There was that in it which was not human, yet here was enough of mankind to make me hope that perhaps whatever magic she believed might be woven by this *would* come to our aid. Though I had never tried to make my mind command my sight, I had learned enough to believe this might be done—whether or no I was taught in the mysteries of Power.

The silver face stared back at me, that alienness, which had at first appeared so marked, was growing less. There *was* power here. This represented a high lord, one who dealt justice to his people with one hand, and defended them against all ill with the other. To ride among the household of such a one would be enough for any man.

I raised the goblet yet higher, closed my eyes, and set in my mind that what washed within was not water and bits of dried fruit. No, rather I prepared to taste such a drink as had filled it on that night when I had sat at the feast board at Gunnora's left hand. Setting the rim to my lips I drank.

And—I shall always swear by all I hold in my heart as right and strong—what I sipped was indeed wine, spiced, mellow, such a vintage as had not stood in the casks of any keep I knew. I pledged with those mouthfuls my service—I who was kinless, and had no honor among my own any more.

We of the clans swear our strongest oaths by blood and steel, and by the Flame. Though the latter is a faroff thing which only the Bards and a handful of believers ever mention. I swore rather by a wine which I drank, by that within me which drew me to this lost lord whose face I looked upon as I turned the goblet upside down as is our custom for honor pledge. There dripped from it (yes, this too I swore to) not water, no knotted ball of sun-dried grape, rather wine light as the sun, yellow and clear. Those drops fell into forest mould and were gone. I threw back my head and shouted aloud words which I did not know but which had come easily into my mind:

"Ha, Kurnous, Ha, Hie Wentur!"

My cry swelled, echoed among the trees, repeated over and over again. About us leaves shook as a wind rushed upon us, wrapping us around. We stood without hurt as branches snapped free and hurtled by us, pieces of the leaf mould underfoot were scuffed up and sent hurtling off.

An inflow of new strength swelled within me. I felt in that moment that I was greater than any man, filled with something I could not name but which made me more alive than I had ever felt before in my life. I could have drawn steel and stood against the open attack of a whole clan, laughing as I fought to victory. Or I might front such a cat as Gruu with none but my own two hands, and it would be the cat that would first give ground!

Above the rushing of the wind we could hear the hoarse cries of the birds. They were screaming, calling to whatever had sent them for aid. No help came to them. I saw the air toss branches of the trees which had sheltered us, and between those whipping limbs, that beat wildly here and there, began to fall bundles of ragged feathers, limp bodies of battered birds. Some still struggled feebly as they struck the ground. Their red eyes were glazed, but one or two still gazed toward us and their furious hatred was plain.

The wind swirled, appeared to gather itself together as if it had just formed a wide-flung net and was now being once more compacted into a bundle. Then it was gone. Only a scatter of torn leaves and the dead birds remained.

My exultation had swept with that wind. I drew a deep, ragged breath, looked once more at the Horned Hunter. The face on the goblet held no hint of any life now. In fact a dulling crept across the silver so that it looked both old and worn, as if a virtue had departed out of it. I held it gingerly. What I had wrought by its aid had left me shaken. Now I wanted to stow it away—to think out what I had done and why I had been able to do it.

However, as I placed it back in the wallet, I glanced at Gathea. She was farther apart from me, her back set against a tree, her eyes wide. Between us she held up the wand, as if to ward off blows she half expected I might aim at her.

"He *came*—" Her words were low, shaken. "He truly came—to your calling. But you are a *man*, a man of the clans, of the House of Garn, how could you do this thing?"

"I do not know—nor even what I did. But you expected it—you told me—"

She shook her head. "I only had some hope—because you possessed the cup. Now you have done what even a Bard would not dare to try—you summoned Him Who Hunts and have been answered! This is—I must think on this! Now, let us go before that which sent the Black Ones can seek us again!"

She began to run along one of the more open aisles of the wood, leaping over fallen branches here and there. I followed, catching up just as we came out into the open.

I expected that some of that vile flock might have survived the killing wind to spy on us. There was nothing to be seen there except one winged thing (too far to say whether it was bird or something far worse) flying at speed away from the wood. So, relieved of any need for immediate action, I turned to Gathea, caught her arm and held her by main strength. The time had come for answers to my questions.

"Who is He Who Hunts? The Black Ones? Ord? You will tell me now what you know!"

She twisted in my hold, and she was strong, stronger than I thought a woman might be. Still I held her, and, when she half raised the wand I promptly struck out at her wrist as I was only too wary of what she might do. I had never so roughly handled a woman before, nor did I like this trial of strengths between us. However I was through moving blindly when I believed that she had knowledge which might save us both from new and unknown perils.

Gathea glared at me, though she stopped her struggle. I saw her lips move, though they shaped no speech I could understand. So I swept her closer to me, clapped one hand over her mouth for I believed she might be summoning up some new aid—against me.

"You will talk!" I said into her ear as I held her prisoner against my body. "I have gone your way too long—you have drawn me into sorcery—and I will have answers!" She was like a bar of sword steel in my hold, though she no longer fought for freedom. What further steps I might take to make her answer I could not imagine.

"You are no fool," I continued. "To go farther into this land without knowing how we may arm ourselves—that is folly past believing. I do not want your secrets—but I am a warrior as you know. I will not go blind if you can tell what will aid me. Do you understand?"

I thought that her stubbornness was going to continue. If so I did not know what I could do, for I could not hold her prisoner forever. When she would not speak, another idea came to me, even as had that invocation which had entered my mind. I spoke again and did so in a voice which demanded an answer:

"By Gunnora I ask it!" For I felt that to invoke whatever power had answered the cup ritual would not make her yield. She spoke so much of women's knowledge and of things which were not of a man's world at all—proud in the fact that this set her apart. Gunnora had been all woman and I was sure a person of no little power—in her own time and place.

I was certain that I had done rightly when Gathea made a last plunge for freedom without warning. However I was ready for such a ploy and gave her no chance. Only I repeated:

"By the power of Gunnora, I ask this!"

She as suddenly went limp in my hold, her head bobbing against the hand which gagged her. I released her then and stepped away, but I kept a wary eye on the wand. She was grasping it tightly, the burned part down, and she did not face me even now, only her voice, cold and hard, came:

"You meddle still. Once you shall go too far, and then you shall learn what comes to those who invoke what they do not understand. You are the fool!"

"I would rather be a live fool, than a dead one. And I think you know enough to let both of us walk this land with some weapons besides steel to hand. You know where we go—"

"Where *I* go!" Gathea corrected me. Even now she kept her face turned away as if she had been shamed by my handling and was thus lessened even in her own eyes. But I kept rein on any sympathy—I had treated with her fairly from the first, she could not say the same and be honest.

"Where we both go," I corrected her calmly. "Also, you have a guide—one unseen—I saw you speak with such a one. Is she—or it —here?"

"These are Mysteries, not to be spoken of by those who stand outside," she retorted.

"I have been involved in them. I have spoken to Gunnora. I have called upon the Hunter—and did he not answer me?"

She still would not look at me, rather her eyes went from side to side as a cornered animal might search for some hole of escape. "I have given oaths. You do not know what you ask—"

Again I was visited by inspiration. "Call upon that which cannot be seen—ask then of it whether I should be left blind among the sighted. I demand this in Gunnora's name!"

The wand quivered. "*She*—why do you speak of *her*? She is no voice for a man's hearing!"

"She is for this man. I sat at a feasting board at her left hand and she spoke to me with far better grace than you have ever known. The cup was her gift—"

"I cannot tell—"

"Then summon what can," I pressed her. "Your invisible one."

Now she did look at me and there was a flame which could be either rage or hatred in her eyes.

"On you then be the consequences!" She drove the wand butt down with a vicious push into the ground at her feet, stepped back a pace or two to settle herself beside the charred branch cross-legged, her gaze now concentrated on the half-burned wood.

My own hand fell to the wallet in which I had put the goblet and I pictured in my mind my amber lady as she had been, full of life, as ripe and bountiful as the symbol she wore.

There was a gathering chill, though the sun had been warm on my helmless head only moments earlier. I felt as if the breath of the Ice Dragon was spreading outward from the half-consumed rod which meant so much to my companion. Every passing moment I expected to see that light fan out to hide it. Only that did not happen. Just that cold grew greater, as if to banish me. I stood my ground and thought of Gunnora, and the cup I carried. Also I fumbled in my wallet and brought out that gem-leaf. Perhaps, as once it had been a growing thing, it would prove now a talisman.

Gathea spoke, in that other tongue which held a singsong cadence. She could be reciting some bardic invocation. The chill increased. I might have been encased in ice from head to foot, only under that hand which lay upon the wallet and within the hand which closed upon the leaf there was warmth which spread outward, fighting that chill which perhaps could be deadly. Whether Gathea deliberately summoned harm I had no way of telling. Perhaps what answered her had its defenses against the interference of an outsider.

I heard no voice out of the air. However Gathea stopped her chant, to speak directly to the source of that cold. Again I summoned to my own mind my most vivid memory of Gunnora. That began to fade in spite of my efforts. Another face took on substance in place of her amber and golden beauty. This was of a younger woman, one I had never looked upon. Her hair was held straight back by a band with the new moon in silver mounted over a brow which was austere, remote, where Gunnora had been well aware—and forgiving—of human frailties. The eyes beneath this other's wide brow were gray as winter ice, holding no more warmth than that. Night black as any winter sky was her hair, and the robe which was girdled about the straight figure of a very young girl was white as the light of the burning wand.

There was no humanity in her. She had been frozen away from every warmth known to my kind. Still there was in the lift of her proud head, about her face a trace haunting of memory. I did not question that this vision in my inner eyes was that of the entity Gathea had summoned, and that there was nothing in her which would move her followers to seek out aught but sterile knowledge which would serve to wall them yet further from their own kind.

There was no escape for me from her inspection. I sensed a kind of impatient contempt—not for me as a person—but because to her no male was of consequence.

"Gunnora!" Had I thought that, or had I cried the name aloud?

The saying of it broke the calm. She did not frown, she did not draw back, yet I sensed that, in some way beyond my comprehension, she was disturbed, shaken. There might well be a feud upon another plane of existence which touched this land, in which power strove with power. I had chanced upon one such power, Gathea had found another, and they were far from allied.

That I had thought before the change began. The white garment took on a tinge of color, the girl's body beneath it ripened into curves, the crescent moon of her diadem grew into a circle, the same sign at its full zenith. That halting resemblance I had half seen—this was also Gunnora! But in another guise. Maid, woman—both the same, but possessing different gifts.

The cold which had tried to freeze me warmed. I would smell scents of full summer, that of ripened fruit, the dusty aroma of grain falling to the harvest. Two natures: That which abode in Gathea had summoned one, that which lay dormant in me had drawn the other.

Only for an instant did I see my amber lady. Then she winked out of my mind's vision. However as she left I felt that I was indeed accepted by her and that there were more gates open to me, giving on stranger lands even than the one I now walked. I need only reach for what I wished with the full strength of my mind, and my desire would come to me bit by bit in answer to the force which I exerted.

"Gunnora!" I called as she vanished, my whole being longing once more to hear the richness of her voice. My lips burned again, as they had when I had received her kiss.

"Dains!" My own cry was echoed by another name. Gathea reached up into the air, as if she would catch and hold the intangible. For I knew that we were now alone. The Power she had called up had answered me as well as her.

Her voice had a desolate ring as if she had called upon near kin who were leaving her forever. Then her hands fell down upon her knees, her head drooped forward.

I did not move to her, for I knew at that moment she would resent bitterly any touch of mine. But I spoke:

"She was Gunnora, maid—wife—"

"She was Dains who knows no man! She was—" Gathea lifted her head. The tears in her eyes astounded me as much as if one of the tree trunks about us wept. "She is—the Moon Lady. Then—then—" Again that hawk fierceness shone in her eyes as she raised her head to look at me. "Gunnora is for women also, but only for women who put off their maidenhood to follow the path of submission to some man."

"Submission?" I countered. There was nothing in my amber lady to suggest submission. "I think not so—unless the woman so desires. She is of the harvest, the coming together of those who would produce new life. She is warmth—your Dains all cold—"

Gathea shook her head slowly. "It is true that Gunnora answered your thought-call. I do not know why or how she lends favor to a man. Her Mysteries are not for you. But it seems, past all belief, that she has indeed chosen you for some reason. Only—it is to Dains's shrine that we go and that is another matter."

I noted that her "I" had become "we." However, I was wise enough to make no comment. She arose slowly, as if that invocation had worn her hard. Now she plucked the wand from the ground to lay it across her palm which she held out well before her.

Though I could detect no movement of the flesh on which it rested, the wand did turn, pointing to her left, out into that green land. Gathea nodded.

"We have our guide, let us go."

That this land was inhabited I was sure and I had no mind to meet with any in possession until I learned more of what we might expect. The coming of the birds was warning enough to tread with caution and keep well away from what we did not understand until we could judge it good or evil.

These who had withdrawn from the dales were, I suspected more and more, of many different species. I remembered the glimpses I had had in that feasting hall of those who were far from human in their seeming. Though all had been in harmony there, much time must have passed. Having been raised among a people who were often torn by clan feuds, I could understand that some such disputes might well have rent apart the dwellers here.

"You spoke of the birds as Ord's." Now that I had broken through Gathea's barrier against explanation I determined to make the most of it. "Who then is Ord?"

"I do not know—save he is a Dark Master—and those are loath-some things which are hunting prey their master wishes."

"That winged thing which I strove with in the mountains?" Swiftly I told her more of that battle and of the strange statue which had guarded the entrance to the foul hole from which it had crawled.

"Evil, yes—but twisted from another way long ago. There was some great warring here once. Those who chose the Dark were changed. Then there are the ones who made no choice, who with-drew. They changed in another way—drawing farther apart from either good or ill into a state where they acknowledge the power of neither and cannot be summoned to a quarrel."

"You have learned a lot," I commented.

"Do you not understand even yet?" she asked. "I was born knowing that I had in me powers, talents, which I could not use because I lacked the key which would unlock them. I came here and there were keys! Zabina wanted me to walk slowly, to creep as a babe who has not yet found the way to rise upon its feet. I am young, but my years do not stretch so far ahead that I can wait, and wait, and accept humbly scraps of knowledge when I know there is a full feast provided for those who dare seek it! The Moon Shrine—that gave me the key. Through it I would have been able to fly where now I stumble foot over foot, although the magic which lay there came only now and then. Before I could draw upon it your keep girl blundered in. I hope she will or has learned what it means to steal another's hopes!"

She spoke with a twist of lip which made me think that she would rather have framed a curse to hurl at Iynne.

"I know Gunnora—she is another phase of your Moon Lady— though she goes in guise of sun warmth. Who is the Hunter who came to my calling?"

"What his name tells you. In a woman lies the right to hold the seed, to nourish it, to watch it grow, to harvest when it is ripe.

In a man lies hasty action, the seeking for prey, the hand on sword, the readiness to cut down growth. The Horn-Crowned One hunts—and slays—"

"So he is evil?"

I could read in her face a desire, or so I thought, to agree. But, at length, she answered reluctantly:

"All things must balance in any world. There is light and dark —moon and sun—life and death. For the most part one is neither better nor greater than the other. The mother sows, the man reaps, she gives life, he grants death when the proper hour turns on the everlasting wheel. To her all the harvest rooted in earth, to him dominion over that which runs four-footed, flies two-winged, unless the balance is disturbed and there arise those strong enough to challenge the proper order of things and bring about pure evil. For that is the true nature of evil—it is power which is used to pull apart the smooth weaving of life and the world."

"So the Hunter is the opposite of your Dains, of Gunnora, yet he has his place."

I thought of the fact that she assigned death as the task of the Horn-Crowned Man and that I did not like. Even though it was part of the scheme of life. For my blood mostly look upon Death with dread—unless life has beaten them so cruelly that they do indeed welcome him as a friend. That I had summoned Death incarnate to our help made me now uneasy and I longed to throw from me that unlucky cup—perhaps the leaf also—and have nothing more to do with them. But Gunnora had given me the cup, and if she stood for the abundance of life why would she present me with the visible image of death? Unless (the woman of the forest had also life coursing in her, strange though that might be—I could not believe her leaf a promise of ending) unless there had been a dire message in both gifts.

Only never would I admit to Gathea my doubts of the Amber Lady and what she stood for. Since I was bred a fighting man I should not shrink from the idea that I had indeed called upon Death as an aid. In that moment I decided to live for one day only. What came I would face without flinching. If Gunnora had meant that cup as a warning—no, that I would not believe. She had spoken of a future for me, and I would hold fast to her prophecy.

Gathea could not read my thoughts. Now she frowned. Not as if she held me to fault, but rather as if she faced a puzzling task.

"The Horn-Crowned One is not the opposite of Dains." Her words came slowly, her frown grew more forbidding. She plainly spoke against her will. "He is honored with the Maiden, and the Mother—he is in turn, brother, and mate—even son to the Old One—"

"And this Old One?"

"The Wise One, she who finishes life as the Maid begins it, the Dark Moon we cannot see. Yes, the Horn-Crowned One is their equal. Save that he does not answer to the Shrine—he has his own place. And—"

What more she might have said she never added for there came a silver flash through the air. With one great leap Gruu was again with us. Behind the cat coursed something else. To me it looked like a streak of black lightning—if one can conceive of lightning as being that, instead of the brightness which we know. It cracked in the air as might the lash of a whip—

The lash of a whip! That was what it was! Out of the country-side rode at a gallop three robed figures and one of them was reeling back, as he came, a black lash, both hands busy with that while his mount, unguided, came forward, its huge fanged jaws agape, its scaled legs in such motion as I thought no living creature might achieve. For these were no steeds of the common world which the three riders bestrode, rather they raced upright on pon-derous hind legs, their shorter and thinner forelegs dangling as they came, while their riders balanced on saddles strapped upon those mighty shoulders.

I saw that black lash coiled, ready to come flying out at us. Gruu had turned at bay once he reached Gathea's side, his fangs showing white and sharp as he roared. I drew steel and thrust my-self before the girl, knowing that there was no time for us to flee back into the forest. Death-bringer indeed. I had summoned the Hunter and now I was faced with his price for playing a game I could not understand.

14

Our attackers made no attempt to close with us, rather they set their monstrous steeds to circle, penning us in. I pivoted to watch, while Gruu crowded back against us both, his head up, snarling, his tail lashing in rage. The lizard things these dark strangers rode hissed, shot out forked tongues as if to impale us. Why the trio did not ride us down straightway I did not understand.

There was no time now for any invocation such as I had used back in the wood. Nor could I even be certain at this moment that the threat I faced had not been drawn upon us because I *had* called on a power I had no ability to order.

At length the three of them came to a halt again. Their faces I could not see for they wore hoods after the manner of my own people in winter, and those were drawn so far forward as to conceal their features, though I caught glimpses of pallid skin on sharply pointed chins. One stopped his slavering mount on the right, matching his fellow to the left. While he who had first used the lightning flash was directly before us.

They have said that the best defense is sometimes attack. I knew in that moment without being told that such an act would avail me nothing. Why they did not simply cut us down with those lines of flame I did not understand.

In spite of my attempt to shield her, Gathea had moved out, her shoulder near touching mine, even though she held no sword, just the shortened wand. We waited, the only sound now being the rumble of Gruu's growl, the hissing now and then of one of the mounts.

I remembered what my companion had earlier said—that iron in itself was a menace to some forms of Dark life. Could it be my sword that they feared, not because of any skill of mine in using it, but because it was wrought of that metal? If so—then perhaps attack might still be possible—

From the very air over us there came a voice, deep as thunder in its way, so startling that it shook my attention away from our captors, making me look up to hunt its source.

Save that there was nothing there.

No! That was not so! There was a troubling of the air, like unto a ripple which a pebble might cause in a pond. If sounds could have visible substance. . . . And those did! There were trails now of something like the thinnest smoke. These did not vanish, rather curled and circled over our heads as the riders had encircled us. While we moved to the ordering of that near invisible ring in the air.

I struggled hard to counteract the compulsion which sent me walking forward, even to use the sword I had in hand. My body was no longer under my control, I was a prisoner within my own flesh and bone. Both Gruu and Gathea must have been the same, for they, too, moved in a stiff, jerky fashion, as if they were being pulled along by invisible ropes.

He who directly faced us turned his scaled mount, heading outward into the open land, with us drawn behind him, paced on either hand by the other riders. Though there was sun above us and the land still looked fair and green beyond, still it was as if we walked prisoner within a shell which was subtly foul.

We crossed a road, but he who led did not turn, kept rather in a straight line over open fields, while always that faint circle over our heads continued to hold.

"What do you know of these?" How deep Gathea's knowledge of this land might run I had no idea, but any hint which she could give me might be of service—had to be of service! I might be helpless now against some witchery, but there could also come a moment, a chance—

"They are of the Dark," she answered me shortly. "Their

master is a strong one. It is his voice which holds us in spell. Save that they are the enemy, I can tell you no more."

She had pressed both hands against her breast, the wand resting between her palms and her body as if she would somehow shelter that thing of power. I did not sheathe my sword as I was urged onward. It was better that I go prepared.

Thus we were taken captive, and thus we passed over green and pleasant lands to come into another strip of country. The growth was as luxuriant here, perhaps even more free and full. Still it seemed unpleasant, darksome. There were flowers which looked like avid scarlet mouths ready to fasten greedily upon anyone who passed too close, others stood pale, possessing ugly-looking stamens of green-yellow which caught and held struggling insects, and from which spread a charnel reek. The trees were twisted, with lumps upon their trunks which were like masks of dread, or rather the heads of men and women who had died in agony and despair. While their leaves were few, the green of them was overlaid with ashy gray as if disease had so marked them.

The ground was also gray-dark and with each step we took there arose a stench of mouldy decay. Fungi grew in patches, looking like the sloughing flesh of things long dead but not decently buried.

Things lived here. We could hear rustling in that mass of growth. Now and then eyes peered at us and we caught short, very fleeting glimpses of stunted misshapen creatures which could be animals twisted by some strange magic from their proper forms—animals—or worse!

On this blighted ground stood a wood of trees, so interwoven and matted that I did not see how any living thing could force a way through. Still from the midst of those dark trees arose a tower.

The stone of its fashioning was a dull black, making a smear against the clear sky to outrage nature. It was toward that tower that our captor rode, we being forced along in his wake.

I saw no opening of path but, as the rider approached, that wood, so much of a barrier, thinned, drew back. It, too, could have been of smoke or an illusion. Yet I somehow knew that it would prove very real to any who had no dominion over the power which had set it there.

Thus the rider moved within its boundaries without any halt and so did the three of us march after him, compelled still by what had taken command of our limbs, if not our minds. I glanced from side to side as we went on into that dark and more noisome place. There were great thorns as long as my belt knife on branches. In other places gray flowers with red veining across their petals, like the veins which brought life through a true body, dripped from their hearts sluggish yellow drops I was sure were poisonous. Strange it was, but also there was about it a daunting aura of evil and of vile life. I made myself face my own fear and ride above it. Sight and smell and sound—these had been used, yes—and witchery worked in them. Only inside I still was myself and that I must hold to in this place. I might be helpless of body, but my mind—

Why it was necessary to remember that at this moment, I did not understand. Save that thought was the one way remaining that I could fight, holding out against my captors in so little.

We came into that opening in the wood where the tower itself stood. There was no outer wall, no other building of any true keep —only that upward pointing black pillar. In the side facing us opened a doorway which gaped darkly, no barrier seeming set in it to deny any entrance.

Our mounted guide came to a halt before that doorway, raised the staff from which his lightning lash had shot in a salute. He did not speak. Now even the hissing of his mount and of those other two ceased. It was very quiet in that tower-centered clearing —hot, oppressively so, and the air so filled with a variety of stenches that no lungful one drew seemed to satisfy the body's craving for air.

No voice spoke this time, but the rider, as if he had received an order we could not hear, drew his mount to one side. He did not dismount though I saw his cowled head turn as that which controlled us now pushed us on, straight into the waiting, open door.

The dark appeared to reach out for us. I had been in unlit rooms, in the dark of storm-clouded nights. Yet nothing could equal this complete and utter absence of light. Even as we were marched through the arch we were encompassed by it and lost in a thick black.

Lost— I strove to command my hand by even this much—that

I could reach out and touch either Gathea's flesh or the fur of the cat. Only no command I used to signal that action reached my muscles. I might well have had both arms tightly bound to my sides. The dark itself was smothering so that I heard my own gasps for breath, knew within me a stir of panic.

We no longer—or at least *I*—no longer moved. Nothing of the day's light penetrated here. Nor could I even guess where we now were, for I had a strange sensation that in passing within that doorway I had entered no hall but a vast space of another existence, that there were no walls about me—only long, unseeable distances.

How long did I stand so? I will never know, for in this other place there was no measurement of time. That had been suspended. There was only the here and now, the crushing dark which was forcing, with a slow, sadistic pleasure, the spark of my life into nothingness which would leave me forever caught like an insect in the sticky gum of a fruit tree, trapped and encircled.

My species fear the dark. That is born in us. Still is it also born in most of us that we must fight fear lest we vanish into nothingness. No man of the clans might have faced such an ordeal as this before, still I found, a little to my astonishment, much to my heartening, that I could hold the fear at a distance—for this moment, and the next—counting time by the breaths I drew as shallow gasps. If I could do it for this instant, then I could do it again, and once more, and—

The dark—there was a change in the air ahead—the stenches of the humid hotbed behind us no longer tormented our nostrils. Instead there was a puff of scent, heavy, musky—not entrancing—rather with a sweet hint of the beginning of decay.

That was accompanied by a faint, very faint lighting of the complete dark. A spot of the same smoky gray as had formed to take us prisoner grew slowly there, hanging in the air equal with our heads. Pale it was, in this utter gloom glowing wanly.

It enlarged from a disc into an oval, spreading downward and its gray became a sickly white—tinged with yellow—as the flowers we had seen without. Now it resembled the surface of a mirror, though it reflected no part of the three of us. Complete in its growth it remained, forming a second doorway, though the force which had compelled us here did not now move us toward it. No, rather that which had its being on the other side approached.

Just as the doorway had grown so did this come slowly—first a shadow on the oval, then deepening in substance into a blurred figure which was like us in form. Only about it there was a hint of ill-shaping—of distortion. The rest of it came with a rush. In the blink of an eye it was there sharp and clear.

I saw a woman, her skin pale, her hair long and dark, loose and flowing nearly to her knees. Her body was as ripe as Gunnora's and she stood flaunting it in a way which a part of me understood and responded to, just as I had responded earlier to Gunnora's womanhood.

Only—

Was my mind playing tricks? When I thought of Gunnora in connection with this female there was a blurring for an instant of that perfect body, the eyes which had been green-yellow, like Gruu's, had held a red spark. I had sensed a small flash of rage.

Still I took a step forward in spite of myself. I was aroused now, as I had been by Gunnora. I was not aware that I could move freely until I found myself sliding my sword back into the sheath; I wanted my hands, my arms free, I wanted—

My swinging hand scraped across my bulging wallet. Again the figure awaiting me—promising me—blurred. The cup—

She might well have read my confusion. Now she held both arms to me, and lustful hunger almost overwhelmed me until I was on the verge of taking those steps between us, reaching out my hands to stroke that satin smooth skin, to caress, to possess. . . . She was all a man could want in a woman and it was me she wooed! She was—

Something moved before me. Gruu flashed into the air in one great leap. I cried out, hurled myself after the cat. The figure in that oval of light blurred again. Somehow, as I swung my weapon —I must save her from the beast if I could—I brushed against the wallet. Brushed, no, my hand clung to the leather above the bulge of the cup, fastened there, in spite of my violent efforts to free it. At the same moment I did not see the dark lady savaged by the beast as I had thought. Rather Gruu rolled with another cat, one which matched him. I heard him cry out and saw him bowl over the newcomer. There was no woman, only the two cats.

Then Gruu and the other were gone, the woman stood there again, her enchantment reaching once more for me. Only there was a wrongness in her image. It strove to fit itself into the pattern it had made earlier, yet it continually flowed beyond the bounds here and there. So at length I knew—this was an illusion. What awaited me there was no woman but something which used witchery to bring its prey peacefully into its hold.

I pressed my hand harder against the wallet. If there was any power radiating out of that I needed it now! The Horn-Crowned One! Gunnora! I grasped at fragments of memory, sought to weave those into a shield.

There was a woman—there was swirling substance—there was a woman—back and forth the struggle of the Dark One who ruled this nest of evil went. Perhaps she—or it—was not aware at first of what small defense I had. The lure was still strong, my body pulled me forward, the lustful heat in me arose high and higher. I fought both myself and that illusion, tearing myself apart with a fear that I would never be able to find words for.

Once I was on my knees, crawling like the animal which more than half of me had become, toward that light and her who had managed to wholly materialize there for a longer period. Only there was no woman there—that I held to, as a dying man holds to the last spark of life. For I truly believe that had I been conquered by my body then, I would have been dead after a fashion which is too evil to think upon!

The Horn-Crowned! Kurnous—Kurnous—! I had no wine to summon him; I had nothing but a part of me and memory. To summon Gunnora in my thoughts—no! Hastily I walled that away. Gunnora, herself, had a small part of this kind of magic. To think of her would open the door again. The Hunter—the Killer —the slayer—

That figure in the light changed. No woman postured and beckoned there now. Instead there was a man, tall, well favored, and wearing on his head a crown of interlaced antlers. He had the calm, proud face of a great and well beloved lord, and he held out his hand to welcome me. Me, the kinless, the clanless. Never alone again. I need only take that hand and I would not be just liegeman, but sword brother, close kin! This was not Garn, but one infinitely above him, a lord one would follow eagerly on great quests, joining to rid the land of the shadow which lay upon it, to serve in glory! This was he I had called upon in ignorance, now come to me in all his—

Still, with my eyes fastened on him, I fumbled with the lashings of my wallet, to take that cup forth—prove that I was one pledged to him! This was how he had saved me again from the prowlers in the dark. This was—

I had the wallet open. My fingers reached in and touched the cup, my forefinger slipping into the bowl.

The man wavered. No! Not to go! I could prove—I could—

Once more he wavered. Then I saw her—that girl—she was pushing ahead of me. Her hands were up, out, she was reaching. . . .

There was no man, no Horn-Crowned warrior. There was a woman, not she who had nearly drawn me into her net, no, this was a girl, slender, lithe, her body partly covered by a moon-silver tunic which fastened on one shoulder and came to mid thigh. On her head she wore the crescent of the new moon. She was gone. The man began once more to form.

I had pulled loose the cup, held it beneath my chin, awkwardly. What ancient wisdom had come out of the past to make me aware that this was what I must do? There was nothing in that cup, still there came to my nostrils from its interior a sharp, clean scent—the leaves of certain trees, under the morning sun, the sharpness of herbs crushed beneath foot.

It was as if a veil had been swept away and I really *saw!*

Cloud bubbled and frothed within the oval, veiling and then revealing the form of Gruu, who lay on his side unmoving. There were streaks of red in that murk, darker shadows, as if small things wavered back and forth through it. Still Gathea moved toward it, her hands outheld. She had already passed me. However, that hold upon us which had kept us from any movement was broken now. Still cradling the cup close to me with one hand, I threw myself forward and flung out my other arm across her path when she came close to that coiling matter.

Her face was rapt, her eyes all for the frothing within the oval. At first she simply pushed against my hold as if she did not expect or know what it might be. I knew that thus, one-armed, I could not hold her back. I dropped my arm, laced fingers of my left hand instead in her belt, jerked backwards myself, so brought her with me, even as a tendril of the mist reached for her.

She tripped and fell and I went with her, my body rolling over her as she began a frenzied struggle for freedom. I do not think she even knew me for who I was, but rather only as a barrier between her and what she must have. With fist, tooth and nail, she fought me, and I could but use my strength to pin her to the ground, attempt to dodge those raking nails. For I knew that the cup was my salvation and only while I held it to me, and breathed in that strange scent which still arose from it, would my head remain clear and that weaver of illusions could not take me to its self.

Somehow I held, and then hoping that it would serve her as it had me, and because I felt a little safer with my back to that oval of light, I forced the cup itself closer to her face where her head turned from side to side and she snapped teeth as if seeking to tear my arm, as Gruu himself might do in a frenzy.

We were still caught in that struggle when—

My grip on Gathea became desperate, my hold on the cup even more. We no longer lay on the pavement of that place of darkness. There was cold so sharp that I believe no living thing could have stood it for more than the instant. Then we were in light again, a red light which leaped and flamed. As the cold had struck at us, so now did heat lick out to sear our bodies.

Gathea lay still, her eyes closed. But I could feel the quick rise and fall of her breast under gasping breaths. I raised myself to my knees and looked around. The heat was so intense it seemed that every breath I drew must blacken and char my lungs. There was rock under us—that, too, blistering hot, so I hastened to pull Gathea up from it, hold her against me lest she burn. I smelled singeing of hair and as I turned my head I saw Gruu, still stretched motionless nearby.

We were surrounded by a wall of flame which burned red and yellow. Now and then, as if blown by a breeze we could not ourselves feel, it sent long tongues reaching for us. The fire was bright, its wall held no breaks, so I could not see what lay beyond it. All I could think now was that our defiance had angered the tower presence so that it had abruptly banished us through some mastery of power into this prison which was like to complete the matter by reducing us swiftly to fire-blackened bones.

"Dains!" Gathea opened her eyes. They still did not focus upon me, but searched beyond. I was sure she sought whatever vision the tower presence had formed for her beguiling. She frowned as apparently true sight returned. Then she looked at me with an anger that would send me hurtling into that blazing wall if she could aim it rightly. "Dains—she was there! She called me—at last!"

She raised both hands and fended me off so sharply that I was indeed pushed too near the fire, had to jump away and to my feet. The cup I kept hold of with a fierce grip.

"It was all an illusion," I retorted. She had claimed to know so much of sorcery, why had she not seen that for herself when Gruu had been drawn, when twice I had faced what was intended to bind me also to the Dark?

"What did you see?" I continued, fronting her and speaking with the heat which was not of any flame wall, but arose out of my own spirit. "Gruu went to another cat. I saw first a woman—" I was not going to go into detail there—"and then the Horn-Crowned One. You—did you see your goddess—your Moon Daughter?"

I think that Gathea had no mind to listen to me at first, that she was still so bemused over the illusion that she had only anger for me and used it to drown out my voice. She raised her hand, balled into a fist, as if she would beat me, and then as she took a step, she snagged her boot on Gruu's limp body and fell forward, sprawling over the cat.

"Gruu!" Her cry was loud. As she lifted herself, she gathered the cat's head into her hands, stared into his half-closed eyes. I wondered if he had died, his life sucked out by whatever lure that thing had set for him. "Gruu!" She was smoothing the fur about his throat. Then her eyes wide, and with all the bemusement gone from them, she looked up at me.

"He is—no!" she added, her fingers dug deep into the fur at his throat. "He is not dead! You—" Still cradling the cat's head against her breast she gazed at me again.

"You saw Gruu—what happened to him?"

That she had not seen the cat leap into that enticement should

not have surprised me. I had already reckoned that the presence
had set for each of us the most suitable temptation. Gruu had
gone to another cat, doubtless a female of his own species. I had
fronted that which had beckoned to me first for the body, as if my
senses were like Gruu's—and then touch on a more subtle line.

"He was drawn to that thing by sight of another cat, a female!"

"Dains—Dains was there!" The girl shook her head as if still
she could not rid herself of that dream. "I had found the shrine—
I was—" Then she stopped, though her hands still caressed the
head of the cat. "You did not see her. You saw others—" Gathea
looked at the flames now which sent waves of heat against my
back, not at me.

"One who deals in false illusions." She shivered as if her own
fear chilled her enough to banish those flames. "And one of the
Dark! But why—? And Gruu—" She looked down at the quiet
head pressed against her.

"How did we get here?" she asked after a long moment, her
voice steady now as if she had accepted what had happened as
fact and then put it behind her, ready to face what might come.

I told her—of the cup and how the scent from it had banished
all illusions for me, that I had prevented her going into the light
and then we had been transported to this place. She listened. I
believed she not only understood what I said, but was able to
build upon it a little from her own strange knowledge.

"Three of us," she said slowly. "It had to control three of us at
the same time. That spell which its liegemen brought to us—yes,
that could be held. For it was set to control our bodies together,
and the wills of the three riders would help feed it. But when we
fronted it alone, that control no longer worked. Poor Gruu, wise
as he is he would have no understanding of a spell of illusion;
therefore he was first trapped. And you—you were guarded in a
way it did not suspect."

"You did not see what it fashioned for me?" I asked as casually
as I could. Why had she stood so silent and aloof while all that
had been pictured for me? Or had her vision of Dains been pro-
duced at the same time as mine?

"I saw a shrine—a Moon Shrine—with the light full on the
altar. I waited, for I knew that *she* would come—that that was the
place I have searched for. No, I did not see what was made for

you. Only, that spinner of vision could not hold two illusions steady, one for each of us. When you defeated its aims with your cup, then it wrought Dains—as I waited for her. It could not hold for the three of us at one time. Your cup power shook it, and you were freed, enough to free me—

"But," she gave a sweeping glance which took in the flame wall, "where did it banish us when we would not yield?"

"Into some strong evil of its own," I returned. "I do not know where anymore than I know how. If there is any way to win out of here we had better seek it before we are dried and cooked and so barred from all hunting entirely."

Gathea laid her cheek against the cat's head. "I no longer have the wand," she said. "My learning is nothing here. Nor can we hope to reach the Light if we are deep in the realm of the Great Dark, for there is no passage between the worlds of the two. They meet at boundaries and there they struggle one with the other. Only I think that here we are well past that debatable land and no moon magic will come to my calling."

I could not believe that she was resigned to whatever fate awaited her. I had learned, I was sure, that she would not give up, no matter how high the odds against us. That we had defeated in part something which seemed to have power far beyond my imagining at least heartened me.

Gathea was busy now, loosening the latching of her wallet. She brought out a packet of dried leaves. Sorting out seven of them she put them into her mouth and began chewing quickly and thoroughly.

"What—?" I began a question.

She shook her head and pointed to her mouth, signalling that she could not speak. Then her hand went once more to Gruu's head and I realized that what she strove to do was for the sake of the cat.

15

GATHEA TOOK A PAT OF PASTE FROM HER MOUTH, AND, PRESSING
the cat's eyelids down gently, she spread the mixture across the
closed eyes. When she had finished she touched fingertips of both
hands to Gruu's skull between the ears. The girl appeared to take
no note of the flame wall about us. The breath of that was, I
believed, growing stronger. I strove to win some measure of sight
through the play of the red tongues, but they seemed to stretch
solidly.

Flame has been man's tool for years uncounted, but it is also
his bane. Now I felt that that space about us might at any moment narrow to consume us all. While Gathea sat supporting the
head of the cat, her eyes also closed, using some inner power of
her own to summon back whatever life essence our enemy of the
tower had forced from its victim.

Gruu moved a paw, unsheathed claws. A mewing such as might
issue from a bewildered kitten came from his mouth, which hung
open to display his formidable fangs. Gathea caressed the fur
behind his ears, rubbed along the line of his jaw.

"It is well. He is waking."

"To what?" I retorted. "If he escaped this," I waved toward the
flame, "through illusion, why summon him back?"

My mouth was dry; I longed for a long pull at the water bottle
hooked to my belt, except that I had no mind to waste the small
store of liquid it contained. Sweat plastered my hair to my skull,
ran in trickles within my clothing, making both linen and quilted
jerkin cling tightly to my skin.

"Illusion," Gathea repeated. She still soothed the cat. "It would seem that the weapon of this Power lies therein. And—"

She looked beyond me to the play of the flame wall. There was no need to put into words what thought had come into her mind.

"Perhaps that is an illusion," I conceded. "Yet it is tight woven and I think we cannot break it—"

"As above, so below—" she said then, and the meaning of her words I did not understand.

"Illusion," she continued, "means the drawing of thought from an enemy's, or victim's mind, building upon it. Then one summons from another plane the substance of that which is most feared—or desired—and the subject transposes it into life himself."

"You mean, we feed this flame?"

"As long as we believe we see it, then our belief feeds it." She nodded.

"And if you are not right, if we have indeed been dropped into a real place of fire?"

"Even reality can answer to Power. What can be summoned can also be dismissed. Have you not already proven that?"

I saw the trickle of sweat down her own cheek. Then Gruu's head raised from her knee; the smears of dried herb paste cracked and fell away as his eyes opened; his gaze centered on her face. He made a sound between purr and growl.

Yes, I could accept the changes I had witnessed for myself as well-woven illusion—but this was something else again. For I was sure if I put out a hand those flames would sear my flesh to the bone.

My companion closed her eyes again and the great cat seemed content to stay where he was, as if he drowsed. In the red light I saw movement of her lips, though now no words were spoken aloud.

This playing with minds! No wonder my clansmen had fought shy of the ways of the Wise Women, much as they had depended upon the fruits of such delving into the unknown. I wanted no more at that moment than an opponent I could see, one with a sword in his fist, ready to do battle in a way which was open and of my own world.

I was not even sure that where we were now pent *was* in the world I knew at all. Certainly we had been snatched here in a way that suggested travel through a space not meant for those of my species. Even if we conquered the flames by whatever sorcery Gathea could summon—what then? If we were not in our own place—or time?

She opened her eyes to stare straight at me. "You hinder!" she accused. "You withhold unbelief! Oh!" She made a fist with one hand and pounded it against the hot rock of the floor on which she had hunkered as if that were spring cooled. "If I but had one who was fitted to this task! You—you fight me with your belief in the wrong things!"

Her emotion passed into the cat. He lifted his heavy head well up for the first time to snarl at me.

I was stung by her words. She owed me a little. I had kept her from answering to the false Dains, had I not? Once more I felt for the cup and raised it, hoping that I could again sniff that cool rich air which had served and saved me. There was nothing there now. Gathea looked at what I held and her eyes narrowed. There came a faint change in her expression; she might have been looking at some object she could put to better usage.

"If you only knew more—"

"Tell me, then!" To my sight those flames which sprouted from the fire wall were moving closer.

Gathea raised her hand to push back the hair plastered against her forehead.

"What you ask is impossible. You cannot compress years of learning into a few words here and now!"

Then she gave a jerk as a flame tongue nearly licked her hand and I saw the shadow of fear arise in her eyes.

"We may not even have time for a few words," I pointed out grimly.

"Those who have the Power," she answered hastily, "are said to be able to transfer objects from one plane of existence to the next. They look into the thing and see its innermost self. For each thing, born or made, was once only a thought, therefore it remains partly a thought. That thought being the substance we on the plane can see, does exist elsewhere in another form. A mistress of the Mysteries can seek out such a thought, reduce the object once more to its beginnings. This is what we are taught—"

"You have seen it done?"

Slowly Gathea shook her head. "It would take one who knew much to see the innermost heart of a thing and so use it."

"But you have said that if I knew more," I persisted, "you could help us. What should I know?"

She shook her head again slowly. "We do not know the innermost being of the force that sought to entrap us. And—"

"This—" I pointed to the flames again flaring inward at us. I was *sure* that the circling walls were coming closer—"is fire. Fire is born of fuel—wood—some liquids which burn fast if a striker spark ignites them. What is then the innermost part of fire—that which it feeds upon?"

In this fire I could see no sign of either wood or a trough for the oil we used for long-lamps.

"That which it feeds upon—" Gathea repeated thoughtfully after me. Then an expression of excitement began to grow on her thin face. "Yes, it could be that the food for the fire exists elsewhere."

A statement which did not seem helpful to me, but which appeared to awaken new life and purpose in her.

"Come." She reached upward, holding out her hand to me. "The cup—have you a measure of water to pour into that?"

"A very little."

"It must do. I cannot do this thing, for the cup is yours. Only you can evoke the power it exerts. Pour water into it—hold it steady. Then link hand with me. Perhaps Gruu also can give us of his strength, since his own bespelling is broken. Do this—it may be our only chance! For my power cannot rise alone."

I allowed a trickle of water to moisten the bottom of the cup, hardly enough to be seen. Holding it in a grip tight enough to cramp my fingers, I sat on my heels, my left hand firm clasped in hers.

"Now, close your eyes. There is a fire, it is burning—from wood —just as it would on a keep hearth. There is water, a spring of water and it is rising, rising. *See* this! You must *see* it!"

There was urgency, force in her words. Yet when I closed my eyes, my mind rebelled, I could not build such a picture. When I tried it was a pale thing which winked out of mind as the lack in me allowed it to vanish.

Somewhere a voice was to be heard—but far off, sounding in

such need that I strained to hear better. No, it was the fire picture not the voice—not anything but a fire burning in the pocket of a forest clearing. A fire, laid on wood as might be in any hunter's camp—a fire!

Something built within me, a strength of will which I had never known I possessed. It was as if the force of the water and the fire had themselves transformed their substance, and all the energy which both held now filled *me*. My weak and fluttering picture of the fire firmed, I could hold it longer. There were the rocks of a basin into which the water of a spring flowed. Fire and water—ancient enemies!

That fire, that basin of water, became the world. Nothing lay beyond them, no action mattered save that I hold them in mind's eye as steady and clear as I could. Fire—and water!

Into me continued to flow that strength which made clear my sight, which now allowed me not only to visualize the fire, the stream from the basin, but enabled me to use that stream, to draw the water higher and higher in the basin. No, it was a full well of water, very deep. The water which filled it to the brim overflowed —toward the fire!

The fire flared, was gone. I held firmly to my thought-picture. It *was* there! And once more it was. The water had fallen away as I had concentrated on the fire. No, up water, up—over—down—I saw the rise of it like a wide sea wave, issuing forth from the mouth of the well, splashing, flowing heavier. Again, when my picture wavered, there was a renewal of the other strength so that I could catch and hold.

Down poured the water, it lapped at the wood, then engulfed it. The flames sputtered, fled to far ends of the brands which were its food; the water advanced upon those also. There was a last flicker of my picture as if the fire I watched knew its force was failing. Only *I* held, and the water flowed on in full flood. There were no flames left. I released the flood. It was gone. But had it, for a moment, mirrored a head crowned with horns? I could not be sure. I opened my eyes. The head was there, shining on the side of my cup. For the rest it was dark; we were no longer surrounded by the blistering heat of that wall.

I blinked and blinked again. The only source of light came from the dim glow of the head on the goblet, and that was slowly fading. If there had not been the firm stone under me I would have thought we had been whirled out of life itself. As the interior of the tower had been so was this blackness thick enough to swallow one, pressing against the body with a stifling hold. I heard a sigh from the dark and knew it came from Gathea.

"It—it worked!" I found my tongue. "The fire is gone. But we are not yet back—or is this still the tower?"

Somehow I did not believe that. There was an otherness which was like the Dark, pressing in. Now that we had lost the fire which had held my mind, I realized that one step could not mean a journey. Out of the thick black came Gathea's voice to awaken my unease yet further.

"We are still trapped," she said. "This is not of our time or place. . . . And—"

What she might have added I will never know for at that moment the darkness changed. There was no oval of light piercing it —rather we were being sucked, pulled through it at such a speed as to nearly tear my breath from me, so I gasped and fought to fill my lungs. My hold on Gathea's hand was vise tight. At that instant I feared more than anything that we be separated, each whirled to a different fate.

My body seemed weightless, as fragile as a leaf caught up by the wind's blast. I even closed my eyes, for the pressure of the dark through which we were drawn seemed painful against them, as if it would strike me permanently blind. We were drawn and that which drew us gathered strength, lapping us as lightly about as if we were encased in a net of ropes which drew tighter and tighter across and around our bodies.

Then—that feeling of rushing through the air vanished. We hung, still prisoners in the Dark, for I ventured to open my eyes to see nothing. There was a purpose; I could sense it. Within me something marveled at how quickly I was able to sense the unknown. I had no teaching, as Gathea had pointed out. Then what had awakened me to this knowledge of things-which-were-not and the patterns wrought by Power?

We hung, as I say, helpless, waiting the need—or the pleasure— of a pressure so beyond my comprehension that I could not begin to guess at its nature. All that linked me to the real was my hand interlocked with Gathea's. I wanted to ask questions; my words were smothered before they reached my lips by the heavy pressure of the black upon my chest and throat.

I think that I was not far then from retreating out of myself, seeking even death as a shelter, if one's will can carry so far as that. The faint light which had outlined the face on the cup had vanished, perhaps blown from us during that wild journey. I could still feel it, know that, like Gathea's hand, it was locked to me for good or ill.

There was another wrenching, we were on the move again. Once more I experienced that icy cold, that sensation of blasting through some unbelievable barrier. Now there was light—dim—gray—yet still enough to cut through the curtain, making me blink. It was below, as if we were aloft in the sky, but it grew larger, brighter, and we were falling toward it being wafted downward, upheld by will—whose will and why?

There was a shock, wrenching my body with such force that I was torn loose from Gathea. That power which imprisoned me carried me away at another angle. Now I might have looked through the eyes of a bird or some winged thing which held itself aloft by swiftly beating wings.

Below stood a circle of stone, silver bright, for there were moon's rays across it. In the center was a block of shining white, so vividly aglow in this light that I would have hidden my eyes from its glare had I had the ability to raise my hands. Again no part of my body would obey my will. On the stone lay someone, a woman. Her hair was outspread behind her head, flowing back over the edge of the stone. She wore no clothing and at first I thought that she might be dead, for I could determine no sign of life in that quiet shape.

Now I saw that there were four pillars set at the four corners of the pavement, each bearing a moon sign—even as there had been in the shrine among the dale hills. Under each of these wavered a thin form which seemed unstable, wraithlike, weaving in and out of human outline. They thickened, became more stable the closer I was borne to their stations.

As bare of body as the woman they were plainly masculine. Each held a staff within his hands, and they did not stand steadily, but changed from one foot to another constantly, as if they marched or danced, still keeping their places. There was a shadow of excitement building here, it reached out to me, sought to enter my mind, my body.

Out of the shadows beyond that place of gleaming silver came a fifth shadow, dark, a body like a black blot which soiled the silver, tarnished the fresh cleanness of the moonlight. In my hands the cup came alive, it was warm, growing hotter. It might have been filling with anger, with outrage.

I was to be a tool, a weapon in the hands of the Dark to forge a needed spell, to turn Light awry. And I could not fight against the pressure.

That black shadow wavered and weaved in a dance which led from one of the pillar men to the next, halting for a moment before each one to throw skeletal arms high in some invocation, while each this shadow so visited became more and more real as if fresh and powerful life were drawn into it. Still all this time the woman lay on the altar bespelled or in deep slumber, knowing, I believed, nothing of what chanced.

Downward the compulsion which had pulled me here forced me now. I was close enough to see their faces—all save that of the moving shadow who made the circling about, raising the power. That I could feel, streaming about me like a swift current.

If the dancing men saw me they gave no sign of it. I had reached the ground now, my feet were on the pavement, those moon silver blocks by the altar. I looked down and saw—Iynne!

Gone was the girl who had ridden in Garn's train. She was changed in a manner which I did not understand. Her lips, dark against the pallor of her face, showing not red, but black in this light, curved in a slight smile. I could believe that she was dreaming, finding in sleep some great happiness never experienced by the timid maid I had always known and who shrank from others, perhaps so cowed by her father's strong possessiveness that she dared not lift her eyes unless he might order it so.

Iynne! A—sacrifice. I needed no one to tell me that. Whatever was being wrought here was no act of the Light, rather of evil—of a Dark as black as that place from which I had been drawn.

I stood, the cup between my hands, feeling its growing heat. Its metal heart might have been filled with leaping flames, so did it burn my flesh. This was its defense against what would happen here. That silver face on the side blazed, from its eyes shot brilliant spears of light—white as the moon above us—yet in their way different.

That dancing shadow, still formless in its many swaddlings of night black, save for the skeletal arms, turned from the last man and came jigging and prancing toward me. The head was hooded; I could catch no sign of a face within that shadow. Still I knew that this one was aware of my coming, that it was in league with the presence which had sent me here.

Once more those arms were flung up and out, the wide sleeves fell away from arms which were skin over bone—ancient skin, ancient bone—to uncover them near to the shoulder. The crooked fingers which might be of extreme age, long of nail, knobbed and twisted, swooped down, reaching at the cup across the sleeping girl. I held to that fiercely, knowing that in my hold alone was this talisman safe.

I set my will, not against that which brought me here, for I believed that opposed to that I would have no chance at all. Rather I strove to center what strength I had upon continued possession of the Horned Man's goblet. To that I bent every effort.

Fingers drove nails into my flesh and I jerked free. Perhaps I had taken by surprise whatever power had sent me here as a captive, perhaps the goblet I held, and determined to go on holding, roused in me strengths I did not know that I had.

The thing which would grasp the goblet made a second attack. Now its efforts loosed the full cowl over its head. The material fell away. Another woman—a travesty of her sex. She was very old and her aging had not been by good and well sought ways. Thus her deeply wrinkled face was a mask of ancient hatreds, imprinted by vices beyond reckoning. Across a nearly bald skull straggled a few wisps of greasy white hair, and, as she opened her mouth to spit and curse at me, I saw but one or two yellow teeth, more like Gruu's fangs than those grown in any human mouth.

She was malevolent and she was powerful. What she desired to do moved her to greater strength than I would have thought possible, judging by her bony body. Having failed in her first grab at the cup, she rounded the altar on which Iynne slept, coming straight for me, her eyes pits of a rage, born of both cunning and madness, her crooked hands out to rip my face to tatters.

To move against the power which had sent me was like struggling through thick sand. I could not avoid her leap at me, nor would I loose my hold on the cup. I strove to lessen her attack, take the force of it against my shoulder, my raised arms.

There was spittle at the corners of her mouth as she shouted forth strange words. To my amazement I could *see* those words. They were both red and smoky in the air, swirling up and about my head, pressing down as if they would scorch me like true fire.

It was then that I flung up my head and once more cried aloud.

"Ha! Kurnous— By the Name of the Horns!"

She might have run full against a wall, for she staggered back one step and then two, striving to keep her footing. Her mouth worked, spit dribbled down her chin. Now her hands moved, sketching out signs. Those, too, carried the red-black of the Dark weaving in the air.

The cup within my hands was almost too hot to hold; still I brought it level with my own mouth as if I were about to drink down what it held—though it was empty. From those eyes on the side the beams of brilliance were like the heads of spears set to bring down the charge of enemies.

They struck at that black-robed crone, met resistance, sprayed sideways, lapped across the altar stone and the sleeping girl. I might have loosed a fountain of light, for this radiance did not fade. Instead, the beams mingled with the moonlight, grew sharper, brighter.

The crone, with an agility which I would have thought beyond her years, hurled herself backwards once again, withdrawing from the outer wash of that light. She screamed, and the sound of her voice within my head made me cringe in turn, for it was pain such as I did not think I could bear.

Yet I stood my ground. The pressure which had brought me here was gone. I could if I wished have thrown aside the cup with its torment of fire, run from that confrontation. But in my heart I knew that I would not do. What strange battle was mine I could only guess. But I held as the light washed on and farther out.

The crone stumbled back and back. She stood now on the very edge of the pavement. There she halted as if determined to make a last stand. I well knew that she was summoning up the full force of her power. Though I had been long the prisoner of something beyond my comprehension, I was still warrior-trained. I caught that small motion of her head, saw that, for a moment, her eyes did not hold on me, but had flashed to the girl.

It was my turn to attack. I so discovered that I had not lost all the ways and skills of a swordsman. An instant and I was between the crone and the girl. Also I shot a glance at the nearest of the men—would those four now move in upon me at the service of this sorceress? They were bare of body and had no weapons I could see, save those staffs they held. However, who might tell what other arms they might have which were not of my knowing at all?

The two I could see had not moved. Still they stood by the pillars, dancing from foot to foot, their eyes not for me, nor for the crone, but facing inward, though I could not be sure whether they watched Iynne or not—

A bolt of light flashed at me. I again swung up the goblet. Not only from the eyes of the Horned Lord did the answering radiance stream now, it welled from within the cup itself, fountaining into the air, sparking outwards, forming a veil between me and the crone. While on the pavement the flood of light also swirled outwards. It reached the bare feet of the nearest man. For the first time he awakened to what was happening. He twisted, his gaze breaking as he looked down at the stream now about his ankles.

Handsome he had been beyond the common; now his features writhed and moved in a sickening manner. His fine body might have been caught in a furnace of heat, shriveling, becoming stunted. He cried out like a wordless beast in agony as his staff turned into a silver flame ignited by the flood. He hurled it from him.

No man stood tall there now. Rather there crouched at the foot of the pillar a hairy, crooked thing with a great toad-wide mouth, a mixture of beast and reptile. He strove to hop or throw himself away from the flood of light but that held him full captive.

I looked to the other man. He also had been wrought upon. What struggled in the morass overflowing from the cup I held was part bird, such a bird as lived in no land I knew, tall as the man had been, rapacious of beak—bearing resemblance in part to those black fowl which we had seen in Garn's dale, save that this was a giant of their species.

The crone—she retreated another step, off the moon-drenched

pavement. The creeping flow of light halted at the edge of the stone, did not reach her. She was in a half crouch as if trying to overleap that rippling spread of light, still coming at me. For, though I might have baffled her for a moment, I knew that she was far from defeated. Nor was she done with whatever game she had attempted to play here.

Her mouth worked as it had when she had thrown at me those fiery curses. Only this time there were no words to be seen. Instead she brought her two hands together, and the sound which followed that gesture of flesh meeting flesh was as loud as a clap of thunder.

She was gone!

I backed against the altar. The two things at the bases of the pillars could not move in spite of their struggles. I swung around to view the other two. The radiance was creeping in their direction also. But it was not to reach and entrap them. Though they showed no sign that they could see the danger seeping toward their feet, they both suddenly snuffed out as had the crone.

Leaning back against the altar stone, I tried to view what lay outside that silver square. That I had been borne out of the other place where the Presence in the tower had sent us, I was sure. This was my own world—though what portion of it I could not begin to guess. This was certainly not that shrine in the hill above Garn's dale. While Gathea and Gruu—where were they? Had they been left behind in that nothing place? If so—how might they be brought forth?

There was a sigh from behind me. I swung around. Iynne's eyes were open, she was waking up, that shadow smile still on her lips, her eyes languorous, as if she had come from such a dream as no true maiden might hold in her mind.

16

"IYNNE!"

That we must get from this place filled with a play of unknown forces was the first thought in my mind. The cup I clutched had cooled, no longer giving forth its own glare of light. Even the face on it was fading back into the dulled markings which concealed the power it wielded, in spite of my inept handling.

The girl pulled herself up on the altar stone, her motions still the slow ones of a person aroused from so deep a sleep—so far a venture into dreaming—that she did not wholly focus on what lay about her.

Her hands stroked down over her body to lie below her waist, clasped there as if they pressed against her some treasure past all believing. She began to croon softly, her eyes never lifting to mine, a soft murmur which spun me across years and distance. Just so had I heard long ago in my first childhood remembrances Iynne's nurse soothe her charge—a sleep-song for a babe.

"Done—" Still she did not appear to see me, her gaze was either turned inward or flew out beyond this place, to fasten on a promised future richer than the moonlight, which was all that clothed her slender body. "It is done! The god has come to me and I shall bear his will. A child who shall be greater than any lord—greater—greater—" Her voice trilled away once more into that croon of a cradle song.

Were her wits utterly cleaved from her? I placed the cup carefully on the ground, shuffled from my shoulder the roll of travel cloak which had been buckled about the wallet cord. Shaking this loose I dropped it around her shoulders as she sat still on the altar stone, smiling so gently, her hands protecting the new life which she believed must lie within her body.

"A son—a son who will ride forth in time to summon Great Forces, who will draw power into his two hands and make of it what weapon is needful for the hour. Greatly have I been honored—"

"Iynne!"

I made her name as sharp a call as I could, wanting to shake her into awareness of where she was and that I was with her. Now her head jerked, turned in my direction. I saw her eyes widen and knew that the illusion which sleep had left her was breaking.

"Elron!" Recognition at last. Her hands went to the cloak, wrapping it about her swiftly. "But—" She stared around her, as if looking to see who had accompanied me here. Then she must have seen those monsters who still writhed, if now feebly, in the hold of the cup's overpour. I saw her shock. She screamed, her voice shrill and high in the night.

"Elron! What are those?" Contentment was wiped away by a look of fear and loathing mingled. "There is—" I saw her nostrils expand, her head lift a little—"evil here! I must not be touched by that. I bear a god—a son of power within me!"

She scrambled down from the altar to draw back, away from the creatures who snuffled and uttered cries, not of any entreaty, rather of bafflement and weak rage. I eyed the dark beyond the borders of the Moon Shrine. Though the crone had vanished from sight, I could not altogether believe that she had been so easily bested. Anything might lurk out there.

"Elron!" Iynne held the cloak close about her with one hand, now seized upon my arm with her other. "Get me away!"

"Presently. When I am sure there is nothing out there waiting for us." I could not shake off the grip of her fingers. Holding the cup before me as I would a sword—for in this place perhaps it was a greater weapon than any blade, I edged still farther away from the altar, striving not only to keep in sight the two struggling beast things, but also to make sure that those who had stood by the other two pillars did not return to deny us passage.

There was an odd feeling of lightness, of emptiness, here now. Was it that I had won freedom—if only for a space—from the sorcery that had sent me to take a part in these labors? I could only hope that this was true.

Though Iynne kept still her hold on me, she moved without urging to match her pace to mine. We reached the edge of the shining pavement without any interference. I took one backward step, drew her safely with me, and then half faced around to stare into the darker ways of the night.

It took a moment or two to blink the glare of the Moon Shrine from my eyes, to see what lay in the softer light where those silver rays did not focus so brilliantly. Unlike the smaller shrine I had seen in the dale hills, this was not surrounded by trees or growing things but by pavement, though not of the silver-white. Raying outward like the spokes of a wheel were low buildings also of stone.

I half expected to find life there, gathered to watch the ceremony my own coming had so abruptly ended. Nothing stirred. This was a dead place—a long-deserted place—in which only the shrine had life or purpose left.

For the first time Iynne dragged back, twisted away. It was my turn to take her in hold.

"Raidhan!" she called. "Raidhan? Where is she? Why is she gone?"

"Keep quiet!" I did not like the way her call was echoed hollowly back from those silent buildings about us. That we were really free of any company I could not quite believe, and my wariness was warning enough.

"Let me go! Raidhan!" Again she called, and, short of stuffing one end of the cloak in her mouth, I did not see how I could silence her. The cup I must still keep in my hand; I was beginning to trust it all the more than any ordinary weapon. Also I feared if I freed Iynne now she would run from me. I had no desire to hunt her among those dark and empty buildings before me this night.

"She is gone," I made what answer I could. If that was the name of the hag I had driven out of the shrine, with the Horn cup's aid, then that was the truth. "Listen." I shook her a little, to gain her full attention. "You saw those monsters by the pillars, did you not? Well, their like may prowl here. We cannot draw them to us."

Her answer came fretfully: "I do not understand you. What are you doing here? Raidhan said that the god would take me, that his power was meant to be born again from my body. The Moon Shrine drew me here for no other purpose. That is true! The god came—he took me—"

I had to choose and quickly. "You dreamed. They must have drugged you and you dreamed! There was no god—the Moon Shrine is not his—" I could only hope that what I said was the truth. What had happened before I had been thrust into the midst of that ceremony I had no way of telling, but I believed that it had not been carried to its intended ending. Had those monsters in the temporary shape of men been summoned by the Dark to father on this girl some greater and more evil thing? That appeared to me to be the reason for the rites.

"Let me go!" She was twisting like a serpent in my hold. "You cannot know the truth! Raidhan told me—"

Luckily she was less strong than Gathea. Even with one hand I could hold her.

"If Raidhan was that black-cloaked bag of bones back there," I retorted, "then she is gone. I would like to hope to some distance! It is best that we go also—"

She fought me hard, I was forced to thrust the cup beneath my belt and use both my hands. Then I managed to turn her, spitting and crying out against me as she was, and march her down the nearest open way, hoping with all my heart that her continued cries would not bring upon us some attack.

The road we followed was paved, while the buildings set along it were low, one story only, and small, with gaping, dark doorways but no windows. Also the way under us slanted upward, past the length of thirteen buildings before we came to open ground.

Iynne had fallen silent at last; she was crying, sobs which shook her whole body. I could not think but that she was frailer than I had known her. Her body in my hold seemed to be slighter, and I thought that her dragging steps now were not from her desire to remain but rather because she was weak and tired. Then she stumbled and fell against me, so that her head came against my shoulder as it drooped, and I felt her go limp.

This might be a ruse. But I needed a chance to get away from this place of ill omen. So I swept her up in my arms, and went on, climbing up the road at the best pace I could hold to. We reached the rim of the valley and there I was forced to rest, letting Iynne from my arms but keeping her supported against me as I looked back down into that strange place.

The gleam of the Moon Shrine was still bright. But I could no longer make out the two caught against the pillars. Nor were there any other lights, or stirring, in all of that town. The buildings squatted dark and heavy and the roads running between them were open and free. Nothing moved.

Iynne's heavy sobs had become sighs; she hung in my grasp as if all will and strength had gone out of her. I moved slowly, bringing her with me, to see now what lay beyond.

The road we had followed ran out and on, a dim white line, into the distance. There was moonlight enough, now that my eyes had adjusted from the greater glare in the shrine, to see that the country round about was well covered with vegetation. Trees formed copses, even a small grove or two. There was brush which cast pools of shadow I eyed with growing dislike. Too quickly my imagination could conjure images it was better not to see at all. Though the road might be watched by evil forces, yet at this time it was safer, I believed, than striking off into the open land.

"Can you walk?" I demanded of my charge. To go on carrying her, unable to use my hands for any sudden defense, was folly. Nor had I the least desire to remain where we now were, so close to the shrine.

"You had no right!" She struck out at me and the cloak half slipped from her body. She gave a gasp and caught at it clumsily, huddling it around her. "Raidhan will come—she will not permit you to take me."

"Can you walk?" I dismissed her warning, for that concern was already on my own mind.

"Yes," her assent was sullen. But if she thought that I would release her so that she might elude me to flee back to the shrine, she was mistaken. I kept one hand heavy and tight upon her shoulder, pushing her a little before me down that road.

For a time we went in silence. Since Iynne now gave me no trouble, I paid more attention to the fields stretching on either side, alert as I could be to any movement there. So far there was none, save that brought about by the wind which brushed the trees and swept across the ground growth in a steady whisper.

"Why did you come?" The question from my unwilling companion surprised me a little. I had come to think of her as a burden which must be borne, and not a living person.

Why had I? I had never aimed for this place. I had swung off into the unknown because I still owed Lord Garn a debt, repayment for my own folly. That I had found Iynne had been none of my own doing. Nor did I understand why the forces which I perhaps could never truly understand had summoned me here.

"I am kinless, clanless," I answered. "Rightfully my lord has judged me. Had I not kept silent when you sought the hill shrine you would not be here."

For a long moment she was silent. Then, when she spoke again, her voice was very low.

"Thus you have come to clean your honor—as a liegeman would say."

Her speech was not that of the Iynne I knew. It was sharp, quick, with a sly sneer in it.

"I am no longer liegeman, and, as you know, for the kinless there is no honor. I failed at my guard—there is no erasing that."

"You think to take me back—back to those who do not look beyond the labor of their own hands, who have no power and do not know what witlings they truly are!"

Her voice was becoming louder, more shrill. "I am not a bond maid to be pushed here and there as if I had neither wit nor desire of my own. I am—" She fell silent and I was caught enough by her sharp protest to ask:

"You are what then, Lady Iynne?"

She surprised me with a laugh, again there was slyness, a sneering note in her voice: "Wait and see, kinless, clanless one. You have meddled with matters you cannot touch no matter how far and how high you would reach. I bear within me now—yes, I a virgin—carry a child! A child of power, and such power as will make him ruler of this world. I was chosen—I am fulfilled! You cannot win me out of this land—try and see! I am a part of its greater force now—"

I thought of that crone and her evil mouthings, of the two things the cup flood had revealed at the shrine pillars. That these were allied, if not in a common bond, then in general spirit, to the Presence of the Black Tower I did not doubt. That Iynne would rejoice in such an evil possessing her was a thought I could not hold. She must be truly englamoured; she had not openly chosen the Dark.

Now I slowed pace and taking from my belt the cup, never far from my hand, I held it out before her, turning it so she could look upon the Horned Man's face. In the moonlight that was bright enough, as if the cold metal of its fashioning somehow sensed what I would do and would aid me in the doing.

"Do you know this, Iynne?"

"Yes, it is Kurnous—the Hunter. But what have you to do with him, Elron?" I caught sheer surprise breaking through the former harshness of her speech. "He is the warden, the protector of the Moon Lady. It was she who summoned me, whose bidding made me thus—"

No, that memory, foul as any stench upon the night air, which I had only partly understood, had certainly not been of Gathea's Dains, nor of Gunnora, nor of the Horned Lord. Someone had perverted a rite to ensnare my companion. How deeply she was caught within that net I must discover, perhaps for the safety of us both.

"Dains summoned you?"

"Dains?" She repeated that name as if she had not heard it before. "Who is Dains? It was Raidhan—she who is the Elder, the ruler of the moon's shadow. She is the Wise One, the one who would bring the Great Lord to life, calling me to form a body which he can use."

"And Gunnora," I tested yet further, "has she also spoken?"

"Dains, Gunnora!" The petulant tone was back in her voice. "Names which mean nothing—where did you learn them, kinless one? But more important, why do you carry the Horned Hunter's cup?"

"It was a gift to me. Listen, Iynne, you have been used by Dark Ones. Dains—Gunnora—they are the rightful ladies of the moon. It is their power which this Raidhan of yours has usurped. Could you not tell when you looked upon those monsters back there that you were dealing with the Dark?"

"Your wits are awry!" Once more her tone was shrill. "*You* are of the Dark—not I! I tell you, I was summoned—*I* was chosen. I have slept this night in the arms of the Great One. I am his beloved—his chosen vessel—"

Almost she won free of me then, for she swept about and clawed at my face so suddenly I was not prepared. I was left holding only folds of the cloak. Then I lunged forward, pinning her arms, holding her so close to me that I could see the expression of fear and loathing which distorted her face.

"I will not argue with you." I knew that at this moment she could not be touched by any reason which I might offer. Gathea—Gruu—at that moment I would have given the sword at my side to have them with me. That they could still be caught in that place of complete dark gnawed at me now that my struggle at the shrine was over. "What remains is that we are alone in a land which is full of ensorcellments and we must stand together or we shall be pulled down."

Her hands, which had been attempting to fight me off, fell to her sides. She looked from right to left and the moon was bright enough to show me that the shadow of a hunted creature had fallen upon her.

"I was safe—I *am* safe—Raidhan shall find me!" Only that did not ring as confident as she might have wished it to.

Still she seemed to be through fighting me, and I had no desire to stand in suspect openness on a road which ran directly into a place which, Moon Shrine or not, was befouled by evil. Thus once more, hand on her shoulder, I urged her on and she went without a struggle.

I needed some sanctuary. Everything behind me, dreamlike though some of that seemed to be now, had drained my strength. If I could find a temporary campsite, could I be sure that I might keep Iynne with me if I slept? Perhaps I must go to the limit of binding her hands and feet, thus making sure of her. Nor did I see any wrong in that considering what I had witnessed at the shrine in that forgotten town.

The road took a curve ahead and, out of the land, casting some very dark shadows, stood a series of hillocks which, to my mind, bore an unpleasant resemblance to grave barrows such as the clansmen will raise to a lord whose rule has proven safety in the midst of great disaster. If these were such memorials, the lords of renown here had been many indeed.

The wind, which had caused that constant whispering in the grass and among the leaves of the trees, changed its pathway. Now it came once more from my right hand which I star-judged to be the west. It brought with it a scent which was like that I had once found refreshing in the cup—keen, clear, and clean. Instinctively I faced in that direction, seeking what might promise some link (for so bemused by all that had happened was I that I would accept even scent as a guide now) with the Horned Lord.

A dim track broke away from the road, winding out among the barrows—westward. With no more promise than that scent on the wind should we take that way? It was dappled with shadows as I brought us both to a halt and looked down its length, for the barrows threw their half dark across it.

Again Iynne showed resistance.

"Where do you go?" she demanded. To me it seemed that she was two persons—sometimes the girl of Garn's House, biddable, meek, but more often the other who was no friend to me and who lusted for strangeness and freedom of another kind.

I was right, the scent I sought was heavier down the vale between the looming mounds. Daring to loose my two-handed hold on Iynne, I brought out the cup and on impulse turned the face of the Horned Man to face in the direction of the path.

I had my answer, and, so accustomed had I now become to things outside my knowledge appearing to help or hinder, I was not too surprised when there was again an awakening of light in the eyes of the face. A twin set of faint beams picked out the direction which lay on into the heart of what might be a vast memorial to long-vanished lords—perhaps even armies who had battled here and buried the slain within the land for which they had struggled.

I heard a swift intake of breath from Iynne, but she made no more objection when I brought her with me from the smooth pavement of the road unto the beaten earth of the side way which was far more like the trails I was used to.

A shadow swept above us. I pulled her up short and against me, looking to the sky. There was a winged thing there, large—that Vark which I had fought and which would not die came into my mind. It passed above us, seeming not to pay attention to anything below it. I could not make out its shape clearly; still there was an ominous suggestion that it was no true bird. Though it had been flying straight, it swerved suddenly directly above a barrow ahead, made a quick flapping turn northward. It might have run into some obstruction invisible to us. But the fact that the thing had been so deflected gave me heart, even though I could not be sure that was what had happened. When it had winged some distance away in a burst of added speed, I brought Iynne along as fast as she would follow, though she complained that there were stones which hurt her feet, and that we had no need to hurry.

In and out among the barrows wove that way which had plainly been made since the earth mounds were raised. Now as we passed I could see that great stones crowned some of these. From those there streamed skyward a thin bluish haze, though not enough light to aid us on our way.

I knew that we must find a refuge soon. My thirst was great, and also my hunger. I did not know whether Iynne was in a like state, but I felt her falter, and it was past my powers to carry her.

At length we came to a barrow which topped the others, stone-crowned, with the bluish radiance rising from the four corners of that stone as if candles stood there, as was done among the kin, set at the four corners of the burial bed for our lords. Looking up I could find no other place where safety might be.

From that crown we could well view the land about, and there was a kind of rightness in it. He who lay there might be long dead —but he still had his protections, and those who were of a like heart with him could well call upon such in their time also.

Iynne objected to my suggestion that we seek a camp place on the barrow, saying that it was well known that the restless spirits of the dead resented encroachment on their final resting places. Yet when the cup swung in my hand as she strove to pull free, and those twin beams of radiance not only turned toward the mound but grew stronger, she cowered and pulled the cloak tighter around her body, as if it were armor set against some stroke she feared. She said no more, but, at my urging, began to climb the slope.

We found the top of the mound had been squared away, with

the stone set in the middle of sodded earth like a low altar. As I
came those candles of light bent like flames in the wind, pointing
toward the cup.

Iynne cried out, falling to her knees and hiding her face in her
hands, her tangled hair about her like a second cloak. But I stood
tall to listen. For there came sound out of the night. I heard the
ring of sword upon sword, the clash of blade meeting shield,
shoutings, very distant and faint, some of triumph, some of despair. Then, above it all, rang the notes of a horn—a Hunter's
horn, not such as a keep lord carried as a battle signal. Excitement
fired in me; my weariness of body, my hunger, my thirst, were forgotten. With one hand I held high the cup and with the other I
drew my sword, not knowing why I did. I was not prepared to
face an enemy. No—the enemies here were long gone, and only
the triumph remained, clear and steady as the lights which lit the
barrow tops. Rather my blade came up in a salute such as I would
give an overlord to whom I was a liegeman, the hilt touching my
lips as I held it so.

To what—or whom—I pledged myself then I did not know.
Only that this was right and fitting. Around me the blue light
swirled and spun, and the cup blazed sharply bright, though no
liquid flowed from it.

Then it was gone. Swept away perhaps by a wind which was not
chill, which carried with it the scent of the Horned Lord's wine. I
felt a loss, a pulling at me—a desire as strong as pain to pass on, to
find those who had shouted, him who blew the Horn. Though my
time was not yet, so I was left behind.

Slowly I let my sword slide once more into its scabbard. The
blue of the candle flames had thinned, only the faintest trace of
them remained. Iynne raised her head and stared at me. Her eyes
were wide, there was both awe and fear on her face.

"What are you?" she asked.

I answered her with the truth. "I am Elron, the kinless,
though—" My voice trailed away. The bitterness of being an exile
—it had somehow been leached out of me by all I had met since
my feet had been set on the path to the west. I looked back at that
Elron and he seemed very young and very empty of mind. Though
I knew but little more than he now, still I was aware of my ignorance and that was a step forward.

Iynne pushed her hair from her face as I hunkered down beside her and brought forward my water bottle, the little food which still remained in my wallet. She ate hungrily, making no comment that the food was stale, the water tasted more of the jar than fresh from any spring. We ate together there in the night, the moon and the grave candles giving us wan light. Each of us had our own thoughts, mine turning once again to Gathea and Gruu.

So when I had done I took the cup once more into my hands, brought it breast high and stared down into its hollow as if that were a window—or a mirror. I fastened my thoughts on the girl who had been with me in the Black Tower. This time I strove with all my powers of concentration to bring her to life in a mind picture, as I had the water and the fire of our ordeal in that other world.

It was so hard to hold the picture of her face. She was here and then it faded and was gone. I had finished the quest I had set myself in the beginning. Iynne was with me. Gathea had chosen her own way of her free will. I had no ties upon her nor had she any upon me. Not so! cried another part of me. There will be no rest for you until you are sure that she is again in this world—that she is free to reach for her desire. No rest—yes, that was true.

17

"ELRON!"

At first that cry arose out of my own memories—I never had heard that note in Iynne's voice. My companion was on her knees, staring out over that land of barrows lighted with their thin and scarcely discernible grave candles.

The moon was well down the sky, its clear light muted. Iynne pointed to the west. In a moment I caught sight of them, too. Shapes were flitting among the barrows, only to be sighted as they sped from one patch of shadow to the next. I grew tense for it seemed to me that perhaps as many as a lord's meiny might be purposefully encircling us.

They remained remarkably difficult to see, even allowing for their love of the shadows. Thus I could not get any clear idea whether they were some hunting pack of large animals—men—or another unpleasant and dangerous life form loosed in this wilderness, perhaps by that Presence which had already played a part in my life.

"I see," I returned in a whisper. Though as far as I might determine the closest of those moving forms was still well away from the barrow where we sheltered, yet I had no desire to make any sound which ears perhaps keener than my own might hear.

The girl moved closer to me, her shoulder brushed against my thigh as she knelt beside the great stone. In this subdued light she looked older, drawn and pale. Girlhood and that human aspect which was her birthright might have been rift from her during these past hours. Now she stared at me.

"You see—" there was a malicious glitter in her eyes. "They come for me! I—" Her hands came together on her belly, protecting, covering, what she declared she carried. "I hold their future lord—and they know it! Run, kinless one, save yourself while still you can! Not even my words can stand between you and *their* vengeance!"

Plainly, she believed this to be the moment of triumph for the forces with which she had so mistakenly allied herself. I had no intention of running. Nor was I as certain as she that what slunk through the night were the Dark minions in their might.

The cup moved in my hands. I would have sworn that my fingerhold on it had been tight, that it could not have shifted so by chance. It bent backwards; its hollow no longer displayed. Rather I looked down to see the face again uppermost. While the eyes in it—they saw! They caught and held me though I felt it was dangerous to turn my attention from the drawing in of those who came among the barrows.

I had believed that I had changed in a manner, was no longer the raw untutored youth who had failed his lord and been sent into exile. Now—now indeed I was becoming—

No! I strove to cry that denial aloud, to break the compelling gaze of eyes which must be—*must* be—only metal. Cunningly wrought so that they looked alive, yes, but still metal—not real, not reaching into my mind, fashioning a place—a place to hold what?

Strength was pouring into me. Not strength alone, but something more—an intelligence which strove to fit its identity into mine. Save that I was not the vessel it expected, it needed. There remained a barrier. To that small wall of safety my own person, whatever remained of Elron, clung, a last defender, determined to die rather than yield his post to a stronger unknown.

Whatever will sought so to encompass me and found that it could not enter in as it would, made the best of what I was forced to abandon. I was well aware that I now housed a power which I could not understand but which was determined that I serve its purpose. Or was it another that was prepared to serve mine? I distrusted that last thought. Such might be only an insidious second attack launched by this invader. I was no sorcerer, no Bard, who could open his mind, surrender his will to the unseen.

Iynne was on her feet in a quick sideways movement which took her farther from me. Before I could move, she flung aloft her arms and, facing where those hiding shadows appeared the thickest, she cried aloud:

"Holla, moon-born, light-bearer, I am here!"

I thrust that bewildering, dangerous cup again into my belt, reached for her. This time I did not try to spare her, rather threw one arm about her just below her throat and dragged her back against me, while once more she became one with Gruu's clan, clawing, spitting her hate, striving to reach me with her finger-nails. Thus we fought a wild battle until my greater strength triumphed. The cloak had slipped from her during that struggle, catching at our feet, so I tumbled backwards over the slab of blue lit stone, still holding to her flesh, now slippery with the sweat raised by our battling. I did not let go, nor was she able to break my hard held embrace enough to turn full upon me. This was like holding a maddened thing, for my prisoner was no longer the Iynne I had thought I knew.

A wind bore down upon us even as clouds closed overhead so that the only light was the ghostly beams of the "candles." Twice I realized she strove to call again, and only a quick shift of hold to her throat choked off that summons.

I must have rendered her near unconscious, for finally she went limp. Then I released my hold a fraction to see if she was playing tricks. She did not move so I scrambled up, drawing her with me. Her heated body gave off a strange, heady fragrance as if her skin had been anointed with oil. She was panting, drawing deep, heavy breaths, as if she could not get enough air into her lungs.

Above that heavy breathing I heard something else. Far away the sound of a horn I had heard once before when I had been pent with Gathea and death sniffed about us—the first time I had sought the aid of the cup. High and clear that rang out.

The clouds above began to loose a burden of chill rain. I jerked Iynne to her feet, stooped and caught up with one hand the cloak to thrust it upon her.

"Cover yourself!" I commanded harshly. That soft and fragrant flesh in my hold, it brought back that temptation which the thing in the tower had striven to use as a weapon against me. Were I to loose a man's hunger here and now—that would indeed open a doorway for my opposition.

The horn sounded closer. I tried to measure the position of the shadow force below us. All one could sight were the blue lights of the barrows—and not all of those were lit either. That which had flowed into me when I looked upon the cup, which had, for the moment, left off its struggle to become *me*, supplied a bit of knowledge. Those gathered below would not dare to climb the Har-Rests. For good or ill I had made a choice when the cup came into my hands. The force I had so allied myself with—mainly unwittingly—had protections as well as dangers. We stood on ground which had its own defenses and those were not of this world.

Iynne was sobbing again, more in anger, I believed, than for any other reason. She snatched the cloak, dragging it around her, turned from me, crouching down by the stone again, peering into the dark, her body tense with expectation. For the third time the horn sounded—still afar. The wind-driven rain pelted us furiously.

Garn's daughter lapsed into sullen silence. I could not see into the dark valleys between the barrows but I had sensed that the menace there had withdrawn in part. It could be that she also knew. In spite of the clouds and the rain the sky was growing lighter, morning was coming. The candles became fainter, were gone. Now I could see that there were deep graven markings on the stone by our camp—runes beyond my reading, far different from those of our clan records. On the upper end of the stone toward the east—where it might even be above the heart of him who was buried here, there was the outline of a cup. In shape it was like my gift from Gunnora, save that there was no head upon it. However, above the picture of the cup there was also set in the stone the antler "horns"—these plainly formed the crown of some ancient lord.

"Dartif Double Sword—"

I raised my hand, palm bare and out, as I would to one whom I followed into battle, even though we knew little of each other.

"You name a name." Iynne, huddled deep into her cloak, looked at me, still sly and sullen.

"I name a name, I greet a great lord," I replied, knowing that that greeting, that naming, came from that other within me.

"This was Farthfell." I looked out over the crowding of the barrows. "When the Dark Ones following Archon came down from the north and the war horn called in all of the Light, there was here a battle of the last days. They slew—they died—their world was finished. From that warring came no victory—only memories of a better time—"

Those words arose out of me, yet I did not understand them until I spoke. Now I bowed under a deep sadness such as I had not felt before—a faraway sadness like that which can be summoned by a skillful Bard when he plays upon the thoughts of men and sings of great deeds and great defeats which lie hidden in the past, building so the belief that men of other times were stronger and better than any who now walk, giving us heroes by which to measure ourselves—goals toward which to strive.

For men must have such heroes, even though they look about them and see only lesser men, mean and petty things. Yet if they can be led to believe that once there was greatness then many of them will seek it again. That is why we can listen to the Bards and some of us weep inside, and others feel dour anger that life is not what it once was. Still there is left the core of aroused memory to strengthen our sword arms, make us ready to fight when danger arises even in our own day. It is the gift of the Bard to tie the past to us, to give us hope. I was no Bard, I listened to no hand harp here. Still I looked down upon the semblance of that Horn Crown, knowing that I was far less than he who lay below, yet I was not altogether overshadowed by him for I was another man and I might have within me the seeds of some small gift of service which was mine alone.

The gloom of the morning lay heavy, but we could see out over Farthfell and nothing moved among the barrows. What had crept upon us under the cover of the dark was gone. I reached a hand down to Iynne to help her to her feet.

Where we would go I was not sure. The horn had cried from the west and something pointed me in that direction, though it was eastward I should have turned to return Iynne to the dales.

"Where do you go?" she demanded, refusing to move until I set hand on her arm and drew her with me, half expecting that I might once more have to struggle with her and not liking that idea.

"West—"

She looked beyond me, seeming to consider the land around Farthfell, which was open enough, though there were groves of trees here and there. "Have you thrown the luck stones for the trail?" she asked.

"I have not yet heard my name called in the battle morn." I returned one folk belief for the other. "Thus I do not think that this day, at least, I shall die. And while a man lives, then anything is possible."

"You do yourself no good by holding me. I have those waiting for me and for the child now within me. Let me go. I am no longer Garn's daughter—I am she who will mother greater than any man now living."

I shrugged. That she nursed some delusion the hag had set upon her I could well believe. That indeed she was no longer any maid—might also be the truth. I only knew that, for good or ill, our fate lines were woven together for a space. And that I would surrender her back to the forces I had fought in the Moon Shrine I would not do.

When we descended from Dartif's resting place I found deep tracks all about the winding path which had brought us there. Some were of cloven hoofs, some of great paws, more were misshapen—humanlike but with the imprint of long claws extending beyond, or even booted, yet all so deeply pressed it would seem that these had been left behind as a warning—or a threat, insolent in its very openness.

We followed on the path until we came to a stream and there we stopped and filled the water bottle, ate a little more from my fast-shrinking supplies. I would have to turn to hunting this day if we were to have any relief from gnawing hunger.

Farthfell was a widely open stretch between two ranges of heights. I thought that those to the east might be the ones I had crossed before the adventure of the Black Tower. Viewing the western rises, I did not relish the thought of another such passage ahead with no more purpose or guide than an inner feeling that this was the road we must take.

The rain lightened into a damp drizzle which plastered clothing to the body but did not beat on our uncovered heads. Though shelter was offered by any of the copses of trees I had sighted from the barrow, still I wanted to remain in the open. I had met too much peril within just such stands.

When I shouldered the water bottle and got to my feet Iynne appeared in no haste to push on. Her hair lay in wet strings across her head and shoulders and she looked like a fetch out of an old tale. I wished I had better to offer her in the way of clothing, but one could not conjure a robe, or a shorter riding dress, out of grass and brush.

"Folly!" Her hands, tight curled into fists, beat together. "Let me go! You achieve nothing, only raise their hate against you—"

"I do not hold you now," I answered in weariness, for this struggle had become such that I would have gladly turned and walked away from her, save that I could not.

"You hold me—with that in you now, you hold me!" Her voice soared. "May the Death of Kryphon of the Dart be upon you—and it!"

As one who is tired to the point of limbs heavy and body worn, she arose slowly, faced westward, and began to walk, her white face set in the grimace of one being herded against her will.

We had not gone more than a short distance from the stream which we had splashed through before her stooped shoulders straightened, her head came up, turned a little to the north. There flowed back into her, so strongly that I witnessed its coming, new energy. Dropping the cloak as if the covering of her body meant nothing, Iynne broke into a run, her slender legs flashing at a sprint like a horse's gallop.

I paused only to catch up the cloak and then pounded after her. It seemed that whatever purpose moved her gave her energy past my own, with the weight of mail and heavy sword belt upon me. Still I kept her in sight, and, now and then, even gained on her a little. She kept to the open, luckily, for I feared that she might dodge in among one of the stands of trees to hide until I had passed her. Rather she appeared now to have forgotten me altogether and I could only believe that she was again in a net of whatever had entrapped her from the first.

The ground was rising again. Iynne took the slope easily, even leaping now and then across a pocket of earth to the top of a rock and then ahead. Over the crown of that hill she went as I ploughed doggedly after. When the other side of the ridge came into sight I nearly stopped short as I witnessed what awaited us a little below.

There was that dark-robed crone who had been working her spells in the Moon Shrine. She was partnered, not by any human kind. Rather one of the flying monsters such as I had fought by its lair stood on her left—this being a female and much taller than the crone, its wings fanning the air lazily, but its clawed feet firm planted on the ground. To her right was another figure—and at the sight of that I slowed pace.

It was both man and beast in an evil mixture of the worst of both. The body from the waist down was covered by a bristly pelt, the feet were hoofed like those of a bull. Huge and bull-like also was its masculine organ, so fully visible that it would seem it flaunted its sex, or was prepared to use it as a weapon of sorts.

Above the waist that bristle hair thinned, though it still grew thicker on chest and along the shoulders and upper arms. The arms themselves were overlong, its huge hands dangling low. But it was the head and face which had startled me into slowing pace.

There was a resemblance, a horrible and fearful resemblance to the face on my cup. That representation was noble; this was vile. A single being might have been split in two, all good in its nature to one side, the evil pulled to the other. This man-beast was the reverse of the Horn Lord—and he was not crowned. No entwined antlers rode on his thick tangle of curly hair.

His head was thrown back, and now he mouthed a roar which was part a beast's cry, part laughter of cruel triumph. While the crone by his side flung high her arms, her fingers moving like a weaver's shuttle. The winged woman thing smiled, her lips parting to show fang teeth.

Iynne, seeming to see no threat in those before her, was still running eagerly toward them, though she slowed when she nearly tripped over a stone set in the grass. I was too far away to reach her. Taking a chance I flung the cape after her, aiming as well as I could with that roll of the dank cloth.

It uncoiled in the air, and I saw that I had done better than I had hoped I might, for it whipped over her head, then dropped about her. She took only one more stride; then, blinded and startled, she fell sprawling, still well away from the waiting three. I spurted to her side as she still fought with the cloak.

The laughter of the beast-man died away. What rent the air—each word she uttered was like tearing open the very sky over us—was the chanting of the crone. She called on Powers, that much I knew.

The beast-man stood, grinning now, his wide fists resting on his hairy hips, about him all the confidence of a bully, a victor in many battles. His confidence was very sure and his eyes held a glint of red fire as if there were no natural orbs within those hollows, rather some other means of seeing the world and bending what he saw to his own purposes.

Back and forth the winged woman teetered, rising now so that only her toes were fast upon the ground, her wings beating with longer and stronger strokes. I felt she was about to launch herself straight at me and I drew steel.

Seeing the blade bare in my hand moved the beast-man to more open laughter. I had thrown my left arm about Iynne, held her as tightly as I could. If she went to them, if that hag laid hand upon her, I knew that she would be utterly lost, that this time no power I could summon would bring her free again. All that was still good, clean, and human in her would die and what was left was far better dead. Death itself might be the greatest gift I could give her now—when I sensed that they could take her at their pleasure. Better far to draw the edge of my blade across her throat—

"Do it, young fool!"

I saw the beast-man's flare of flame within his eye pits. "Give her to us in blood—we shall take her more gladly so."

So their power could reach beyond clean and sudden death. That was a new and chilling thought. I kept glancing at him, though I willed myself not to. He was so like in part to the Horn-Crowned One, yet so dark and lost. It is human nature to be a mixture of good and bad—perhaps what was better in me had been drawn one way by that image in the cup. Now the lowest inclined to this being.

"True—you think straight and true, fool. You are mine, do I desire it so." He gestured.

Fire burned in my loins. I was caught up in just such a wave of lust as I had been when the Presence of the Black Tower had faced me. To toss aside the cloak—to take this girl I held to—! I clamped my hand so hard about the hilt of my sword that the guard brought sharp pain. It was that small pain which aroused me. I was able to tear my gaze loose from the hold of his stare.

There was a pulling about me, what the crone wove, that net of her sorceries, was closing about us both. I would go to death—if I was lucky. Iynne to much worse.

Then that strength which had come to me among the barrows moved. I could accept or deny it. There would be only this one time of choice at last. If I accepted what it was I must do so fully. But I was a man. As a human I went my own way. To allow myself to become a tool of any power—good or evil—was I not then surrendering all that made me what I was?

Time—I wanted time! But there was no time left. I flung up my head, looked up into the dull cloudiness of the sky which closed us in as if we stood in a dungeon of a keep. Even all the land about us had taken on a grim overcoating of gray which denied even the fresh green of the growth, all that I knew as life.

I moistened my lips with my tongue. For a moment more—just one moment—I held on to the Elron I knew—the Elron I had always been. Then I called: "Hi, Holla, Kurnous!"

It was like being caught up and twisted in a mighty hand, my blood sent to run in another fashion, my bones altered in a torturous grip. I was filled with an overpowering sweep which shook me from side to side, as if buffeted by the greatest wind of any storm. Still I did not fall. There was a sharp, agonizing pain in my head. I could only think of a place with many doors long closed, all being battered inwards—or outwards—at once. So that which had been hidden behind them was freed and came flashing out.

What was I? I could not have said. I saw and heard things for which no man of my race had words, could have given name to. The tearing, the rending grew less. How long had it lasted? It had seemed to my tortured smaller self to have gone on for days out of time.

Then I was standing and Iynne crouched beside me, looking up at me with dazed eyes, a thread of spittle running from her slack, open mouth, while those other three still fronted me. Only, the winged one had lost her smile, the beast-man no longer laughed. Rather, he too, showed snags of teeth, and there was such fire blazing not only from his eyes, but the whole of him, as to set the grass about him blazing, save that it did not.

While she who Iynne called Raidhan stood with her hands upraised, yet her fingers had stopped their weaving, hung limply downward, as if all strength had been drawn out of them. What the three saw in me I could not tell. Only my heart warmed and leaped. I had thought that in this surrender I would lose all. Rather all had been drawn in to me. I must make haste now, forget my wonderment at the richness I had been shown which had been locked within a child (for all men no matter what the tale of their years were children if they knew not their strength). There would be time now to savor all I had gained—later.

Once more I looked into the curtained sky and called:

"Holla, Kurnous!" Those talents which had been body bound linked within me, so more than my voice rolled across the land.

My answer came—the fluting of the horn—not in search, but in a peal of triumph, as if a quarry was not only sighted, but had been brought to bay. Though I was no questing hound, rather the sword of the hunter.

Then—

He came out of nowhere. No, not out of nowhere, but from the other place which marched beside this world, and which in time might become mine also. He was as tall as Garn, but his mail was a coat of shifting light which glowed about his body in green, and brown, and blue. I had been right—though the head on the cup was but a very dim imagining of what the Horn-Crowned Lord was—still his features were not too far from those of the beastman. There were the Light and Dark. And I remembered in a flash then something Gathea had once said:

As above, so below. Each Power must have its light side and the dark—they were balanced. Save when that balance was disturbed and one grew the greater, then the fates—the need for all things being equal—took a hand. The righting of the balance might be bloody and dire, still it must come within all existing worlds.

The three before us gave no ground. Instead they began to swell, to take on stature, more and greater substance—striving to balance even now against the Horn-Crowned Hunter.

There was another disturbance of air.

Longing caught at me even to look upon her. Rich gold and amber light made her garment as she fronted the crone, her head high as a lady of power giving judgment. Yet—there was that in

Raidhan which was a withered, far-off remnant of the same bountiful richness my amber lady wore as the body she had chosen now to assume.

A third coming—there was another winged one. But the brightness of this hurt the eyes. I could not look at her directly. The air raised by her wings blew against me, bringing the clear scent of small spring flowers, among last year's dead leaves.

"As above, so below," I said softly. There was movement beside me. Iynne pulled upward, her hand groping out as if she sought some support. I took her fingers into mine. They were cold and she was shivering as one who stood beset by high drifts of winter's snow.

18

THUS THEY FRONTED EACH OTHER—LIGHT AND DARK. THOUGH Iynne and I were not part of this meeting, I understood, through that path to the past which had opened within my mind, that this was no new struggle. In this haunted land there had long been a swing of the balance, favoring now the Light, again the Dark; and I knew that the coming of my own people might well set it once more atilt and so bring forth such warfare as men of the kin could not conceive.

Gunnora—her spell held for me; I would ever, I realized, cleave to that which she ruled—for she had brought part of me alive. Part of me—the rest—that was liege to Kurnous—the Horn-Crowned Lord. I was sworn to him by my own desire, and did not regret that choice. In him there appeared that quality which I had seen in the Bard Ouse, opener of gates, and in the Sword Brothers. At that moment I began to wonder if all our journey had honestly been a matter of choice, or had we, in some manner, been summoned into this world, that we might supply the opportunity to rebalance again the immortal scales.

How did the gifts and talents of these who confronted each other appear? Did they indeed need others, outside their own kin and kind, outside their knowledge, to bring about the proper time and place, the action for rebalancing? This was largely a forsaken land; had the numbers of the Old Ones become so few that now they would struggle against each other for possession of those of our own blood?

As I thought this there was no speech between them. I put my arm about Iynne, for she had half fallen against me as if her legs could no longer support her; her strength might have been sucked away to feed the greedy need for power that abided here. Raidhan's bony arms dropped to her sides, hidden in the black sleeves of her robe. The winged woman's grimace became more pronounced. She spat and the spittle landed close to the feet of the shining figure who was her opposite—whose brilliance was too much for mortal eyes to pierce.

"It is again the hour—"

Did that ring in my ears, or, rather did the words marshal within my head? Kurnous spoke as he moved a pace toward the beast-man. "You have challenged, Cuntif—so I answer. Your gate is not about to open again!"

His opponent snarled. "But *you* have opened gates in plenty, wearer of horns. Now you bring others into the game—was that not forbidden of old?" He pointed directly at me. "Because the blood has grown thin, the heroes have all died, you summon these lesser ones and strive to fashion new liegemen. That is against the Oath—"

"Against the Oath? When you would have made use of him—or your companion would have. Who summoned him with the *cup* —to put that to a foul purpose? We shall have no devil child born in Arvon!" It was Gunnora who spoke before her tall companion. "And you, Raidhan—your trap is sprung, your victim has been brought forth out of that bondage of deceit you wove. She is still a maid, in spite of your enchantments, and no vessel for evil."

From the shining one came lilting notes, like the clear song of a bird—a wondrous trilling which made the heart glad to hear. She, who was the gross parody of that presence, hunched her shoulders, allowed the tips of her wings to trail among the tall growing grass.

"Yes, the gates have opened," the Horn-Crowned Lord said calmly. "When there comes a time for the shifting of forces, then we must summon those who can be aroused. From these so called there may be a new beginning. We have been long alone in a deserted land. Not all can we deal with—but there is always fertile ground waiting for the right seed. They shall be given their choice, and that shall be freely made, as is the right of all living things."

"That girl has chosen!" Raidhan pointed a bone-thin finger at Iynne.

I tightened my grip more on Garn's daughter. She was not going to that infamous three.

"Not freely, not with true understanding," countered Gunnora. "Do you think I do not know how you entrapped her? She has not within her that spark which should have flared of itself for a real choice. Look you, is that not so?" She turned a little toward the two of us and held out her hand.

I felt such a hot desire that I thought I might sway as I stood. But Iynne cried out as one stricken by a sharp blow, slipped about in my hold, to press her face against my shoulder. She might be turning from a sight she could not bear to look upon.

"You would have used her—not by her true choice!" There was pity in Gunnora's eyes. "You would have brought about the Great Secret coupling between your evil forces and an empty one— debased that which is of the Light!"

Once more she looked to the crone. "Three we are, nothing in the Lore binding can make it otherwise. But also we are pledged, you, I, Dains, to keep the faith—or there will be a reckoning."

"Once before," Kurnous took up that attack of words, "there was the strife of Light and Dark—there followed death, in spite of deeds for good. Harm and destruction rent wide this land and we were near spent—near banished because of it. Freedom of choice must remain."

"I have my place, my power, you cannot deny me!" flared the beast-man.

"Have I denied that? Freedom of choice. Those you can openly win—they shall be your liegemen, for there shall be that within them which can only answer to *your* call. These two have chosen—"

"*She* has not! You yourself have said it!" Raidhan snarled at Gunnora.

"In her way she has. She is not of those who can be touched because their minds closed to us. Ensorcellment is forbidden; those who come wish it more than their other lives. Call her now without those spells!" ordered Gunnora.

The crone's expression was as thunderous as the heaviest of storms. I saw her sleeves flutter as if her arms moved, but she made no ritual gesture. Perhaps she was forced to accept the truth of what my amber lady said.

"You see?" There was an odd note in Gunnora's voice—could it have been a tinge of *pity*? Did she feel a little warmth for this twisted, wasted, ugly female creature? "What was done, must now be undone— Now!"

There was a force about her, a deepening of the warm gold light which I saw outline her figure. A point of this swept out like a well-aimed dart. I saw the crone stumble back a step. Her face was truly venomous. Her mouth twisted as if she wished to spit poison in return.

Then her shoulders drooped. If she could have taken on a heavier burden of years, she would have done so at that moment. Her hands arose, jerkily. I could sense her own will fighting a stronger force she could not withstand. This was not Gunnora's doing—the division lay within herself, bringing her back into balance against all her greed for more power of her own.

She spoke, four words—those rumbled, thundered. I felt as if both earth and sky answered with a shifting, as if two worlds overlapped for the space of a breath. Then we were once more in a single time and place.

I held—nothing! Iynne was gone, leaving empty space between my arm and my body. Then I cried out and Gunnora looked to me quickly.

"Have no fear for her, she has been returned to her own people. Nor will she remember. That she does not carry within her a dread child which would have been a bane for all of us—that is because you stood firm. Be glad!"

"You have not won!" The beast-man roared, his voice promising blood and savage death. "This is not the end—"

Kurnous shook his crowned head. "Neither of us can ever win. You will continue to try through the years to gain your will, but there will, in turn, always be one to stand against you—the balance will remain."

"Not forever!" The beast-man swung his arm across his body in a furious gesture of repudiation.

He was gone!

The crone showed a straggle of yellow teeth in a sneer. "Not forever," she repeated in turn. Her black sleeves whipped about her body as if there were a wind blowing, though I did not feel it, and it did not even ruffle the grass where she stood. Enwrapped in the blackness which covered her spare body, she dwindled until she was like a sere leaf which that wind carried away with it into nothingness.

Now the winged woman gave a harsh cry, unfurled her pinions, and leaped high into the air. Then she too sped away across the sky, the shining one flying after her.

The other two turned to face me fully. Enough remained in me of the earlier, more youthful, unfinished Elron so that I asked:

"The Dark is then loosed to work its way here? What then will be the fate of the clansmen?"

"No land is all light without dark. For if there is no Dark how could the Light be judged and desired?" Kurnous asked in turn. "As it has been said—this is a near-empty land. There will be born among those who came with you some who are open to us—light and dark. Choices will be fully theirs. Others shall remain unknowing, for they will be of another kind and not seekers—"

I thought now of the presence in the Black Tower and it seemed to me that good might well be termed evil if such was allowed to have its way with its foul lures—without hindrance of those who might help.

"Not without hindrance—"

I began to believe that there was no need of speech between us. This was the lord I had chosen indeed and by that choice I would live from this hour on. Still there might come times when I would be troubled, when it would seem that good could do much and yet did not.

"Power—it rests upon the balance of power," Kurnous continued. "Do you not understand that whoever gathers too much power, be it of the Light or the Dark, tips the scales and only chaos will fill the land? We learned that lesson long ago—and found it hard learning. This land was once great and strong until the balance was upset. Rebuilding will take very long—and many times that will seem beyond the strength of those who attempt it. They will try—for in your people lie the seeds. You will grow beyond your own belief that such can be achieved."

Some part of me knew the truth of his speech. Yet human impatience remained.

"My lady Iynne is truly safe?"

"She will awake in the same place from which she was taken. Raidhan laid there a snare at the coming of your people. But her purpose was defeated because when she summoned the cup, you, who had set your mark already upon it, came also. For this lifetime it is yours," Gunnora said. There was a difference about her. That overwhelming impact which she had on me appeared to have ebbed. I could look upon her and feel content, happy in a way I had not known before, but that fiery longing no longer moved me. I saw her smile.

"Not now—that is a hunger you shall know, yes, but in the proper time and with the proper one who will share it."

"Gathea—and Gruu?"

There was no smile on Kurnous's face. Rather he looked at me as if surveying a liegeman about to go into battle, to make sure that his man was properly armed, well prepared.

"The cup is yours, the rest must lie with you. Again free choices —for you both. Do you choose to face a trial knowing that you may be denied? Or do you accept what will come—good or ill."

I did not understand what he would tell me. But I had an answer for what I wanted most myself.

"Gathea—Gruu—they may need me. I would go to them."

"Very well, so you have chosen. Go then and do what your heart tells you to do!"

It was no whirlwind which bore me away, nor any wings set on my shoulders. Rather there came a moment of dark when I believed I was back with the Presence—in that place where no light ever reached. Then came light—moonlight once more, as if the day were left behind.

Before me was a Moon Shrine. Not that of the dales, nor that sinister place in which Raidhan had tried to muster her helpers for foul witchery. This had a brightness of pure light—perhaps another part of the balance—standing to equal that other shrine where Iynne had waited defoulment and death of spirit.

She whom I sought was before the altar stone, and her body was silver white, for she had thrown aside all clothing, bathing in the radiance, drawing to her the power alive in this place. In the air above the altar stone hung a column of brilliance, veiling a figure I could hardly see.

Arms upheld, Gathea worshipped, her eyes closed, yearning open and avid in her face. My fingers went to buckles, to latchings. I put from me, first the trappings of war and death, and then all else so that I, too, had only the light, the light and the cup, and with it, as memory stirred and impulse ordered, that leaf of the forest woman.

As I moved to the shrine the light gathered thick before me. I felt it resist me, that resistance also attacking my mind—offering a sharp protest, a denial of what I carried, of what I would do. There arose out of the light, where he had been lying across the space between the two pillars before me, the silver body of Gruu. His lips wrinkled back in a soundless snarl of warning.

Then his eyes, as brilliant as any gems in that strong light, rested on the cup, before again meeting mine. Out of what had awakened in me I spoke to him mind to mind, reassuring that cat, who was more than cat, his place in my life which would be ours for the future.

"This is my right—and her choice."

So Gruu moved aside and I entered into the Moon Shrine.

So much power! It beat against me, I could feel the cool pressure of it against my skin. My flesh prickled as if tormented by thorns. I felt an urge to hurl myself forth, but I took one step and then the next. The cup I held at the height of my heart, the leaf warm in my other hand.

Gathea turned suddenly, as if some warning or uneasiness had struck through the serene sorcery which filled this place. I saw her eyes widen. She raised a hand to ward me off.

But I knew what was to be done, I had made my choice—hers lay yet before her. I dropped the leaf into the hollow of the cup. It lay solid for only a second or two, then it melted, swirling down and then up, to near fill the cup—the bounty of nature herself summoned to bless this hour.

As a liegeman might do in high ceremony before his lady I went down on one knee. Was there a slight feeling of pressure on my head? Light indeed—yet I was ready for the crown—though that would not be of my summoning.

Gathea pointed a finger at me.

"Go!" There was force, was it also colored by a faint fear? That command heightened the pressure on me. If she held firm I could well be swept from this place, and neither of us would ever be whole. Always we would know a lack to keep us hungered until we passed through the last Gate of all.

"Dains!" When I had not obeyed, Gathea turned again to the altar, to that pillar of light above it.

I could see, but not clearly (I do not think any man would ever see that presence as she was). But there was the shadow of a slender maiden there. The face she wore, misty as it was, had a kinship to Gathea's—closed, proud, keeping to vows which held against the fullness of life.

"Dains!" the girl cried again.

The face grew colder, showing a ghost of enmity. I remembered out of my newfound knowledge that Dains could kill a man who tempted or forced one of her maidens against that maiden's will.

I called upon nothing, no one. This struggle I must win for myself.

"Dains!" Was there a questioning rather than a foreboding in Gathea's voice now?

There formed above the cup, spiraling upward from the leaf's bounty, a golden mist—the color of Gunnora's harvest robe. Then that became amber and there was a heady fragrance to fill the space between us.

"Dains—" Gathea did not call; she murmured. Now she half turned from that silver figure to look at me. I spoke and my words came from a ritual older than a time any of my race could reckon:

"The field awaits the seed, the Power of the Lady opens the field to the seed. There comes the other to whom is given the duty of awakening—that the harvest may follow—that it may be for the nourishment of body, mind and spirit."

Gathea came to me, one reluctant step and then another. The struggle was plain to read in her face. I held the cup, waiting. Choice, the choice was hers—I would not bring it to her, she must come to me—willingly.

For a long moment she stood so close that I might have stretched out my hand to touch her soft flesh. Only that was not the way. Yes, the power passed from man to maid—from new-made woman back to man. Only when the pattern was done so would the whole be greater than the parts. Still, the choice was Gathea's.

"Dains—" a fleeting whisper. Around us the silver light pulsed, now hot, now cold, as if the struggle which was within Gathea was measured thus.

She was looking deeply into my eyes. Nothing passed between us. I do not know what she sought to see, or if she could indeed find it. Slowly her hands arose from where they hung by her sides, and— Would she dash the cup from me? Or was her choice otherwise?

Above mine her fingers curled around the bowl of the goblet, curled and held. Then she lifted it out of my grasp. As she took it, I stooped a little more and touched her white feet, the old words ready on my tongue:

"Those who seek shall also find, and rich shall be the treasure found. In the Maiden lies the Queen, and in the Lady's name do I salute her, even as I salute thee."

I raised my hands and laid them to where her slender thighs joined her body:

"In the Maiden awaits the fulfillment of the harvest. In the Lady's name so I salute thee."

Rising to my feet, I touched her small, firm breasts.

"In the Maiden stands another who cometh forth when the time is ripe. In the Lady's name do I salute thee."

Gathea held the cup level now between my lips and hers. In her eyes there was an awakening wonder—a change.

I drank from the cup she proffered, and then she drank also. Between us the cup was empty and she tossed it from her. It did not fall to the pavement, rather was carried through the air to stand upon the altar. That pillar of silver light there was deepening, changing into rich gold. I took Gathea into my arms and the kiss I gave her, even as Gunnora had promised, was to seal my fate and open the last barrier.

The golden light—the warmth—we forgot all else. What remained was priestess and Lady, man and Horn-Crowned Lord. From their union would come power with which much could be wrought. As I took one who no longer would follow the sterile path of Dains, I felt that weight settle upon my head—the crown. Liegeman I had been, in this hour was I Lord.

Kinless—clanless—and crowned!